Manuel Vázquez Montalbán was born in Barcelona in 1939. Joining the Spanish Communist party in his student days, at the age of twenty-three he was imprisoned for four years by a military tribunal for supporting a miners' strike. He started his career by writing satirical articles for a left-wing magazine in the last years of Francoist Spain and then went on to become a respected poet and novelist. Renowned for creating Pepe Carvalho, the fast-living, gourmet private detective, Montalbán won both the Raymond Chandler Prize and the French Grand Prix of Detective Fiction for his thrillers, which are translated into all major languages. He died in October 2003.

Also by Manuel Vázquez Montalbán and published by Serpent's Tail are *The Buenos Aires Quintet*, *Murder in the Central Committee*, *Southern Seas*, *Off Side*, *An Olympic Death*, and *The Angst-Ridden Executive*.

Praise for Manuel Vázquez Montalbán

'Montalbán is a writer who is caustic about the powerful and tender towards the oppressed' *TLS*

'Montalbán writes with authority and compassion – a Le Carré-like sorrow' *Publishers Weekly*

'He is the modern committed writer, entertaining his readers as he reveals what lies beneath Barcelona's glittering carpet' *Guardian*

'If you haven't yet made the acquaintance of Carvalho . . . now's the time. He's the most original detective to come along in an age' *Venue*

'Pepe Carvalho is a true original . . . the plot is less important than the joy of Pepe and his milieu' *The Times*

Other Manuel Vázquez Montalbán titles published by Serpent's Tail

The Buenos Aires Quintet

'A suitable requiem for a character and his writer' *Guardian*

'"The cops guarantee order. All I do is uncover disorder." With these words Pepe Carvalho, Vázquez Montalbán's superb creation, reaffirms his position as the most metaphysical gumshoe on the streets' *The Times*

'With Carvalho's love of fine living, and his always sympathetic eye for the virtues and resilience of the poor, Montalbán manages to make an essentially bleak worldview feel almost optimistic. This is nothing less than world-class crime fiction, packed with three-dimensional characters, honest appraisals of the contemporary world and vivid writing. That you'll want to know what happens comes almost as a bonus' *Big Issue in the North*

'His philosophical discussions, laced with cynicism and humour, climax at a dinner party which is sheer, murderous farce' *Sunday Telegraph*

When Pepe Carvalho's uncle asks him to find his son, Raúl, in Buenos Aires, Pepe is reluctant. All he knows about Argentina is 'tango, Maradona, and the disappeared' and he has no desire to find out more.

But family is family and soon Carvalho is in Buenos Aires, getting more caught up in Argentina's troubled past than is good for anybody. As he gets nearer to finding Raúl, he begins to realise the full impact of the traumas caused by a military junta who went so far as to kidnap the children of the political activists they tortured.

A few excellent tangos, bottles of Mendoza Cabernet Sauvignon and a sexy semiotician are no compensation for the savage brutality Carvalho experiences in his attempt to come to grips with Argentina's recent history: a history with too many skeletons in its closet.

See also pages 219–220

The Man of My Life

Manuel Vázquez Montalbán

Translated by Nick Caistor

With the support of the
Culture 2000 Programme of the
European Union

First published as *El Hombre de mi Vida* by Editorial Planeta, S.A., 2000

First published in this English translation in 2005 by
Serpent's Tail,
4 Blackstock Mews, London N4 2BT
website: www.serpentstail.com

Printed by Mackays of Chatham, plc

10 9 8 7 6 5 4 3 2 1

Chapter 1

When Charo burst into tears, it dawned on Carvalho that seven years had gone by and she was probably not the same person. The other Charo would have given in to tears, but this Charo performed them; she felt them, but was putting on a performance as part of a previously imagined scenario. The setting was the same as ever: Carvalho's office, and Biscuter was the same too. Carvalho had not permitted the slightest change in himself over the past thirty years. But Charo? Charo had changed. Even though when she had left in 1992 she was no longer a young woman, she still looked like one, but now she could pass for a comfortable middle-aged matron returning after a long absence with a changed status and silhouette. Thicker all over, although not by much. Perhaps the oval of her face had become rounder, she had more cheek than cheek-bone, and yet there were fewer rings under her eyes, as if she had spent seven years resting from the accumulated fatigue of a life of whoring, which in her case was true.

'Doesn't she look beautiful?' trumpeted Biscuter, who as usual was crying from his eyes and the tip of his nose. Both of them were staring at Carvalho, offering him or demanding from him an emotional response he did not feel. He needed to be left alone with Charo to find out whether he really wanted this re-encounter. To rediscover a space of their own and see whether the old reflex actions of the past were still there, to see whether he still needed her. But the presence of Biscuter as theatre director feeding him his lines annoyed him. Charo pointed at him, seeking Biscuter's approval.

'You'd think he was greeting a girl cousin from his home village.'

'The boss is sorry, but that's how he is.'

For a second, Carvalho thought of saying something that would help create a more cheerful atmosphere – welcome home, for example – but he mentally rejected lyric and epic formulas and was about to laugh instead when it suddenly occurred to him he could say: Seven years of solitude stare down at you from these walls. Fortunately he controlled himself, and when he finally coordinated sounds and silence sufficiently, what came out was:

'When are you going back to Andorra?'

Charo and Biscuter looked at each other, stupefied.

'He's throwing me out!'

Biscuter gestured with one hand as though trying to snatch Carvalho's words out of midair before they reached Charo's ears, and vice versa. But it was no use. That wasn't what I meant, thought Carvalho, I should explain, but he was annoyed at having to do so, and decided instead to thank her for something.

'Thanks for the cassette you sent me a few years ago.'

'They're really cheap in Andorra.'

In order to speak properly to Charo he would have to sacrifice Biscuter.

'I need you to go to Fuster's office so he can give you some papers I can't go and fetch myself.'

Biscuter's face recovered its enchanted expression: he was sure that when they were alone, Charo and Carvalho would rediscover each other. Within two minutes he was on his way out, though not before planting a big sucking kiss, more from a snout than a human mouth, on Charo's cheek. She stood up, and smoothed her skirt down, preparing to leave as well, then picked up her bag and turned to Carvalho. She went up to him, took him by the arm, pulled him towards her and kissed him on the lips lightly, but with a moist, dense, noisy intensity. A kiss that hit home. The man and woman stared at each other. The slamming of the door behind Biscuter made them jump apart, as if their two bodies were afraid of being so close together when they were on their own.

'Do you still love me?'

Carvalho did not answer. He wondered whether he had ever said to Charo: 'I love you'. No, he had never said it. She did not respect his silence.

'Well, I still love you. You're the man of my life.'

Carvalho rushed over to his swivel chair and buried himself in it while Charo was examining all the details in the room. Her eyes lit up with amusement when they added the fax machine to her inventory.

'Everything's the same, apart from the fax. You're modernising.'

'Biscuter is modernising. I've no reason to. I don't believe in modernisation. Everything is always modern. Today is more modern than yesterday. And I won't even mention tomorrow. But it's true, you look very modern.'

'More than before?'

'As I said, it's hard to judge. But you do look very modern. You can be modern, like everyone else, or even very modern or supermodern. Just don't ask me for an example, because I'm making it up as I go along.'

So Charo sat down and told the story of her life for the previous seven years. I crawled away, Pepe, because when you went chasing after that French tart, I realised how little I meant to you. I had no contacts in Andorra apart from Quimet, a solicitor from Barcelona who had a house there. He had been a client of mine for years. Every Boxing Day, when he was fed up with having to eat a second Christmas dinner, he used to say Prime Minister Pujol had called him, leave his family and come and visit me. A real gent. Better still, a real person. Don't laugh at the mention of Pujol. Quimet is a true Catalan, and in his youth he used to go climbing with the head of the Generalitat. They were Catalan nationalists, Catholics, and hikers. Quimet gave me a helping hand in Andorra: he found me a job as a hotel receptionist. It was a godsend, Pepe, from one day to the next I was in a proper job, and I no longer had to spread my legs to be able to buy a bottle of Dior Poison or eat a real French omelette with lots of fresh parsley. Later Quimet made me an associate of the hotel, a part-owner, and so the days and years went by. I sent you that cassette, and a few letters, but you never bothered to answer them; I guess you were enjoying your freedom after having got rid of me. But Biscuter tried to encourage me whenever I phoned him: 'Don't lose heart, he loves you, Charo.' So she and Biscuter talked on the phone; how modern of them. There was little more to tell to bring the story up to date. Carvalho raised his eyebrows, waiting for the rest, but Charo fell silent, looking across at him with increasing, embarrassing affection.

'Well then?'

'Well then what?'

'You send me a note, you disappear and I don't see you for seven years. It's only natural for me to ask: well then?'

'Did you read the note?'

Carvalho opened a desk drawer. He knew exactly where he had kept the note, and made to reach for the envelope, then thought better of it.

'Yes, I read it.'

'Did you keep it?'

'I don't think so.'

'I don't have clients any more. Quimet is a true friend. An important friend, but he's not my kind of man. There's only one man in my life, and that's you. You don't look too good.'

She criticised his appearance in such a tender way that Carvalho thought she was talking of the passage of time, of how although he might not realise it, they had both aged. It was not the kind of thing he liked to hear; it made him so uncomfortable that he wrenched himself up out of his chair, but he did not want to return to the chill of the first minutes of her return, so he listened patiently as Charo went on philosophising on the passage of time.

'So one day I said: Quimet, I'm very well regarded here and I'm earning a living. But I can't live without Barcelona and without my Pepe – he knows all about us.'

'How did he manage to visit you each Boxing Day in Andorra? He could hardly leave his family sitting at table and shoot off there.'

'They don't celebrate it any more. His elderly in-laws have died, his children have got their own families now, and he and his wife don't even speak to each other in the lift.'

'Have they separated?'

Charo shook the whole of her head and all the air round it to deny any such possibility. No. Prime Minister Pujol had asked him as a personal favour to avoid the political scandal this would cause.

'In short, Pepe, I'm back in Barcelona and Quimet has helped me open a shop.'

'A cigarette kiosk?'

It was Charo's turn to be patient, and instead she listed all the reasons why shops selling tobacco should not be allowed. Smoking was on the way out anyway. Quimet had been working on a Catalan anti-smoking campaign that left the American one in the shade. It had a wonderful slogan: *Som sis milions però cap fumador.** She ignored the fact that Carvalho chose that very moment to light up a Hoyo de Monterrey cigar just waiting to be smoked in his top drawer. She stayed calm, and took a business card from her hand-bag.

'He's opened a diet foods and organic cosmetics boutique for me. Here are my details: don't tear the card up. I was thinking of you. You're getting old. You don't have a future, or enough money to live through what little future you do have left. Quimet could help you. I've already talked to him about it.'

Then Charo leaned impetuously across his desk and stuck her tongue in his mouth, feeling her way as though rediscovering its hidden contours, and as she straightened up and walked backwards towards the door, her eyes were full of promise.

'We can still be happy, Pepe, sort out our problems and have somewhere to end our days.'

'Are you really interested in where you end your days?'

'I'm interested in how they end, and that's why I'm thinking of the future.'

'Thinking of death is not exactly thinking of the future.'

'How do you intend to grow old, my little Pepe? I asked myself that question in front of the mirror in my Andorra hotel: "How do you intend to grow old, Charo?" It's one thing to die of cold if you haven't got a cent, it's very different to carry that cold inside you if you don't have any feelings, not even self-respect. Who loves you, Pepe? Do you still have any self-esteem?'

Self-esteem. Charo's vocabulary had improved. Self-esteem. She had always expressed herself well, but used simple words; she would never have dared used a phrase like 'self-esteem' with him. It must be a word her 'friend' Quimet had taught her.

'Does Quimet have a lot of self-esteem?'

'He deserves to. He has made his own success. Quimet is an important man in Catalonia, one of those "building the country", even though he is hardly ever in the limelight. It was thanks to him I got on in Andorra, and now I'm back because he has helped me

* There are six million of us, but not a single smoker.

open this little shop and because I feel secure in what I'm doing. Can you say the same?'

So Charo was a member of two sects: the Theology of Healthy Eating and the Theology of Security.

'What links do you have with NATO?'

'What's NATO got to do with organic foods?'

'You can only feel secure if you have the backing of NATO.'

'I don't follow you. I think you're trying to pick a fight, but I can understand that a few minutes can't compensate for seven years. I just want you to get one thing straight in your mind: Quimet has helped me, and he wants to help you.'

Charo did not give him time to think up a sarcastic response, in words or gesture. She floated away from him, leaving her business card on his desk. She headed for the door, and her back announced:

'You'll be hearing from me.'

Just as Carvalho was coming to terms with the fact that he was all alone again, with Charo's card in his hand and an erection between his legs, the fax machine started to chatter.

I can understand you are not responsible for what is said about you, but you must be aware that you have become some kind of social hero – or rather, an anti-hero. I was surprised at your surprise, because you must be used to being stopped in the street and asked for your autograph. I didn't dare ask you for it myself, so I sent my eldest son instead. I was close enough to say to him: Look, it's that man over there, and I saw you weren't very happy about it, both by the way you reacted and by your inscription, which said next to nothing, but had an outsize signature to go with it. 'To satisfy a client . . .' you wrote. Definition: CLIENT: of a professional person, someone who uses their services. Of a commerce, a customer. I realise you have no shortage of definitions, which makes this one even more wounding, because I suppose you knew what you were writing. So yes, I am upset, because I don't think that was a correct definition: a client returns the goods if he or she is not satisfied with them, but I'll keep your signature lovingly, because one day I discovered that Pepe Carvalho was a human being who could make mistakes, and for that very reason perhaps the things he does well, very well, 'divinely', are all the more valuable. At least that's what I think, even though the experience we shared long ago doesn't seem to me to have been very human on your side: or was the lack of humanity or maturity all down to me?

It is not just me who is concerned with what you are up to. Everyone around me (by which I mean basically my husband and two children) knows how I feel about you, and they frequently tell me what is being said about you, as someone lots of people talk about but very few know. To show you how generous I am, I'll confess I'm not only offended on my behalf, but on yours too. I really do not see you as being in commerce (stores like El Corte Inglés buy to sell at a profit), and I don't think being a private detective is having a profession, not a lucrative one at least. Well, I see I'm already lowering my guard, which must be because of the 'unruly passion' I feel for you. Anyway, now every time I look at your huge signature I feel sad. Not sorry, but shaken; everything you stir up in me is equally outsized.

I think I should admit I have been searching for your address (electronic, telephone, postal . . .) everywhere, so it is quite possible that you hear about it from someone or other. Finally I discovered you are exactly where you were when I first knew you. I don't know why I was surprised you didn't have email (you see, I even searched on the Internet); of course, given the way you are, I should have known you were more likely to communicate by tom-tom – much closer to magic, to the arcane. Ah well, it's obvious I adore you. You'll just have to accept the responsibility, you can't avoid it.

MORGANA (the witch)

As soon as he had finished reading the fax, Carvalho could not prevent his eyes seeking out the details of the sender: 'SP Associates', and a fax number he was not interested in retaining. He did not want to reply. He did not want to become intrigued by the personality of this correspondent who was so fascinated by him, or worry about what the supposed 'experience we shared long ago' might have been: besides, the Morgan of Arthurian legend was not really a witch, she was a straightforward fairy, although perhaps a fairy and a witch are the white and black versions of the same transgression. He imagined this particular witch as a fat old woman built like a brick, a frustrated wife who turned to literature in search of paper heroes because she could not find any in real life. It was true that the press had written about some of his cases, but between Carvalho and Julio Iglesias there were a million paper heroes more deserving of a fax from some fat, neurotic cow. He was surprised, though, that he did not want to tear the message up. Also that he put it away in the desk drawer he could lock, as if to protect it from indiscreet eyes, which could only mean from Biscuter. He had no wish to dredge up all the experiences he had shared with women, not even those most capable of the kind of fantasising and syntax evident from the fax.

He went out into the street with his bad temper lodged in some corner of his brain, but it was obviously not well enough hidden, because every few steps he would pause and ask himself: Why are you in such a bad mood? And the immediate answer was: that fax woman. He was still holding Charo's card, and he headed for the address of her dietary foods and organic cosmetics boutique in the Olympic Village. He felt a need to re-read Barcelona, to reconcile himself with its desire to turn itself into a pasteurised city, with the smell of fried prawns coming from the metastasis of restaurants in the Village. How could there possibly be enough prawns in all the seven seas to supply the quantities of them being cooked in Barcelona, changing the smell that had characterised the sinful city from one of cordite, armpit and groin to one of pine freshener and grilled prawns? All the old metaphors for Barcelona were out of date; it was not the city widowed from power any more: now it had all the institutions of autonomy; it was not the anarchists' fiery rose, because the bourgeoisie had won its final victory by the simple trick of changing its name; it called itself the 'emerging sector' now, and how on earth could anyone throw a bomb or build a barricade against an 'emerging sector'? Like some statues, Barcelona had become beautiful but soulless, or perhaps it had a new soul that Carvalho was searching for as he walked, until he was forced to admit he might be too old to uncover the spirit of this new age, the spirit some pedants had baptised as 'postmodernity', but which Carvalho himself saw as a brief moment of stupidity between two tragic ages. Yet he found himself falling in love with his city all over again, and had to contain his sense of satisfaction as he walked down the Ramblas, came to the port and turned along the Moll de la Fusta towards Barceloneta and the Olympic Village. Despite all the new shopping and leisure malls, the sea was there, and had finally become one of the four constituent elements of the city: Gaudí, grilled prawns, the telecommunications tower built by someone called Foster who had a private jet and was married to a Spanish sexologist, and the sea. Quimet had set Charo up in a shop on one of the less busy aisles of the Port Nou mall, in the shade of the Arts Tower. They were completing the fitting-out, and Carvalho watched from a prudent distance as Charo dealt with carpenters and electricians, one hand holding the shop plans, the other on the left hip of a pair of jeans she filled to perfection. Charo's age flashed through his mind like an illuminated indicator board, but he refused to read it. She still had a young woman's figure, even though her face was heavier and it was obvious she dyed her white hair the mahogany colour that seemed to be so fashionable for women. The nearby beaches which on his left stretched along to the breakwater he remembered from his childhood, and on the right down to Maresme, Barcelona's Copacabana ever since the Olympic Games, were strewn with bodies consuming the Mediterranean and the sunshine for free. He imagined the young Charo's graceful silhouette among them, and had to confess that the Charo of today would fill her bikini more fully and better, and that he would need to go up very close to her to see the tango or bolero of her life engraved on her face. He did not want to be discovered in his role as a voyeur, but when he turned round he found himself face to face with a small, thin, grey-haired man who was extremely well dressed, impeccably so, and who gave off far too pleasant a fragrance and had far too intelligent a look about him.

'Carvalho, I presume?'

How original can you get, thought Carvalho, but he refused to satisfy the other man's curiosity, and even took a step backwards to increase the distance between him and the proffered hand.

'Joaquim Rigalt i Mataplana, although Charo will doubtless have called me Quimet.'

Carvalho had imagined him taller, heavier, more anodyne and

obvious, but he had to shake hands so he could get a good look at him.

'Have you arranged to meet Charo?'

'Not exactly.'

'But this is a great opportunity for the three of us to meet.'

Carvalho was about to invent an excuse, but Charo had seen them and was hurrying over smiling broadly, although her eyes were on the detective, begging him to help her out. She kissed Carvalho on the cheek, and shook hands with Quimet, looking to right and left to see whether anyone had noticed. Her cautious greeting made Carvalho decide to stay, and he let himself be taken off to Port Nou for a cocktail in a bar that smelt of prawns like everywhere else, so that the three of them could catch up with their news. Quimet let Charo get the conversation off to a pleasant start, and Carvalho pretended to be listening while he wondered what they wanted from him, and what he could order at that time of the morning: a dry martini with prawns.

Quimet took over the conversation in his role as Joaquim Rigalt i Mataplana, associate of Doña Rosario, Charo to her friends, whose expertise was priceless in the running of Bio-Charo, one of the many businesses he owned.

'One has to spread the risk.'

He winked at Carvalho, who did not respond. Then he leaned towards him and asked, in the voice of a lyric tenor:

'What do you think of Catalonia?'

'What do you mean?'

'Catalonia.'

'I still don't understand your question. Who is Catalonia? What is it? A geographical or an administrative entity, something emblematic, something symbolic . . .'

'A national entity. Catalonia is a nation.'

'I don't doubt it. A collective identity, then, collective and virtual. Because you are a nation too. Everyone is a nation. But I'm very clear that I'm not a nation. I have enough trouble being an individual, and I don't trust collectives. Individuals can feel compassion, collectives can't. I'd find it too complicated being a nation. But I love other people's nations.'

Charo applauded him with her eyes.

'We're off to a good start, Carvalho. But *anem per feina,** and let's not waste time. How is your work as a private detective going?'

'We're going through a bad patch. Globalisation has hit us hard. The multinationals control all the private security business, and one-off detectives like me are seen as anthropological curiosities. There's never been so much Theology of Security around, nor so many crooks and murderers in the market, but we can't compete with the multinationals of repression. What NATO is doing beggars belief. For now, they're just using intelligent missiles, but soon they'll be arresting and imprisoning people with magnets that can detect defeated human flesh from hundreds of miles away.'

'In other words, you're not doing too well.'

Carvalho shrugged, leaving centre stage to Quimet.

'What do you think of intelligence services, then?'

'Do you mean things like the CIA, the KGB, the Spanish CESID?'

'You're talking about specific agencies created by certain historical conditions: the cold war or the Spanish transition to democracy. I'm talking about the intelligence services of the future, a new concept in agencies that will respond to new strategies, new horizons, the new regional conflicts that globalisation is bound to create. The problem for a spy in the service of the great powers is to know who to spy on. But a postmodern spy in the service of the new fragmented power centres will have to spy on everyone. You once worked for the CIA, or at least that's what they say: Did you work for them?'

'It was so long ago it's just as likely to be true as not.'

'Well, anyway, you've got experience that could be very useful to us.'

'Who is us?'

'Catalonia.'

Carvalho's eyes strayed towards a store selling all sorts of gadgets for spies which was opening at the foot of the Arts Tower. Charo intercepted his look, pleading silently with him to be patient, to listen to Quimet, to do it for her, not to be in such a hurry. Carvalho sat back in his chair to hear what Quimet had to

* Let's get down to business.

say about the need for Catalonia to have its own intelligence service.

'We've discovered that not only are the intelligence services of the Spanish and French state operating in our territory, as well as people sent by Bossi's Padania, but that other autonomous regions are busy setting them up, especially the Basque country, where the PNV has had this kind of thing for over fifty years, from the days when Irala and Galíndez collaborated with the North Americans.'

'So the Basques are spying on the Catalans?'

'They're interested in knowing who we're spying on.'

'If you take that to its logical conclusion, everybody would have to spy on everyone else to find out who they're spying on.'

'That's to reduce it to the absurd. But something like that could take place. Concretely, though, what we're worried about is that we've found evidence of spies working for powerful economic groups who could hijack the very idea of Catalonia: have you ever heard of "Region Plus"?'

'Not enough.'

'This isn't the moment, but I can tell you that we are facing a diabolical conspiracy between international popular movements and the Socialist International who are backing Spanish nationalism, allied to powerful financial sectors, all of whom aim to create a new multinational regional grouping which could not only compete with but destroy Catalonia's identity. They want to establish a powerful economic triangle between Toulouse, Barcelona and Milan, a triangle that would ignore the emotional and national borders of Catalonia. That is Region Plus. The French and Italian governments intend to collaborate with the central Spanish government in order to thwart the secessionist threat from Padania and north Catalonia, not to mention the idea of setting up Occitania. Bossi's Padania does not exist, and Occitania could never happen, but Catalonia does exist: it exists and it's in danger. What Franco never managed to do could be achieved by nonnationalist economic forces. If it were to succeed, this new blueprint for an economic powerhouse could undermine the very idea of Catalonia. Destroy our identity. How are we supposed to feel that we belong to a triangle? Does that mean we believe in geometrical patriotism? We need men like you, Carvalho.'

Now it was Carvalho's turn to scrutinise Charo's face to see

whether she thought Quimet was being serious. Is he making fun
of me? Is he a clown? Charo's eyes told him: No. He is serious
about it, hear him out. Quimet handed him a business card.

'Go to this address, and remember that appearances can be
deceptive. When you get there, show them my card and simply say:
De bon matí quan els estels es ponen . . .'*

'Couldn't we just leave it at: *Patufet, on ets?*'†

Charo's eyes were looking daggers at him. Quimet chuckled.
The card was for another shop, this time a health and dietary prod-
ucts pharmacy called 'Lluquet i Rovelló'. Carvalho made his
excuses, and left the two associates to draw their own conclusions.
It was lunchtime, and he wanted to find the Estrella de Plata
restaurant, where they served avant-garde *tapas*, millennium *tapas*,
dreamed up by a chef called Dídac López. He left the Olympic
Village to its cyclists and bathers equally keen on the sea and getting something for nothing, and to its restaurants stuffed with
prawns, with the honourable exception of Talaia, where you could
eat a fusion of Ferran Adrià's cooking with neo-Mediterranean
ethnic fare. He headed for Pla del Palau. He had to fight as hard as
during his days as a karate expert to make room for himself at the
bar of the Estrella de Plata, and to order a choice of artichoke
hearts with a quail's egg and caviar, or a courgette flower fritter
filled with an award-winning foie gras. Although the four canapés
he ate had given him an appetite for more, they also made him
realise he should not do any further damage to his delicate finances
by offering himself even a modest meal in the same restaurant. It
was no longer a case of saving for his old age, but of not having
saved enough for anything. A recent check on his financial situation had revealed that he had ten million pesetas, which at a fixed
rate of interest would provide him with fifteen thousand pesetas a
month. That was all he had, unless he sold his house in Vallvidrera
and went to live under a bridge. Just thinking of it made his head
spin, so he set off for the Señor Parellada restaurant, where
Ramón, who had once been a hero of Catalan rock and now also
ran the Fonda Europa in Granollers, offered him a special price, or
at least served him a drink. Carvalho wanted to eat real Catalan

* At dawn, when the stars begin to fade . . .
† Tom Thumb, where are you?

food so that he could be completely identified with the cause. He ordered an *escudella barrejada*,* and *peus de porc amb cargols*.†
He knew the stew was nothing more than leftovers, and that pig's trotters were low in calories and would not push up his cholesterol levels.

'Are you on a case at the moment?' Ramón asked him, serving him a dessert of slices of orange in orange juice, sprinkled with candied peel.

'I have to finish my search for the murderer of the Lucifer's Witness. You can't imagine the mess I've got into. I don't believe in the true religion, and here I am up to my neck in a false one. Besides that, I could be involved in a major operation: saving a nation.'

'Which nation?'

'It doesn't have a name at the moment. A nation that's been wandering in the desert for hundreds of years loses even its name.'

* Stew with grilled leftovers
† Pig's trotters with snails

When he reached his office, he realised there was no going back. Biscuter had left the object the fax machine had given birth to on his desk.

That's enough flirting, we've got no time to lose (I'm scared in case you go off on holiday, and we're left 'hanging'; the idea that we should put off until September what we could have done before makes no sense to me). So, I didn't like your autograph.

When one could have painted *Las Meninas* – the Velázquez version – one isn't going to settle for a cartoon by Mingote, however good the joke and its author may be. But from what I know or what I've heard, your life has become a caricature: it is obvious you had a hard time in Madrid with the murder of the patron of the arts, not to mention during your long stay in Buenos Aires, when you were trying to escape from yourself. I find it easier to judge what happened in Madrid. You lived the experience and at the same time recounted it to whoever would listen, strangely transgressing the Pauli principle (two bodies cannot occupy the same space at the same time). A crime which according to you was committed by 'the author' of a novel being presented for a literary prize; the novel's theme: the economic, political and literary intrigues behind literary prizes. A looking-glass that could be used to look inwards or outwards, almost without realising it: a real stroke of genius. A recreation of how Velázquez conceived *Las Meninas,* making both the creator and the spectator part of the composition; an unusual concept, but one with magnificent results! It's 'the' painting, not even Vermeer's *Delft* is half as good. And as for the concept: ten out of ten.

It occurs to me that . . . unless you specifically authorise me to, my upbringing prevents me from continuing: is it too much to ask you for a simple yes or no as an answer?

How I would love your fax to play a bolero instead of that screeching noise it has. It would help my 'case' a lot: you'd be bound to give in if it played:

> *I love the things you say,*
> *I love our hours at play . . .*
> ALICE *(through the looking-glass)*

What was the stupid woman thinking? He had the name 'SP Associates' and her telephone number. She deserved a crushing reply. What right did she have to judge his life? How was Carvalho supposed to be responsible for all that was said about him? What was he supposed to say yes or no to? Señora, send me a photo and I'll decide whether or not it's worth me suggesting we go to bed together. He was still hesitating over what to do with the fax when the silence was shattered by the machine once more, and he saw the name SP Associates and their telephone number emerge at the top of a new message.

Returning to the Madrid case, which I at least am concerned with, although you plainly are not. As usual, you sketched in a plot based around the characters you already had in mind, just like you did with me: I had to conform to the lines already traced by all your prejudices. I can just see how you thought up the alleged suspects: you always use the Goya technique, in other words broad, confident brush-strokes wielded with the precision of a surgeon's scalpel in order to bring out each one's individual characteristics. Chromatic. You are a voyeur who paints reality in his own image. What colours am I painted in, tucked away in the archive of your memory? At what moment did you eject me from the bolero of your emotional life, a bolero growing more and more intense but brutally interrupted when you decide to seize hold of the record and smash it? Musical. In the best musical pieces, all the art is in the counterpoint. That's what brings harmony to the composition; the fictional Carvalho is the one who is meant to make reality shimmer in front of us, to make a dense, almost impenetrable human landscape more accessible, more 'digestible'. Mmmm!

The Lázaro Conesal murder case shows you are working on your polyphonic skills. You are trying to develop several melodies at the same time: the economic, the socio-political and the literary. You work exactly like a composer, playing with several themes: you state the first one clearly, only to fuse it with the next one, then it's the turn of the second theme to make its own statement, which is then subsumed in the third . . . and then ta-ta-ta, back to the beginning again. Symphonic.

But at a certain point the symphony starts to fall apart; the sounds continue, and the tempos are respected, but . . . the result is a hotchpotch of themes that jangle, sound strident, unfortunately far too often. Cacophony. I did not want to worry (I told myself: he must be doing it on purpose) about the fact that you lived as though you were trying to prove once and for all that life is a henhouse ladder as in the saying – 'life is like a ladder in a henhouse, short and full of shit'. I knew that in Madrid you had met up again with a woman you had once been crazy about, and I suppose that's all there was to it, because with women you never seem to get beyond the step of being crazy about them. And it was when you wrote about the relationship with her that the first false notes sounded. You seem to see as paradigmatic an eighteen-year-old boy, Carmela's son, and show him talking to you in his abusive slang about his mother's – and your – behaviour, a boy capable of saying that his mother adores Julio Anguita as if he were Michael Jackson, and that in fact Anguita is a bit like Jackson, a whitened-up red, or a reddened-up white. And he ridicules his mother because according to him she has signed up for all the secret societies worthy reds support: SOS Racism, Amnesty International, Hands Off Chiapas! . . . But I talked to that boy. I've followed your tracks, Carvalho; I even arranged a neutral conversation with Carmela to see what role you really played in her life. I can tell you that on two occasions, at the start of the eighties and towards the end of the nineties, Carmela was expecting you to throw up everything and stay with her. She doesn't know you.

Carmela does not know you, Señor Carvalho. I can understand that you may be worried about me investigating your
investigations (the way that painters sometimes paint over an
earlier composition, it's called *pentimento*, or people write in
the margins of a published book). I suspect you will find this
revelation hard to swallow.

Here's the music your fax should be playing now:

> *Farewell little sailing boat,*
> *my galleon of love.*
> *Your flag and my flag*
> *no longer flutter up above.*

. . . Reply please.

TWEEDLEDUM
(still through the looking-glass)

PS: Getting together again with Carmela almost worked –
almost! What would happen if you tried to get together again
with me? Is it so difficult to recognise me, to rescue me from
your memory files? Haven't you collected the petals of all the
flowers you've plucked? Sorry for the kitsch. It's a controlled
kitsch.

Which petal could the fax cow mean? She could not be anything
else but a cow on the prowl, her horns shaven and her udders full
of sugar-almondy milk, cheap Technicolor milk, the kind used on
souvenir postcards for kids. He had arranged to meet the Lucifer's
Witnesses at five o'clock in the new Plaza de Cataluña Zurich
restaurant, a clone of the old one just as the new Liceo theatre was
a clone of its former self. A time of genetic engineering and nostalgia, puffed Carvalho, ready to face a spiritualist session with an
horchata or an iced coffee inside him. As he walked up the
Ramblas, his eyes and the summer heat were stripping the bodies
of the girls passing by, and of some women too. Carvalho did an
age test. Which did he find more attractive, the girls or the women?
The women. He heaved a sigh of relief.

The *horchata* tasted like poor, open frost crystals, and it took
him some time to remember where this metaphor came from, until
a poetic regurgitation threw up the memory of the lines Miguel
Hernández had written in prison while his son was feeding on his

mother's thin milk, the product of eating onions in the years after the Civil War: 'the onion is a closed, poor crystal of frost'. The sociologist Anfrúns was not excessively late. He was a couple of decades older than when Carvalho had met him during the case of the go-go girl, but he still had the flowing locks of May '68, which had turned grey and greasy in the eighties, but which now at the turn of the millennium he wore gathered in a long ponytail. His height was mitigated by his stoop, as though he had been forced to lean forward to be able to talk to humanity on a lower level.

'From sexology to theology, that's some career.'

'We live in theological times, Carvalho. Anything we have to say about the future has to be theological, because nobody has made any plans, and capitalist neo-determinism has done away with hope. That's why the big market of the next century will be the religious one. There will be designer religions all over the place. The idea of sects will be consigned to prehistory.'

Anfrúns ordered a whisky with a lot of water, or a lot of water with a little whisky. Carvalho asked for a small malt with no ice if it were more than ten years old. Anfrúns rambled on about how important it would be for Carvalho to get to know about all these new religions, while the detective enjoyed himself looking at more female bodies and trying to guess where all the foreigners came from, since Barcelona had become a European myth thanks to its reputation as a Mediterranean city inhabited by people whose greatest anthropological desire was to be Swiss or Japanese if they couldn't be Catalan. Logically enough, anyone with dreams like that deserved to be an object of universal curiosity. But Anfrúns had pronounced the word 'Lucifer', so Carvalho had to drag himself back to their conversation.

'What were you saying about Lucifer?'

'That it's a deterrent sect.'

'I don't get it.'

'One pressure group has created it as a deterrent against another. Apparently futuristic deals are on the cards, and the amounts at stake border on the infinite. Precision geo-economic engineering at work. It all started when the son of one of the most powerful industrialists set up a sect so he could screw as many girls as he wanted, then Papa cut off his money because he didn't like the idea of him being the anti-pope and into sex. The father was

Opus Dei, non-hairshirt faction. Pérez i Ruidoms no less. All of a sudden the boy found himself showered with money, said to be from followers and sympathisers, but in fact from the Mata i Delapeu group. You know who they are, they're everywhere, and up to no good at all, if we apply the ten commandments of constructive capitalism to them. They're asset-strippers who've become multimillionaires. They buy failing companies after they have got rid of their staff, then rationalise them or sell off what's left: the land, the factories. Nice, clean business fun, don't you think? So the idea makes sense for them. But it turns out that Albert Pérez i Ruidoms, alias Satan, attracts your murder victim, Alexandre Mata i Delapeu, to the sect and to bed. The death of a Lucifer's Witness, apparently in a ritual killing, puts the spotlight on the sect, and the identity of its leader means his father is involved too, and everything he represents. Soon, you mark my words, false accounts will appear – elections for the autonomous parliament are coming up this autumn, and there's a serious chance the nationalists may lose to the left, so any scandal would damage people high up in the autonomous government.'

'Such as who?'

'Ventolrà, Stijar, Rigalt i Mataplana.'

Carvlaho took in the full name of Quimet Rigalt i Mataplana. He kept his eyes shut to betray no emotion, and carefully calculated his next question.

'Does this have anything to do with Region Plus?'

Anfrúns was too genuinely startled to be able to hide it.

'Don't listen to me,' said Carvalho. 'When it comes to theology, I'm a novice. Tell me who the people you mentioned are.'

'Ventolrà is one of the main hopes for the next generation in the autonomous government – he's one of Pujol's chosen successors, although the worst thing that can happen to an ambitious Catalan is to be considered Pujol's chosen successor. So far, none of them has survived politically to tell the tale. Sitjat knows everything about the premier and his family's finances. And Rigalt i Mataplana knows everything about everybody. He's a very shrewd man, faithful to the prime minister since they were adolescents. He gets things done. He became rich in Andorra, and super-rich in the Cayman Islands, but nobody remembers that. He's never been linked to any corruption scandals. He's married to one of the

Fatjós: I don't know if the name means anything to you. The Fatjó family is Pols cement, which has just been sold to a multinational. I won't tell you how much that made them, because the figure wouldn't fit in my mouth, let alone your brain. I can tell from your face you've no idea of who is who in this country. You're like a Martian.'

'I'm just passing through.'

'How long are you staying?'

'I've always been here, and always will. Let's get to the point, Anfrúns. I find it odd to be talking to you about religions and power. I had you down as someone who delved into the dark areas of sex, and now here you are representing a Satanic sect.'

'I'm the natural-born intellectual of the group. That's what I've always been: I was that with the Socialist Party, the same when I got into sex, as you remember, now here I am still trying to be the one who makes things happen, though I'm not the man I was. Anyway, to get to the point. The boy who was murdered was a newcomer to the sect, but he was well chosen because they say he had sex with the prophet.'

'Wasn't the prophet mad about girls?'

'He's had enough of heterosexuality. It was logical for him to want to try something different. The same happened to me: didn't you find that?'

'Badly shaven women give me the creeps, so you can imagine how I feel about men.'

'And they say that he not only slept with the prophet, but that he's a Mata i Delapeu.'

'Jesus, Anfrúns! Everybody around here is so important they have double-barrelled names joined by that copulative! It doesn't matter if they're a queer, the prophet of a sect, his father, or a murder victim.'

'In Catalonia, as in Spain and the rest of Europe after the Second World War, a new class has appeared which has absorbed the old oligarchies. You know I started out as a sociologist, so I know what I'm talking about. Don't get me started on that, let me finish telling you what I know about this case. The Pérez i Ruidoms boy is still a suspect, but he's out on bail. The crime itself could have been committed by hitmen from the Balkans who don't cost a lot, and by now are probably back slicing each other's balls off in their own country. There's a lot of demand these days for Kosovar killers, because they have to live, and hunger and wars make the best hitmen. We'll soon have ones from Chechnya. The poor people in the world may be poor, but they're not stupid, and they know the rich need people to commit their murders for them.'

'I was asked to investigate the killing by the archbishop of Barcelona's office.'

'If the archbishop's office has come to you, that's because the sects have made a speciality of covering the cathedral walls with graffiti, and also because Mata i Delapeu's mother is behind it. She is Delmira, from the Rius i Casademont family, and she's a devout Catholic who belongs to every Catholic NGO going: she does it to help her forget that her husband betrays her with anything around, even inflatable dolls, whether they're inflated or not.'

'I'm glad I found that out before I talk to the reverend bishop. In fact, it was Caritas that called me.'

'It won't be the bishop you talk to. You'll see someone under him. Don't forget, he's not just a bishop or archbishop, he's a cardinal. What would you do if you were received by a cardinal? It makes me laugh just imagining it.'

'If he were wearing a cassock, I'd ask him to dance. I read that somewhere: a hooligan was so impressed by a bishop's skirts he asked him for a dance. Anyway, let's see if I've understood the satanic-oligarchic organigram of Catalonia properly, and correct me if I get it wrong: this Pérez i Ruidoms kid sets up a satanic sect so he can screw around, and some time later the body of the Mata i Delapeu boy appears. Apparently, Mata i Delapeu liked playing fathers and mothers with Pérez i Ruidoms. Then Mata i Delapeu's mother, who still uses her husband's name even though he sleeps with inflatable dolls, asks me to investigate the murder, and you, the natural-born intellectual of these Lucifer's Witnesses, tell me that although the evidence points towards Albert Pérez i Ruidoms, in fact it's all a plot hatched by one group of oligarchs to destroy another economic group, the all-powerful Pérez i Ruidoms, the Great Lodge or Chief Rabbi of Opus Dei, and father of the satanic prophet. Now tell me a bit more about the different sects and the hitmen.'

Anfrúns briefly described all the sects in Catalonia, kids' stuff compared to the ones in the developed world of North America.

The neo-Nazis are infiltrating them because they don't know where else to go. For the moment they're not needed by capitalism, and they have to be part of something, Barcelona or Español Football Club, Real Madrid or the Church of Satan, the Ordo Templi Orientalis or Orde Illuminati. Anything on the far right, whether mainstream or anarchist.

'The most noteworthy sect is the Church of Satan. It was founded by a Popular Party diplomat, and its leaders have links with the Moonies. The OTO-Authentic sect has got two high priests: a taxi-driver and a park attendant. They're into black masses and sell daggers for ritual sacrifices, but as far as is known they only kill chickens, cats, a few lambs, the odd dog here and there. Our own sect is a modest one, but it's very creative, in all modesty thanks to my own efforts, because theoretical imagination is my profession, and I've tried to make the whole thing a little more left-wing, not because I think we can make the revolution through religion, but simply to give our beloved bourgeoisie a kick in the balls. Although they often enjoy that, because at least it proves they've got them. Remember my theories on sex. We nearly brought the system down by preaching free sex. Everybody wanted to jump on board, but then Aids and the Polish pope came along. I have to go. Here's a list for you, and try not to bother me too much.'

He handed Carvalho a bit of paper and left. On it were: Current 93, DV 69, the Sacred Gene Foundation, the Astaroth Group, Brothers of Lucifer's Halo, Brothers of Xango, the Great Goat, the Temple of Seth . . . Carvalho glanced rapidly at the list, then got up in pursuit of Anfrúns. The sociologist was hurrying along as though he had only a short time to complete a piece of fieldwork. He crossed Plaza de Cataluña, turned into Via Laietana and strode down the right-hand pavement until he reached police headquarters. There he crossed over to the other side, as if he did not like walking in front of the doors of the former Francoist *cheka* – an attitude Carvalho himself often had, and mentally applauded. After Anfrúns passed what was left of the Santa Catalina market (nothing more than a façade awaiting renovation behind it), he disappeared into the Barrio Gótico until he reached a medieval building, where he simply pushed open the door in the gateway and went in. By the time Carvalho arrived, the door had slammed shut, and although he searched on the door frame and the front of the building for some explanation of what went on inside, he found nothing, so he withdrew to the El Xampanyet Bar opposite, from where he could see anyone going in or coming out of the building. Laid out neatly on the bar were plates of Basque rolls, which had spread through Barcelona like a postmodern rash, or 'collage and eclecticism', as one Carme Casas put it in an article he had read in *La Vanguardia*. He had finished his second roll when his hopeful trailing of Anfrúns was rewarded. None other than Quimet entered the building where Jordi Anfrúns, one-time sexologist and now natural-born satanist, had vanished a quarter of an hour earlier.

Starting from the almost cabbalistic view I had of the way you lived Lázaro Conesal's murder, I was torn between conflicting and violent emotions . . . second-degree equations (remember them?), the ones that solve mathematical problems that can have two answers, are kids' stuff to me, as they also are to you, apparently.

I had always seen mathematics as an ethereal, almost seraphic discipline, subject to the strictest rules, spotless, all of a piece, virginal, so solid and consistent that . . . it made me sick. That was until those equations appeared on the horizon (like the 7th Cavalry, in Panavision and with appropriate soundtrack music) to rescue maths from its staleness, its rigidity, its virtuous smell (the smell of moths?). Thanks to them, maths became magic, unexpected, full of surprises, indeterminate, ambiguous; in a word, disconcerting. The fact that the word itself is plural showed me what a movable feast they were.

I realise you always know who the real murderer is, but allow society to settle for the necessary murderer, with his complete agreement. Someone with such a complex personality as yours is capable of sybilline shrewdness that conceives and carries out designs that allow you to continue being a voyeur in both your stories and in life.

That skill is amply demonstrated in all the cases you take on. Even the one I was involved in. Can you still not identify me? Why don't you want to identify me? Are you really so indifferent or so arrogant that you haven't the slightest interest in knowing who I am? You could track me down through the fax address. Aren't you meant to be a detective? Why don't you do it? Are you scared of me? I want to stay hidden so that you'll be forced to uncover me. But let's continue with my deconstruction of your Madrid adventure, typified by that hotel and the mystery of the locked room. From what I heard about what happened in there before it became public knowledge, it was a baroque farce played out to the sound of sad panting, like a lengthy, weary death rattle. As always – or rather, as always recently – you lived the experience passively, like the peeping Tom you are, with the same attitude you have towards my faxes, the same one you once had towards me. I am capable of 'forgiving' you anything, I would defend you in almost any situation, I would even do it now against myself, but the essential element is missing: you have to say or do something. I hope you will understand my disappointment, although it is absolute, and does not depend on your understanding in any way.

TORQUEMADA
(are you sure he was a man?)

The faxes kept coming. Once she had finished with the Conesal case, she started analysing other investigations of his, as though she had been spying on his career and had become the detective of another detective. Perhaps the best thing would be for him to call her and suggest they meet, but the summer was pressing for the closure of winter's balance sheet of truth, promising that everything would be different from now on, and by the time it was over the fax cow would have got over her obsession. The body of Señora Mata i Delapeu's son was given a Christian burial despite his satanism, and she was demanding from Carvalho in private what she had little hope of getting from the public police.

'Justice and peace of mind. Until I can look deep into the eyes of my son's killer, I won't be able to sleep in peace.'

He had to go and meet this woman widowed by her son. Another cultured, rich woman who had given birth to a rich, cultured and stupid misfit. A nice bit of satanism would help see him through the summer; and besides, he had to see Charo again as soon as possible to clear up what might have been but wasn't, or perhaps no longer could be. He was surprised to admit to himself for the first time that he was unsettled at the thought that Charo depended on another man. She was not on the game any more, but had exclusively become the lover or concubine of a respectable man who had set her up in a business. The fax cow. Satan. Charo. Quimet and spying for Catalonia. Too much to leave till September. He pulled open a desk drawer, and under the cassette Charo had sent him from Andorra he found his swimsuit. While Biscuter was busy in the kitchen preparing saffron-perfumed stews, Carvalho slipped into the toilet and put the trunks on under his trousers. Then he got dressed again and went down to the car park to get his car, which was going to be his beach hut. He drove down the Ramblas to the port, then turned towards the Olympic Village and parked his car in the shadow of the Mapfre Tower. He stripped down to trunks and shirt in the car, locked his clothes in the boot, and climbed the steps up to the Port Olímpic, from where he could see the free beaches stretching out into the distance, where greedy bodies were devouring the gift of the sea, offered to them once more after centuries of walls and pollution. To his left, the Olympic Village was beginning to be masked by trees camouflaging its lack of architectural ambition, while on his right was the dazzling sea and the good citizens of Barcelona in their best and worst displays of nudity, all of them gambolling in paradise. Carvalho was back in the world of his childhood, when the 'free' (meaning you did not have to pay) beaches of Barceloneta converted him into a bather amazed at the way his body was freed by the water. Now there was one beach after another, and if he carried on walking he would reach the French border without ever having to lose the blessing of the sea. But what interested him more was trying to understand this new city, this urban extension gnawing at the instinct for survival shown by the enclosed and romantic cemetery that was Poblenou, with its sprawling cubes of houses recycled thanks to the plastic surgery of simulation culture, its despairing chimneys reduced to giving obsolete testimony to what had once been a mixture of Manchester and Icaria, as other previously cheap, protected, badly-built shacks were reduced to a raucous Harlem thrown up next to Malibu, housing for the poor miraculously built on the most expensive land in the city. What was the link between his imagined Barcelona and this Atlantis suddenly rising from the seas? A flight from itself, or a new city open once and for all, a safe, pasteurised city where pickaxes were attacking the groin of the Barrio Chino and the phantasmal

barricades of the memory of the city of rage and the idea of sub-
version, of the city under Franco, the city on its knees, Lord,
before the Cathedral Chapel, where all that was left of love and
truth was kept. Perhaps the link was nothing more than the smell
of prawns, the revenge of the odour of rancid oil, a foul stench that
contrasted with the cleanest of Mediterranean cities, a dense oil
full of memories of post-war days, of defeat.

He decided to plunge on to the beach before the nudist one,
because it was well known this was where the water was cleanest,
and most sheltered from all the sewage blown back onshore when
the wind was from the east. It was filled with the usual couples, the
usual single women, the usual gays, all of them paying homage to
a particular branch of anarchy, as if they were all direct descen-
dants of vegetarian theosophists and sun-worshipping anarchists,
convinced that onions or garlic or above all sea water were a cure-
all. And it was a joyous feeling when he came into contact with the
cool water and could swim just as he had the first time he had felt
confident in the sea after swimming lessons as a child at the
Montjuic Swimming Club, as if the water brought back memories
of how he had learnt to swim as well as of how he had lived the city,
making him nostalgic for the escapes he used to make into the
other element, fleeing the heavy solidity of work days and working-
class neighbourhoods, on board open-top trams, undressed trams,
trams with cleavage and short skirts, operating only in the summer
and filled with young girls who showed their flesh daringly after
the war, sweaty armpits and glimpses down beyond their breasts to
the moist recesses of their sex. He touched bottom again and stood
with water up to his shoulders staring at the young trees lining
the pubescent Olympic Village, the cyclists, adolescent surfers, the
anarchistic couples, the gays in tangas and on a permanent diet.
He felt refreshed, happy, reconciled to his city even though he
suddenly felt like crying because he would never find his way home
again, and anyway had no clear idea of what home he could not
find, as if it were nothing more than a white wall where memory
sketched the shadows of the dead whom only he remembered.

'My debts are paid, and I've buried my dead. The perfect end
to a millennium,' he thought, and as he was thinking it decided he
ought to call the fax cow. She was the only new thing to have happened to him since his trip to Buenos Aires, or possibly since

Claire had made her brief appearance in his life, or even farther back, since the moment he decided not to be taken by surprise by anything that could make him conscious of his own fragility. He did not like sunbathing like a sea lion stranded on the beach, so after ten minutes he dived into the water again, then spent another ten minutes stretched out, before heading for the public (meaning you did not have to pay) showers. Free, he thought, then thought to himself, Pepe, you're starting to think like an old-age pensioner. As he walked back to his car he stared at female bodies and the sporting acrobatics of kids and youngsters playing football or volleyball, which again reminded him of his own childhood and his own body's impulse to rejoice in the freedom of nature. In his mind (or was it from his mind?) he suddenly had the image of Montjuïc hill much less well laid out than it was now, full of wasteland left by bombs or the demolition of pavilions from Expo 29. Or if not Montjuïc, then in countless other suburbs of the city which had been so close then, and were now buried for ever under new buildings. Why was he remembering his childhood so much lately? When he got to his car, he put his clothes on over his swimsuit and once more took on the look of a private detective dressed at El Corte Inglés sales. He wanted the mother widowed by her son to approve.

Delmira Mata i Delapeu was waiting for him in a vast penthouse on a street that, unusually for Barcelona, was lined with acacias, and had service entrances to every house. She lived in an apartment just right for a woman separated from a husband who did not need him to be able to buy herself a luxury flat costing more than a hundred million pesetas. There were lots of books on her living-room table: *The Structure of Reality* by David Deutsch, *Political Order in Changing Societies* by Samuel P. Huntington, *The Information Age* by Manuel Castells, a copy of *Realitat* magazine from the Communist Party of Catalonia, publications and pamphlets from Sal Terrae, and *In the Same Boat* by someone called Sloterdijk. This was a little book of human proportions which just fitted into Carvalho's hand, so he opened it and read: 'Postmodernity is the age "after God" and after the end of all the classic empires and their local offices. Despite this, orphaned humankind has attempted to formulate a new concept that will include everyone in a fresh unifying principle: human rights.'

Carvalho had no chance to read on and discover whether Sloterdijk believed in human rights or not, because at that point the tragic mother came into the room. She seemed to be ageing by the day, and was dressed in the grey sobriety demanded by her inner mourning. Her face was deeply lined by grief. Carvalho drew his hand over his eyes to wipe away the misplaced film of irony, still holding the book in his other hand. The mother spoke.

'It's a big little book.'

'Pardon?'

'The book in your hand is a big little book on disorder and the new chaos.'

Carvalho dropped the book as if it were burning his hand, and followed Delmira Mata i Delapeu's lead in sitting on a cream velvet sofa. She really had aged since their first meeting three days earlier, and her voice sounded strangled and vague.

'Have you found out anything new?'

'What I've discovered has confused me and complicated the situation. Apparently, your son's murder could be part of a plot to undermine Pérez i Ruidoms' father. It seems that it's easy to find hitmen these days.'

Delmira slowly closed her eyes, as though when the lids rubbed against them they hurt because they were raw from so much crying.

'So it wasn't even a human murder.'

'What does "human" mean in this case?'

'A murder inspired by love, jealousy, passion. It was a test-tube murder, one invented in a financial laboratory.'

'I haven't reached any conclusions yet. Perhaps I gave the wrong impression by coming here, but I thought it was important to give you my news.'

'You don't have to apologise. I'm glad you came. I like to hear a human voice. And you have a lovely, deep voice.'

Her eyes were still shut. When she eventually opened them they seemed to Carvalho sad, old and beautiful. The detective no longer felt in any great hurry, and slid back on to the sofa to tell her all he had learnt earlier in the day concerning her son's death. He tried to find words that would not describe the relations between the two young satanists too crudely. When he did so, Delmira smiled, and patted Carvalho briefly on the arm with a heavily veined and mottled hand.

'Thank you for being so polite, but I knew my son was a homosexual. We talked about it quite often. Naturally enough, he thought it was his free choice of sexuality, but also that it was a reaction against his father.'

'An Oedipus complex?'

'No. He was my youngest child. I was already old when I had him, so there was not much threat of any Oedipus complex. He was simply a sensitive boy who could not bear his father. Have you seen *The Silence of the Lambs*? The film where Hannibal the cannibal has to wear a muzzle all the time to stop him killing and eating human flesh?'

'Yes.'

'Well, my son and I thought that was a perfect metaphor for my husband.'

He returned to Vallvidrera after buying food at La Boqueria market. That was being renovated as well, and Carvalho was afraid it was going to suffer the same fumigations that had got rid of all the bacteria and viruses in the rest of the city. He had got the butcher to debone some chicken thighs, and bought some sausage meat to stuff them with, intending to make an up-to-the minute version of a fricassee with chopped walnuts on a bed of artichokes. An expert on TV had recently declared: 'Walnuts promote good cholesterol and help cut bad cholesterol,' although he himself looked extremely ill, perhaps because he had not eaten enough walnuts or artichokes in time. Carvalho himself was an expert on artichokes and how to steam them to bring out all their goodness and flavour; according to their champions, they were an ideal food and non-toxic for elderly people. What is the most toxic thing for old age? Having no money. Artichokes are diuretic, they help prevent rheumatism and arthritis, they cleanse the blood, and yet they are tasty and can be used in interesting recipes. For Carvalho, they brought back memories of the 'rice for one' his grandmother used to make: with one single artichoke, a single squid, one tomato, and one pepper, as if the number one were the expression of her loneliness and the impossibility to communicate, or more simply of how meagre was the pension she received as the widow of a traffic policeman laid off by the Azaña Law.

He did not want to make things difficult for himself by sewing up the thighs round his stuffing, which he completed with a bit of bacon, some more chicken and ham, a sprinkling of breadcrumbs, egg and a truffle, so he stuffed the thighs, added salt and pepper, used a finger to anoint them with oil, then wrapped them in foil to cook them *en papillote*. At the same time, he cooked onions, added some white wine, chopped boiled eggs, garlic, parsley and the walnuts, and adjusted the sauce with a splash of the cognac the truffles had been preserved in. When the thighs were cooked, he took off their shrouds. They had moulded together perfectly, so he left them simmering for five minutes in the fricassee. His very own creation! He could call it 'Fricassee Pepe Carvalho'. Every human being should be able to have a child, write a book, plant a tree and invent a recipe for chicken fricassee.

He was cooking rice in stock to go with his fricassee when the doorbell rang. He went to answer, quickly downing half a glass of red Aillón wine on the way. It was Charo at the door, and Carvalho showed her in as naturally as if they had been together only a few hours earlier, rather than after a gap of almost seven years. She came in exactly as she had always done, and reacted to things as if she were astonished, although she had been aware of them for years: Carvalho cooking, Carvalho with an open bottle of wine. She glanced over towards his bookshelves, as if trying to guess which volume Carvalho was going to burn on the fire like the last blaze of summer. As he intercepted her look, Carvalho started to wonder not only which book he was going to choose, but how he was going to renew contact with Charo's body. She was probably expecting him to grab her right now as she walked past him, and it was quite probable he would seize her from behind and not let her go at all, but precisely because this would be a total embrace aimed at making up for all that lost time, Carvalho shied away from it. Perhaps when she turned to him, he could kiss her on both cheeks. Or perhaps Charo would think that was too ordinary, and would want him to take her in his arms and kiss her on the mouth. The re-encounter was harder than their first meeting because it was difficult to calculate how far Carvalho or Charo wanted to go in recovering the past, and they both feared that any miscalculation in their performance could end in disillusionment. At a first meeting, desire aids the imagination, but in a re-encounter like this, the rubble of former emotions and sensations lies strewn around like a devastated landscape. As soon as Charo spoke, her voice would tell him how far the recovery might go; but all of a sudden she turned towards him, tears in her eyes, and put a stop to his mental deliberations by seizing hold of him and kissing him once, ten, a hundred times on every part of his face her lips could reach. He stood there and felt her kisses like gentle pecks designed to break the shell of time and distance. Mechanically, he took the initiative: he clasped her tightly to him, and their tongues leapt into action before their brains could. Carvalho's favourite son was stirring between his legs, which was a promising sign for the night, because there could be nothing worse than to go over all they had not lived together and never reach the truth of penetration. That would be like never getting to the ground zero of recovery. The ice or whatever it was had been broken, and what was needed now was for the ordinary to free them from any fears of over-dramatising, to move on from tear-jerking melodrama to high comedy. To help the process along, Carvalho filled two glasses of wine and was about to propose a toast, but all at once he stopped, suddenly aware that a toast was too much responsibility – it was bound to be either too intimate or too distant. Here's to us? Here's to meeting again?

'Here's hoping we can always kiss each other with hope,' declared Charo, and Carvalho concurred, still anxious it might be a bit too much to ask. But then his duties as a host took over again, and he started worrying whether he had made enough fricassee for two.

'There's only one dish.'

'That sounds awful, but I bet it tastes wonderful.'

'I'll make a dessert.'

Carvalho peeled two apples, cut them in slices, and quickly fried them in a pan with butter. When the flesh had started to go soft, he added half a glass of Grand Marnier and fructose, then waited for the apples to soften further without becoming completely fluffy. He beat an egg, added flour, whipped three egg whites, added more fructose and poured the liquid into a caramelised fruit mould. Then he laid the slices of apple on top in a symmetrical pattern. As he was putting the concoction into the oven, Charo asked him why he used fructose.

'Are you diabetic? Biscuter didn't tell me.'

'Biscuter doesn't know everything about me. Anyway, I don't have diabetes, but I will some day. Bromuro was right. The enemy is within us, and the son of a bitch is searching every day for where he can get at us. There's a moment when he realises we are growing old, that our defences have weakened, and then he attacks on all fronts. If we're lucky, we can hope he'll allow us a slow death sipping water through a straw or being fed through a tube up our nose.'

'What a man!'

She shouted her old refrain, and at the same time caught hold of him again, searched out his lips, and started pushing him in some direction, doubtless towards bed. Carvalho weighed up the possibility of rising to the occasion while at the same time not letting the dessert burn, and avoiding the sin of abandoning a ripe and ready woman to turn off the oven. If he turned it off now, the dessert would not be done: what was worse, for it to be burnt or under-cooked? As Charo backed towards the bedroom, he started taking off his clothes, still clinging to her. She dimmed the lights and undressed shyly in the dark, as she always had done, so that Carvalho would not think she behaved with him as she did with her clients. To this now was added her fear of the years showing, but Carvalho refused to look anyway. He did not want to accept the ravages of time in case it meant he could not perform, with the result that when a naked Charo rubbed herself against his body he convinced himself it was the Charo he had known the first time around, and by the time he shifted his weight to penetrate her, he had been aroused by their foreplay and felt powerful, and kept his eyes tight shut or only half opened them to see Charo's features in the darkness as she climaxed. So he felt pleased with himself when they disentangled their bodies and Charo clung to him in order to prolong their embrace and murmur once, twice, a hundred times, her voice as it always had been.

'I've dreamt so often of this re–encounter.'

'You were the one who left.'

'But nobody took your place. Not even Quimet. He gave me a different kind of security, but he's not my man. You are the man of my life.'

'You don't need me any more.'

'Why do you say that?'

'You've changed profession. Before, you needed someone to protect you emotionally, and besides, I cost you nothing. But now you're a businesswoman.'

'Did you think of me as a whore then?'

'No.'

'And I didn't think of you as my protector, or that you cost me nothing. You were my man. You still are.'

Carvalho was able to put on some clothes and still manage to rescue the apple fool before it suffered third-degree burns. Charo was still in full flow. She wanted to bring to the table not only seven years of absence but all the future she hoped to have. Carvalho said nothing. He was picking out books. He pulled them off the shelves, then pushed them back. Finally he kept one in his hand: *La vie quotidienne dans le monde moderne* by Henri Lefebvre. As usual, he read a sentence to see whether he would burn the book or reprieve it: *'la théorie du métalangage se fonde sur les recherches des logiciens, des philosophes, des linguistes et sur la critique de ces recherches. Rappelons la définition: le métalangage consiste en un message (assemblage de signes) axé sur le code d'un message, un autre ou le même'*. Too many people to reach the conclusion that to burn a book in a fire was a metalinguistic act, so he tore it up and laid it on the grate to build his bonfire on.

'Why are you burning it?'

'Because we all use metalanguage without needing anyone to explain it to us. Also because Lefebvre took too long to realise how important the everyday world is to history. For a long while, he couldn't see that work days are always the real thing.'

Charo praised his cooking and talked a lot about Quimet, about what a good person he was, about all he had done for her and could do for Carvalho.

'Do you remember that guy Anfrúns, the sex-mad sociologist who appeared when I was investigating the death of that go-go girl?'

'Of course I do. He advises Quimet on religious matters.'

The next morning, Charo awoke alongside him, and he went with her to her shop in the Olympic Village before going on to his office on the Ramblas. All the way down the Ronda de Dalt and then the Ronda del Litoral, she could not help singing and asking him astonished questions about all the changes in Barcelona. It's like another city, isn't it, Pepe? Just like us. We've changed too, haven't we, Pepe? Charo prolonged her goodbye kiss as long as she could, the same with her goodbye clasp of his hand, and her goodbye look: by the time she had finished, it was like the cliff-hanging final moment of a soap-opera episode, filled with premonitions of disaster. But Carvalho knew what he had to do that day, and had no wish to resolve the ambiguity with which he responded to Charo's attempt to renew their mutual dependency, so when he reached his office he took out the cow's faxes and dialled the telephone number that came with them.

'Excuse me, I've been sent several faxes by you at SP Associates, but they don't say exactly who they are from. No, I can't give you any more details.'

The person at the other end of the line must have asked everyone in her office who had sent faxes to someone called Pepe Carvalho. He heard the noise of the telephone being handed to a different person, then a long, deliberate pause before he heard the studied voice of a woman who had obviously been preparing what she was going to say for a long time.

'Carvalho, is that you? Are you sure?'

'Don't start doubting it: you'll only increase my sense of insecurity.'

Now I'm sure of it: the Three Wise Men exist!

Yes, your phone call was a 'religious experience'; I'm still stunned, amazed, tongue-tied (as you will have noticed). I remembered you as a shy, very shy person, but one who gave the impression of being arrogant (you behaved very arrogantly towards me) and someone who was always very busy. That was why I thought that if I was very lucky at most I would receive a fax message with a laconic yes or no on it.

So it came as a complete surprise not only that you called, but the excuses you gave, and the fact you didn't seem to know what you were meant to be replying to. All I wanted to do for now was to make a proposal which if accepted would mean sharing a few earthly pleasures with you (some recipes, a glass of wine or two . . . do you remember?) offered in a spirit of gratitude for your generous attentions to me in the past. I should already be fulfilling my promise, but at the moment I find I can't concentrate enough to give you a detailed description of the secrets of my 'tuna in puff pastry' or my 'orange salad with garlic'. You won't think of me as a cook, far from it, but thanks to you I am one now. You've been the man of my life in so many ways! I'd like to send you some bottles of white wine from El Empordà that my family makes – it's fashionable to make one's own wine these days. For that I'd need to know how to deliver it to your office: is Biscuter still with you?

Do you know that your voice is warmer than it used to be? Imposing, and slightly 'self-satisfied' . . . do all the gods of Olympus talk like you? I'm still under the spell of your call yesterday. That's to say I'm dazzled, my head's in the clouds, clouds, clouds . . . (I wish that could sound like Alberti's 'waves, waves, waves' . . .). Let's just say I'm in a state of grace.

I bought a lovely dress, I am (I feel) so beautiful in it; everything yesterday was absolutely perfect.

Laugh if you like, but we had a family dinner last night, and I was so out of it that they decided to lay a place for you at table, so that it would be more 'natural' for me to carry on with my/our bewildering private conversation; I mean that whenever I looked towards your plate, nobody was supposed to interrupt me/us. I had to put up with jokes of every description, and tell everybody what you thought of the 'cold soup with melon' and the 'grilled cod' . . . you're just jealous, I told them! That was what was on the menu, and even though you don't know it, you're always present at my dinner table and for lunch too, whether I make it myself or buy food for the maid to prepare. You're always with me in all my life and all my dreams; my family knows it, because Mauricio, my husband, is aware that it is thanks to you that we are married and have two wonderful children.

Things got even funnier when I went to bed (the others are already on holiday and stayed up to chat) and they started telling all kinds of stories about you, including the one involving me. The general reaction seemed to be more one of 'ho, ho, ho' than 'ha, ha, ha'.

I'm telling you all this because it's only right you should know what effect your charitable impulse of yesterday had. By now you should know I'm neither shy nor prudent, and since one should never be afraid of asking, I wonder if after the end of the holiday period, as you suggested, we might meet up: in Boadas, El Viejo Paraguas . . . but you decide where, I'm sure I'll love it (no, there's no alternative).

SCARLETT
(sitting on the staircase marking her dance card)

I forgot to tell you I'm going on a rather late holiday. I like to split my holidays up, and take some weeks at Christmas and in the spring. As I'm the boss's wife and one of the owners, I could take as long as I like, but I have to set an example. When I get back I'll personally hand you my final critical observations about your astonishing behaviour in Madrid over the Conesal affair. At least I hope it will be possible, that you'll agree to meet. You and I are accomplices, we share a secret, or at least I think we do. You can't imagine how beautiful life seems to me, I'd love at least to make you smile (you always have such a serious, wary look on your face . . .) Where are you going on holiday? I'm sure you only go away for a few days at a time, perhaps you try to rediscover some landscape of your memory. But that's enough of boleros for a moment (even though I think they're great): just listen to what's on my radio now. Azúcar Moreno is singing:

> *Let your body sway to the rhythm*
> Ay, caramba!
> *You only live once*
> *You only live once . . .*

Now you can put your Vivaldi back on (if that's what you prefer) but as far as listening to waves lapping and birds trilling in the background . . . we'll have time enough, an eternity even.

NB: I hope I'm not using up all your fax paper; but what I'm most afraid of is being tedious, being a burden to you. Please don't think you have to be polite, and if I am, tell me so straight out and I'll rectify things at once (on second thoughts . . . just insinuate it, or I'll die of shame).

Chapter 2

The pharmacy Lluquet i Rovelló was much closer to an old-fashioned herbalist than any new-fangled health boutique. It had fibrous anti-constipation pills, medicinal plants to fight cholesterol, hypertension and sugar in the blood. The walls were lined with cathedral-choir brown shelves on which stood antique or fake antique ceramic pots designed to conjure up a supposed golden age when humans were near immortal thanks to all these life-saving herbs. The shop was like one that had opened in the 1940s in Calle Botella, only to disappear some years later and become such a nondescript place that Carvalho could not even remember what it was – or was it the draper's whose owners had sheltered him when the police tried to arrest him for the first time? The name was obvious to Carvalho, although it probably meant nothing to the new generations, or even any of the older generation who were not as familiar with Catalan cultural life in the post-Civil War years. Lluquet and Rovelló were the names of the main characters in *Els Pastorets* by Folch i Torres, a comedy with carols based on the (not that far-fetched) hypothesis that the baby Jesus had been born in Catalonia, and that the two main shepherds who went to adore him were the fearful Lluquet and Rovelló, two cowardly peasants who were always undone by the Devil's wickedness. It was the period when the Catalan language was undergoing a timid revival, and the Franco authorities allowed the play to be put on in church halls. Despite the restrictions, the actors usually managed to insert a few subversive jokes. Carvalho recalled how the Devil, defeated yet again by the Archangel Michael, and flattened on the stage with the angel's foot on his back, lifted his head a couple of inches and shouted: *'Miquel! Miquel! Sembles el Real Madrid, que sempre vol guanyar!'**

* Michael! Michael! You're like Real Madrid, you always want to win!

To call this front for patriotic spying Lluquet i Rovelló showed that the owner, be it an individual or an institution, at least had a vivid cultural memory. Carvalho did not want to waste the password or his contact, so he started looking around the shop, worried that he could harldy remember a thing about medicinal herbs from his reading of *Dioscórides*, the bible for healing plants that one of his great-uncles, an anarchist who sold peanuts in the Monumental bullring, always had his nose in. The woman in charge looked liked one of those nationalist, north Mediterranean widows who have successfully recovered from their loss but are not as pleased with themselves as those agnostics who rejoice at being freed from their husband's dead weight. She was one of those modest widows who imagine their husbands are in a very Catalan heaven, dancing the *sardana* every Sunday and listening to the rebroadcast of Barcelona football matches with commentary by Joaquim Maria Puyal. Ever since his childhood, Carvalho had been convinced there was no one to match Catalan widows. Compared to those from the south of Spain, they were still Mediterranean, but with a touch of northern sobriety which meant they no longer went in for strict mourning or lamentation. He told this particular specimen of his long-standing curiosity to see what darnel looked like, because he knew that in the Judaeo-Christian tradition it was an accursed plant, which formed part of the forces of evil ranged against the good, a weed that grew in among corn and could only be pulled up when fully grown.

'We're not allowed to stock it because it's toxic.'

'Not even as rat poison?'

'Darnel has got lots of ergot in it, and with a gram of that you could kill a cat weighing two kilos.'

'I haven't even got a cat.'

The widow was growing impatient, but Carvalho continued his examination of the premises. Everything was open to view, except for a dark corridor which led to the back of the shop. At that moment, a couple of youngsters came in. They hardly even bothered to acknowledge the assistants, but headed straight for the corridor, and disappeared into its gloom. Carvalho imagined that behind the counters there were tape recorders constantly on, or phials of curare, always the poison of choice for spies who wanted to kill at a distance.

'The shop name reminds me of a play we used to put on in the church hall when I was a boy.'

The widow looked at him more sympathetically.

'Well, I'm glad someone has realised. Not many people get the connection between the name and *Els Pastorets*. What part did you play?'

'I was the Devil, or rather, one of the demons. I was the *diable golut*, or greedy devil, because I was a fat little kid. I used to come on stage and say: "*Jo sóc el diable golut / I amb les meves temptacions/ no es poden comptar/ oh, no! / els homes que jo he perdut.*"* Every demon represented a capital sin: for example, the boy playing Lust had to put on a lascivious leer – but not too lascivious, because the director, Señor Solé, was a real church mouse. Those were dark days. I got the part because I was on the plump side.'

'And I was the Virgin Mary, and my husband, may he rest in peace, who was already a jeweller, got to play the Archangel Michael, because he was a big lad and the Roman armour looked so good on him. I was a slip of a girl with a wasp waist in those days. The archangels were dressed as Romans, and that always surprised me. Why should the archangels be dressed as the people who were oppressing the Jews, and Jesus even? It was like dressing them up as Civil Guards.'

'In those days everyone was in uniform. They all had one, and I guess that even Catalan archangels had something of the Franco regime about them.'

Then he saw the two youths coming out again, so he quickly apologised to the widow as if he suddenly remembered he had to go.

'I'm sorry I couldn't help you over darnel. In Catalan it's called *zit'zània* or *jull* or *c'àgola*, by the way. Remember that for another time.'

The youths were only fifty metres ahead of him, but they were walking towards two motorbikes parked on the pavement. Carvalho climbed into a convenient taxi, and told the driver to wait until the bikes drove off and then follow at least one of them.

'Like in the movies?'

---

* I am the greedy devil / and with my temptations / the number cannot be counted/ of men I have destroyed.

'Yes, I'm a spy.'

The taxi-driver peered at him dubiously through the rear-view mirror.

'Spying has changed a lot,' Carvalho explained. 'I follow people who arrive late for work, for example, so they can be sacked without compensation.'

'It's a dirty job.'

'Somebody has to do it. That's the modern world and savage capitalism for you.'

All at once the carol they used to sing at the climax of *Els Pastorets* or *L'adveniment de l'infant Jesús* popped into his mind: '*El mes de maig ja ha vingut, sense ser-hi encara*.'* He remembered too the blasphemous version the rowdy neighbourhood boys who had joined Catholic Action so they could play table-tennis used to sing instead: '*El desembre congelat / m'ha glaçat la fava / al matí quan m'he llevat / no me la trobava*.'†

'I think one of them is stopping,' said the taxi-driver.

'You stop as well, then.'

One of the youths got off his bike in Plaza de San Jaume, and Carvalho got out of the taxi. He followed the youngster down Calle Ciutat, but then he turned into Plaza San Just and walked straight on down a narrow alleyway and entered a medieval palace whose huge gateway was wide open. The former coachyard had two staircases leading off it, one to the right, the other to the left. Although there was no noise from the youngster's trainers to tell him which he had chosen, a kind of vacuum left behind by a body moving through space told Carvalho where he had gone, and he started up the right-hand one after him. The motorcyclist was two floors ahead of Carvalho now, and was already going into an apartment, so Carvalho clambered up as quickly as he could, and found himself in front of another open door. He pushed to see whether it was really open, and poked his head into the darkness inside. He felt himself suddenly shoved from behind, and could not prevent himself falling to the floor. He raised his arms to protect his head

* The month of May is here, even though it is not time.
† Cold December winds
Have frozen off my willy
When I got up this morning
I didn't half look silly.

against any blows, and kicked out at a possible attacker. His kicks flailed the darkness, which soon disappeared. A bright ceiling light revealed him on his knees, surrounded by four young men dressed as summer motorcyclists: Calvin Klein T-shirts, jeans and trainers. One of them was carrying a baseball bat, but another clicked the safety catch off a gun, and Carvalho expected the barrel to be pressed against his head or his neck. What he had expected happened: when he felt the pressure of the metal O against the side of his head, he asked:

'Can I stand up?'

Nobody said he could not, but the gun followed his movements. He waited for someone to say something, but when no one did, he felt obliged to introduce himself.

'I'm Pepe Carvalho. I'm a private detective.'

Still none of them said a word, and the silence continued until a door opened on the left-hand side of the room. A man wearing a tracksuit appeared, looking annoyed. He came over to Carvalho and inspected him with a look halfway between neutral and disgusted.

'Why did you follow these boys? Are you a pervert?'

'I don't know why you say I followed them.'

'You followed them here from Lluquet i Rovelló, where you went in to ask about a herb, darnel to be precise. Hardly a very common interest.'

'I had an anarchist great-uncle, who used to sell peanuts at the Monumental bullring, and plants were his passion. I think he was a vegetarian and a theosophist.'

'Who told you about Lluquet i Rovelló?'

'*De bon matí quan els estels es ponen . . .*'*

He had succeeded in disconcerting the man in the tracksuit.

'You didn't say that in the chemist's. All you did was pry. Who told you the password?'

'Who could it have been? What I wanted to do was see the lie of the land, and spot any possible weaknesses. Such as, for example, two youngsters coming in and heading for the back of the shop as if they were part of the family.'

'They are part of the family.'

But tracksuit man was angry, and not at Carvalho. He started

* At dawn, when the stars begin to fade . . .

swearing in Catalan, and accusing someone of being a busybody who had no respect for other people's territory, who had no idea of how to delegate, and . . . *així no anem enlloc.** One of the supposed motorcyclists tried to calm him down.

'*Son coses d'en Quimet. Ja el coneixes.*'†

'*Quin collons de servei d'informació és aquest?*'††

Realising he had said too much, he fell silent, and gestured to the others to leave. When he was alone with Carvalho, he invited him to follow him to a small, windowless room that was empty apart from two chairs and a map of the territory of Catalonia that filled half a wall.

'When were you asked to join?'

'I'm still in the process.'

'Don't you speak Catalan?'

'Not usually. But you go ahead.'

'No, I like to practise my Spanish as well. My father was from Jaén in Andalusia, but to hear him, he's more of a Catalan nationalist than I am. We're all in the same boat, señor . . . what did you say your name was?'

'Carvalho.'

'Of course! You're Pepe Carvalho. You must give me your autograph, otherwise my wife will never believe I've met you. Well, as I was saying, there are more and more of us climbing on board the same boat, but where is it taking us?'

'We live in uncertain times.'

'You're right there. And we'll live through astonishing changes. I can even see the end of the American empire, which would be a disaster because it would leave us without a fundamental deterrent force, and complete anarchy could break out. Before that happens, the new national structures have to be solidly cemented. The crisis of monopoly capitalism can be resolved if small-scale enterprise can take its place, don't you think? The same can be said of the crisis of the superpowers, and the collapse of the nation-states that have enjoyed hegemony for more than four centuries. The moment for small, repressed and delayed nations will come.'

* That's not going to get us anywhere.
† It's just Quimet. You know what he's like.
†† What kind of fucking intelligence service is this?

They heard voices in the reception room, then Quimet appeared. The man in the tracksuit looked annoyed again, but quickly changed his attitude to one of receiving a superior. Quimet asked Carvalho to follow him. They left the building and went into the first bar they came across, with one of the motorcyclists close behind them. Quimet asked for a tonic water with no alcohol, Carvalho preferred a dry sherry, with as much alcohol as possible, he said. Although there was an undertone of lingering reproach in Quimet's voice, he kept it in check when he took Carvalho to task for not respecting the ritual of the password. It's my way of working, protested Carvalho. I want to get to know the location before the filming starts, and besides, what mostly concerns me is the Mata i Delapeu murder, and I just happened to be passing by the chemist. I'll make a proper visit soon, and say the password.

'Why didn't you tell me so before? We have an office that collects information about all sorts of sects: religious, far right, drugs, preventive corruption.'

'How can corruption be preventive?'

'Let's just say we investigate on our own account alongside the Spanish and Catalan police forces. We investigate cases that could give us a hold over high-ranking people, but we're careful not to make anything public so as not to cause problems for our sovereignty and the weak structures of national power that already exist. They're nearly all extramarital affairs: the flesh is weak. Dirty washing should be done at home. The elections are coming up, and we could lose, so we have to be careful not to be stupid and give our enemies ammunition. We can't let corrupt politicians bring everything tumbling down. But as far as the Mata i Delapeu boy goes, we can point you in the right direction.'

'Do you know Jordi Anfrúns, the sociologist?'

Quimet could pretend the question came as a great surprise, and he did so for several minutes while he tried to work out how Carvalho had managed to link them.

'OK, I can see you like to do things your own way. Anfrúns is an expert on religious affairs, and I make use of his knowledge. That's all there is to it. By the way, do you mind riding pillion on a motorbike?'

When Carvalho shook his head, Quimet left him to go and talk to the motorcyclist, who had stayed at a discreet distance and was drinking a tomato juice. The two of them came back over to Carvalho.

'Here's your driver. He'll take you where you need to go.'

The motorcyclist belonged to the Swerving Kamikaze sect, capable of overtaking any kind of car in any situation, even if it meant ripping off all their wing mirrors and putting up with all the drivers' insults. Carvalho gave up trying to anticipate these mini-catastrophes and instead stared straight ahead at the landscape they seemed continually about to crash into. As he did so, he considered the Carvalhian condition of life, by which a respectable man about to be pensioned off could find himself in the theoretical position of pillion rider on a Suzuki motorbike being driven by a near-adolescent Catalan spy, an adolescent furthermore who was probably sensitive and puritanical, with no other vices than tomato juice, bread smeared with tomato, and tomato salad. It was odd that the two distinguishing characteristics of Catalan identity, bread and tomato and the *sardana* dance, had not become social phenomena until well into the nineteenth century. Both of them were part of Carvalho's emotional identification with Catalonia: from childhood, he had been impressed by the majesty of the dance and the quick-witted solution of smeared bread. The motorbike sped towards the Horta neighbourhood, and finally came to a halt in a street where substantial villas in their own gardens still survived, although several of them already had the signs of demolition companies in evidence. But the motorbike pulled up in front of one that looked as though it would survive, and its sign was an invitation to mystery: Enigma Ltd. How could an enigma become a limited company?

They clambered up half a dozen worn marble steps and went into a long corridor off which branched lots of small rooms. Here the signs read: Salvation Army, Pentecostals, Jehovah's Witnesses, Plymouth Brethren, Scientology and Rosicrucians, Spiritualists, Quakers, Children of God, Satanists, New Age Design, Catharism, Islamists, Orientals and EPC. It looked as though they had come

to the floor of religious boutiques in El Corte Inglés, Macy's or
Galeries Lafayette. The motorcyclist asked him to wait, and disappeared into the room marked EPC. He soon came out accompanied by a priest in a cassock. He was a small, plump man who
muttered something incomprehensible that Carvalho guessed was
aimed at him. The priest chose the satanists' door and showed
Carvalho inside. The room contained only two chairs, the
inevitable computer, and rows of filing cabinets. At work in one of
the chairs was a girl who apart from her red hair bore such a striking resemblance to the priest that she could only be his daughter
or niece. The priest had obviously realised this, because he introduced her:

'This is Neus, my niece.'

To judge by the dedicated way she was trying to put something
into or get something out of the computer, Neus was an extremely
hard worker.

'Print the Ruidoms affair out for me.'

Neus's fingers did not leave the keyboard for an instant until the
printer started to spew out the sheets of paper with an asthmatic
cough. The priest picked up the pile and, handling them as though
they were a top-secret report on the imminent bombing of Iraq or
Kosovo, peered at them and started circling some words with a red
pencil. Then he gestured for Carvalho to come over, and started
explaining things in a low, continuous voice that made it sound as
though he were praying.

'Manelic said you can read the whole report.'

Manelic? Who on earth was Manelic? But the priest did not
seem fazed by Carvalho's bewilderment.

'You should pay particular attention to what I've circled in red.
If there's anything Neus can help you with, just ask. And if she
can't help you, come and find me in my room.'

As the reverend left the office, Carvalho sat down, noting that
Neus had given him a quick sizing-up. She had pretty if myopic
eyes, their pupils accentuated by lenses, and a freckled skin.
Carvalho read the short report twice, jotting down what was most
useful to him: Lucifer's Witnesses, a satanic sect founded by
Albert Pérez i Ruidoms based on the theory that with the fall of
the so-called Rebel Angel, the light of the world went out, and will
return only when a new negation is made of a negative civilisation

in which the Good is defined solely in terms of its contradistinction to Evil, which is all that really exists. Lucifer therefore had a symbolically subversive dimension, which in turn meant that the sect called for the creation of a network of civil disobedience and tried to be part of all the anti-globalisation and neo-anarchist movements. After describing Pérez i Ruidoms as its only significant leader, and the murder victim Alexandre Mata i Delapeu as his significant other, the report dismissed the killing as a settling of accounts between powerful economic groups, and left clarification of the case to this Manelic figure. Could he be Quimet? The man in the tracksuit? The priest? The report summarised all this in only five pages, then devoted a further ten to the position of Lucifer's Witnesses with regard to Catalan nationalist claims and stateless nations, with frequent references to Manelic as an authority. In other words, the key to it all was Manelic.

'Do you know Manelic?'

'I beg your pardon?'

The redhead had jumped merely at being spoken to.

'In the report the reverend gave me, it speaks of someone called Manelic, and I was asking whether you might be able to put me in touch with him.'

'I don't know who he is. All I do is look after the Internet.'

'You need to get out of that net: you're very pale. As soon as I find out who Manelic is, I'm going to have a swim at Barceloneta or the Olympic Village. Wouldn't you like to come?'

One of two things, thought Carvalho: either she looks down her nose at you because of your age, or she blushes and laughs. Neus blushed and giggled.

'It's free and it does you good. Perhaps not today, because I have my suspicions that it's not going to be that easy to find this Manelic fellow, but maybe tomorrow . . . what time do you get off work?'

'I don't have a set time.'

'You decide, then. How about two o'clock?'

'Fine.'

She seemed amazed at the words coming out of her mouth.

'I'll come and pick you up.'

'No, no. We're not supposed to meet people here. I'll meet you wherever you say.'

'At the Mapfre Tower at two then. Wear your swimsuit – under your clothes, I mean, because otherwise you'll have to change in the car park. You can use my car. What's your name?'

'Margalida.'

'Your uncle said you were called Neus.'

She raised a hand to her mouth to stifle another giggle.

'It's my *nom de guerre*.'

'I wouldn't mind betting that if you're not Neus, your uncle isn't your uncle either, even though you look alike. How did you manage it? Do you have a genetic engineering laboratory in the basement? Anyway, I like the name Margalida. It's a nice name. In the days when I was a cultured person I knew a song in Catalan about a very unfortunate Margalida. Then I lost all my culture and now all I like to do is go to the beach in summer and in winter to cook meals until late into the night. Do you like to eat well?'

'And to cook. I did the courses at the Hoffman School, and I've been to several conferences on Catalan food.'

So the redhead was more than just a pretty face. But still, her uncle was probably the one to ask about Manelic. Carvalho went and knocked on the EPC door. The priest's voice invited him in. He was no longer dressed like a priest, but wore a tropical shirt, summer jeans and a pair of sandals he looked perfectly at home in. He obviously had a gift for transformation, and Carvalho suddenly remembered a cartoon character called Mortadelo who could change into a lamp–post or an earthworm as the case demanded.

'The report helped clear up a lot of things, but it suggests I need to talk to someone called Manelic.'

'Why would that be?'

'It's more or less public knowledge that the reason for the Mata i Delapeu boy's death is a fight between different pressure groups, but his mother wants me to discover who actually killed her son. She wants to look him in the eye and ask: "Why did you kill my son?" She's someone who still believes in the tragic sense of life, a Spanish belief I thought was already defunct, especially in Catalonia. Apparently, the murderer was a hired killer, but I can't go back to my client and tell her: Señora, your son was killed by a professional. I have to be able to give her something more. Reasons. The people behind the crime. And I was thinking Manelic would be able to help.'

'Manelic is under cover. You must be aware that this isn't a ramblers' association, and we've had enough fun poked at us in the past. We aim to be a serious organisation investigating spiritual groups. But I'll help as much as I can. I'll get in touch with you to put you on Manelic's track.'

The audience was over. Halfway out into the corridor, Carvalho turned and pointed to the letters on the frosted glass door.

'EPC. Is that something to do with the Inland Revenue?'

The transformer grunted and replied tersely:

'Església Països Catalans. If you don't understand Catalan, it means: Church of the Territory of Catalonia.'

The EPC transformer had not been in touch, and there was nothing from his weird fax correspondent. She must really have gone on holiday, and he had no reason to tell her he was not doing the same. That meant at least a fortnight of silence and peace. Perhaps if she had a good holiday, she wouldn't bother him any more. He put on his swimming trunks, and avoided Biscuter's question about whether he had met up with Charo.

'She's called you two or three times.'

That sounded like a reproach. Biscuter was worried Carvalho was going to ruin his vocation as a go-between.

'There's no point forcing things.'

'I understand, boss. I wanted to tell you that when I finish the course I'm taking on "Globalisation and Underdevelopment" I'm going to sign up for another one on the Cathars.'

'On what?'

'It's a great and ancient religion that defends the poor against the rich and rejects all hierarchies. Besides, the Cathars bathed more than other Christians, which meant they were cleaner, and you know what a fanatic I am for cleanliness. And they also hated killing animals: whenever they found one in a trap, they would open it, let the animal out, and pay the hunter compensation. What do you make of that?'

'A religion is still a religion. *Tu quoque*, Biscuter!'

'But according to what I've heard, this one hated evil even more than the others. It was like a religious anarchism *avant la lettre*. I was given a pamphlet on them in the metro by a young Cathar girl. She had long blonde tresses, but you know the saying: *touchez pas la femme blanche*.'

Ever since he had attended a course on soups and sauces in Paris in 1992, Biscuter loved using French expressions.

'Now there's no more communism, boss, and we can no longer expect Khrushchev and La Pasionaria to arrive on a motorbike and save us, perhaps we have to find another way. Do you remember Lausín? The bank robber we met in jail? You must do – he was like Spiderman, he could climb any wall. Well, he used to say that one day Khrushchev and La Pasionaria would come on a motorbike and get us all out of there.'

Carvalho did remember. Lausín had a strange belief that Khruschev and La Pasionaria would come and spring him from jail or help him end his life of crime. What had always been and still was a mystery was why on earth they should arrive at the Modelo jail on a motorbike. Especially La Pasionaria, who always wore long skirts.

'Well, Lausín is getting on a bit now, but he's become a Cathar.'

'It sounds to me as though you ought to sign up for "Citizens for Change".'

'Yes, I have signed up for them too, boss. There are elections coming up, and I'd love to get rid of Pujol and the Catalan nationalists. I'm as Catalan as the next man, but I can't stand all that nationalism. Why do nationalists have to be so nationalistic? Why is that all they ever talk about?'

Carvalho shrugged his shoulders, offering that as a catch-all response to everything Biscuter had mentioned. His nostrils were full of the combined smell of incense and sulphur. Everyone had gone mad, as if the whole world had returned to a deep-seated Manichaeism between God and the Devil, as if any other attempt to explain the horror or the stupidity of merely surviving in order to die had failed, apart from religious or tribal fundamentalism. The appeal of the sea in summer offered him a strictly non-religious pleasure for which he needed no ideological persuasion. What he wanted was a purely tactile satisfaction from sun and water, his only belief being that what was most profound about men and some women was their skin. The fake niece of the fake priest was waiting for him. As freckled and redheaded as twenty-four hours earlier, but liberated from her job as spy in civilian clothes, and therefore with bare shoulders, cleavage and miniskirt. As they headed for the ramps that led up to the esplanade behind the various beaches, it was obvious she was excited at the idea of bathing in such a sociable sea, surrounded by all these ordinary people, the most bilingual she had been among in a long while. When Carvalho suggested they go down to Mar Bella beach, she agreed enthusiastically, and as soon as she had laid out her towel on the sand, she took off her miniskirt and top and was left in only half a bikini and tits – splendid round, bouncy ones that imposed their white and freckle-free presence on the beach, even among the diehard homosexuals. Too young, thought Carvalho. She must look like my granddaughter. He could not help glancing surreptitiously around to see whether everyone looking at Margalida was thinking she was his granddaughter or a geriatric nurse.

'I can't sunbathe too long because my skin is so pale,' she said, smearing on some sunblock that give a bright sheen to her skin and especially her tits, which seemed almost too much of a handful for her. When she was properly protected, she lay on her back and smiled through closed eyelids, as if telling herself something pleasurable. Carvalho had stretched out beside her, leaning up on one elbow and trying not to look at her, until she spoke and he was forced to turn in her direction. Her myopic eyes were open.

'What did you want me to tell you, Pepe?'

So they were on first-name terms.

'What do you mean?'

'There can't have been any other reason to invite me to the beach with you. There's something you want to know. Listen, Pepe, if you want me to be straight with you, you have to be straight with me. I'm not blind.'

'Does everyone who comes to your sanctuary invite you down to the beach just to pump you for information?'

'Not many people get to see the sanctuary. If they let you in, there must have been a reason.'

'What are you doing there? Building a nation?'

'Earning a living.'

'So you're not a patriot.'

'I'm on a three-month contract. If they like my work, they'll renew it. If not, I'm out on the street.'

That's no way to treat any member of the intelligence services, thought Carvalho. Afterwards you get only double and triple agents, disgruntled people who sell their information to the Neapolitan or Andalusian or Galician or Serbian or Ethiopian spy network. Anyway, this was too much of a caricature to be true.

'You have what I might almost call feminine intuition. I'm very interested in Manelic. Who is he?'

'I can't say for sure, I only have my suspicions. Up there nobody is who they say they are, or does what they say they do. Theoretically we're a service collecting information about sects, and we are not supposed to be directly connected to the autonomous police, but I'm not even certain of that.'

Why had it all been so easy for him? Simply because of the link between Charo and Quimet? Or because we are a country of six million people where everyone knows everyone else and it's impossible to hide a thing, even from spies? The girl had no opinion on this, and listened to Carvalho with an attitude of strict neutrality. Margalida spent longer in the sea than in sunbathing, and afterwards he followed her to the public shower, then she allowed herself to be taken for a lobster and rice in Barceloneta at Can Solé, a restaurant that had stayed faithful to the aesthetics of a fisherman's village and prices that corresponded to a standard of living from ten years earlier. Its owner occasionally called Carvalho when he had *espardenyes** on the menu, because they gave the final touch to a substantial rice dish with squid and browned onion. Margalida obviously liked her food and her drink. She looked on amused while Carvalho tried to restrict his own consumption of wine and kept filling her glass instead.

'You've got a bit of the old-fashioned womaniser about you, haven't you?'

'Why do you say that?'

'Because you're trying to get me drunk. To get me to talk. Perhaps to get me to go to bed with you?'

Too clever by half.

'I can't see you and I going to bed together.'

'Why?'

'Because you look too healthy to me, like one of those girls who before you've even unzipped your flies have slapped a condom on you. And I demand unprotected sex.'

That had given her pause for thought.

'You do it without a condom? What about Aids?'

'If love is Russian roulette, why shouldn't sex be too? If I have

* Sea cucumbers.

to wear a condom, it feels so distant I can't even get a hard-on. It's as though they were stigmatising my poor little prick. I can understand that for sexual athletes of your age it's important not to get infected so that you can go on voting in election after election and build a nation, have children and wave banners until death do you part. But I have no urgent nation to build, I don't vote, and I've no banners left. I prefer to eat and fuck dangerously. When I get the chance.'

What seemed to him like an affectionate gleam appeared in Margalida's myopic eyes.

'You're not just old fashioned, you're a fossil.'

Carvalho shrugged, and said:

'You must find out lots of things in your line of work.'

'I only work with the satanists.'

'So you must know everything about the Pérez i Ruidoms or Mata i Delapeu case.'

'Have you heard of Mont Pelerin?'

'No.'

'Even though he's a satanist, the boy is a saint. His father is something else. Pérez i Ruidoms senior is part of a group calling itself Mont Pelerin. It's made up of businessmen, university professors, bankers and politicians, and they're all connected to a sect or something similar called the Trilateral. On the surface, Mont Pelerin is a select private club, for businessmen and their families too. They throw high-society parties: the kind where they charge fifty thousand pesetas just to get in. They're having one soon to celebrate the end of summer. But that's just a cover. So is the Milton Friedman Club, where similar people meet, but ones who support Mata i Delapeu rather than Pérez i Ruidoms and his cronies. The two groups fight for power at every level: in the political parties, banking institutions and even in Barcelona Football Club. Alexandre Mata i Delapeu's murderer is about to be caught, but he's not the real murderer. Have you heard of Dalmatius? No? You haven't heard of anyone. Where have you been?'

'In the transition after Franco.'

'In the Flood, then. Dalmatius is the organiser behind all the hired killers. It's not just one person. It's a group which is in charge of hitmen who are usually recruited in eastern Europe. They bring them over here. They beat people up. Kill. Rape. Set fire to a business. Then disappear. And when the police need to arrest someone to close a file, Dalmatius also has a list of people who will swallow the pill in order to stay in Spain. While they're being tried and sentenced they are here, even if it's only in jail, and so they gain time. But I've said too much. Do you take me for a double agent or something?'

He took her for an easy agent. Too easy. They walked back to the Mapfre Tower car park where she had left her motorbike, and as she said goodbye, Margalida kissed him on the lips and stuck her tongue into his mouth. Her tongue seemed to be as plentiful as her tits, which was something Carvalho found distasteful. Big tongues had always seemed to him spongy and too juicy, as if they were better suited to some cannibal stew, or even a tongue *carpaccio*, than a proper kiss. He waited for her to enter the car park, then ran out to the road. He flagged down a taxi, but kept looking back to the ticket machine to see whether she came out on her bike. She did not appear. So he paid off the furious taxi-driver, and ran to the escalator that led up to the level where the Talaia restaurant was situated. He arrived just in time to see Margalida emerge from the lift and walk towards the beaches and the Olympic Village. Carvalho followed her to the ticket offices for the Icaria multiplex screens, where the inevitable Anfrúns was waiting for her.

He could have sworn that Anfrúns had seen him and smiled a smile meant only for himself. Then the couple disappeared into one of the five thousand cinemas.

He tried desperately to follow the boy flying towards the rockets, with *mistus Garibaldis* in one hand and in the other a stone covered in gunpowder. It was Carvalho himself, half a century earlier. St John's Eve. The smell of cheap, post-war gunpowder. Rockets in the sky, and closer to, firecrackers snapping at the skinny-legged girls. The *Garibaldis* brought sparks from walls, there were a few paper or cardboard volcanoes up on balconies, while bonfires blazed on street corners. Music on the radio:

> *Old gypsy Andres*
> *Got mad as hell*
> *Picked up his wife*
> *Threw her in the well*
> *When asked by the judge*
> *What did this mean*
> *Old Andres replied*
> *She needed a clean.*
> *Oh, Christopher Columbus!*
> *Oh, Christopher Columbus!*
> *What's the world coming to . . .*
> *Oh, Christopher Columbus!*

The gypsies in the Moderno bar paid no attention to the song. They knew they had lost the battle against the white race, the Gorgio to them, around the same time as had the blacks, wolves and ants. Together with sweaty underarms and ginger beer, that smell of cheap gunpowder could well be one of the memories of the Civil War itself. Now in 1999 up in Vallvidrera he could hear a fiesta going on down in El Vallès, and there were rockets shooting high over what was left of the woods at Sant Cugat. That must be the end of the summer party Señor Pérez i Ruidoms was throwing.

But at the same time Carvalho was remembering the celebrations of his childhood, and he could almost taste the cheap nougat señora María made, or the one his mother cooked from a recipe given her by someone who worked in the Sant Antoni market or in the Petitbó cake shop. He came in from the terrace with its view over Barcelona. Charo was fast asleep. There was a half-finished glass of champagne on the bedside table, so Carvalho went back into the living room and found the bottle of Bollinger in its ice bucket. He took a swig straight from the bottle, then put it back into its icy enchantment. He went out through the garden and down on to the street, got into his car and drove to the main square of Vallvidrera. As he was driving past Fuster's place he saw there was a light still on, so he sounded his horn. Fuster's head appeared, looking more tired than in a party mood.

'Having a good time?'

'Pretending to. Where are you off to?'

'I'm on a job.'

'At this time of night?'

'Evil never sleeps. One of these days I must come and talk to you about religion.'

He left Fuster standing there perplexed, and drove on towards the main road to Les Planes and El Vallès. Rockets still exploded in the sky above the woods, like stars of Bethlehem showing him the way. Dogs were howling as if their eardrums had burst, and Carvalho had almost an entire bottle of Bollinger inside him. He passed Vallvidrera railway halt, and turned into the highway towards Sant Cugat. He did not go as far as the town, but ignored the sign and headed along a 'private road', his headlamps opening a tunnel of white vegetation in the black night, with the occasional luminous sign declaring this was the way to 'Can Borau'. The track descended, and almost immediately Carvalho could see an esplanade that served as a car park for up to a hundred cars, with behind it an illuminated farmhouse with a flat roof and battle-ments. This was where the rockets with ambitions of becoming the Milky Way were being launched from. Two security guards came alongside his car.

'Do you have an invite?'

'I've forgotten it, but it was Señor Pérez i Ruidoms who invited me.'

'And your name, please?'

'Pepe Carvalho i Touron.'

They did not seem impressed by the Catalan version of his name, and spoke to somebody on a walkie-talkie. Then they asked him to park away from the other lines of cars, and told him to get out and open the bonnet and boot. By this time another bodyguard had appeared: this one was taller and heavier, and was dressed like the butler from some film about rich people on holiday in the Caribbean. Señor Pérez i Ruidoms was expecting him. It was not true, though: the butler left him in a large room where twenty middle-aged couples were following the rhythm of a small orchestra under a ceiling festooned with coloured streamers, while he went to inform Pérez i Ruidoms. The dancers looked as if they had been hired to dance politely to polite tunes, and their faces were devoid of any sense of enjoyment, much less rapture, even when they occasionally threw confetti or blew on their cardboard trumpets. But the drink and varieties of nougat must be coming from somewhere, so Carvalho followed a waiter and found himself in a hall where the food and drink were being served: a long table full of silver trays of nougat and bottles of spirits and rum, with at each end a cooler where bottles of *cava* were placed and replaced. Carvalho did not know the brand: it must have been one of the new ones that appeared every couple of weeks, the result of an optimistic producer hoping to found a dynasty on the basis of history, land and wine. Since Pérez i Ruidoms had still not put in an appearance, Carvalho ventured down a corridor that led to the quiet room, where couples and quartets were discussing the millennium bug and how they would be spending the end of the century.

'I want to go to where the sun rises for the first time on the new millennium!'

'Wonderful!' exclaimed an elegant lady with that particular drawl of people who have seen too much to be surprised by anything any more. But this was all too normal for a house and party of this size. Carvalho spotted a staircase with a pink granite banister. He climbed it and reached a balustrade looking down on the dance-floor. Beyond the balcony were four closed doors. He opened the first one, and interrupted a meeting of eight men of the sort who are usually given a green light of approval in conservative newspapers. None of them looked like Ruidoms, and all of them made it plain they wanted him to leave, perhaps because they were all sitting with their bare feet in bowls of water. Carvalho went back to surveying the dancers from the balustrade, and soon saw the Caribbean butler emerge from behind a column, obviously in search of someone. Him, probably. He went downstairs and waited for the butler to move on before heading in the direction from which he had first appeared. The column concealed another corridor, at the end of which was a lit flight of stairs. Carvalho started down them, becoming more and more cautious as the sound of voices from down below grew louder. At the last bend in the stairs he stopped to observe the scene in front of him. In the dim light he could make out several figures in dinner jackets grouped in a semicircle around an armchair. Here the Pérez i Ruidoms he knew from the television was seated, the most powerful of the powerful. He was staring up at the skylight in the centre of the ceiling of the circular room, as though waiting for the divine voice to issue forth from there. What it concealed in fact was a small closed-circuit TV camera that Carvalho had not noticed before. Ruidoms had a mask-like face, as if his narrow, bony skull and his beak of a mouth were all fake, and he was so concentrated on what he was about to say that all the others could not take their eyes off him. All at once, however, he turned his head to Carvalho, still half hidden on the stairs, and shouted:

'Come on in, Carvalho, we were expecting you.'

As if this were a signal, the dinner jackets also turned towards Carvalho. They all seemed to have exactly the same features – in their case because they were all wearing the same mask. Carvalho advanced to the centre of the semicircle and came to a halt opposite Pérez i Ruidoms, who was smiling and waiting for some comment on the setting from the detective.

'What do you think of the stage set?'

'It reminds me a bit of the independent theatre I saw when I was ideologically green. Or perhaps a performance of the *Ramayana* I saw in Bali more than thirty years ago. I think it was an assembly of monkeys, who spent the whole time going hu-hu-hu.'

At this, the masked figures stood up and started chanting the hu-hu-hu from the *Ramayana* until Pérez i Ruidoms signalled to them to be quiet and sit down again.

'You asked me to tell you about Mont Pelerin, and here you have it. These gentlemen and I are Mont Pelerin.'

The butler had appeared, carrying a chair. He placed it for Carvalho next to Ruidoms' swivel-chair. As he sat down, there was complete silence, which suggested it was up to him to take the human initiative in what he had called a monkeys' assembly. He could sense the hostility behind their masks, the hostility of important people, and so decided it would be unwise to provoke them still further.

'As I have already informed Señor Pérez i Ruidoms, Señora Mata i Delapeu has hired me to investigate the murder of her son Alexandre. The prime suspect is of course Señor Pérez i Ruidoms own son, who is on bail for a very high sum. As far as I can determine, the crime was committed by a band of hitmen with the aim of discrediting all of you – because as I understand it, I am in the presence of a collective subject which is struggling for control of the world or the presidency of Barcelona Football Club, which amounts to the same thing, especially in a country that has no precise frontiers or easily definable patriotic ambitions.'

'We didn't come here to have you laugh at us.'

One of the masked dinner jackets had stood up, but their host calmed him with a gesture that also invited Carvalho to continue. But the masked marvel had already launched into a refrain:

'Jo sóc català i porto barretina / i a qui em digui res / li tallo la sardina'*

Satisfied, he sat down again obediently, and Carvalho could go on.

'I asked to see you on your own. I had no idea I was being invited to an end-of-summer party.'

'This is not exactly a party. While our families and staff are enjoying themselves upstairs, down here we're discussing the difficult situation we find ourselves in. This is no innocent battle, Carvalho, and our intelligence services have warned us we could be facing another attack.'

'Which you will respond to one of these days, I presume. I don't know whether to be amused or bored by the way this farce is being played out; on the whole I think I find it amusing. But I need a

---

* I am Catalan and I wear my cap / if anyone objects / I'll give him a good slap.

murderer with a face. I need to be able to go back to my client and say to her: this man and that man killed your son on the orders of these others.'

'Is that all? You'll never find out who gave the orders, but we can supply the other information you're after, provided you promise to stop snooping around. We know what you're up to, Carvalho, and we think you're getting out of your depth.'

'I have realised that everybody belongs to one sect or another. And that there are two sorts of sect: the destructive ones, like the satanists, and the constructive ones, like you, the Catholic Church or Opus Dei.'

The masks peered at one another. Only Pérez i Ruidoms kept aloof. Then the masks started chattering in a language that sounded to Carvalho even more exotic than Korean, if in fact he had ever heard Korean being spoken. Pérez i Ruidoms was staring intently into a shadowy corner of the room, a worried look on his face. Then he turned back to Carvalho, and when he spoke, his voice was cold and cutting:

'To be brief. This is not exactly a sect, more a club of friends and followers of Friedrich Hayek. His name will mean nothing to you, but he was one of the most outstanding figures of the twentieth century, one of its most lucid ideologists and strategists. In 1997 he got together a number of intellectuals and politicians in Mont Pelerin in Switzerland to draw up the guidelines for the rebuilding of capitalist pride in the face of the onslaught from communism and Keynesianism against the freedom of initiative, man's most precious freedom. Nowadays there are clubs in Hayek's honour all over the world: at first they showed the line of resistance, then the progress of our reconquest, and now they are the symbol of our victory over the shadows of Marx and Keynes. That is what Mont Pelerin is, and nothing more.'

Another masked marvel stood up and recited his lines as if they were a Christmas thanksgiving speech.

'Two spectres are haunting Europe: communism and Keynesianism. Both of them attempt to destroy mankind's spirit of initiative, that spirit which has made of man the master of creation! If communism had its way, pigs would be our masters; the triumph of Keynes would mean bacteria held sway in the world!'

Carvalho nodded in appreciation of the speaker's oratorical

prowess, then leaned over towards Pérez i Ruidoms so that only he could hear what he wanted to say:

'What does Mont Pelerin have to do with Region Plus?'

For the first time the human mask looked unsettled, and then it was Ruidoms' turn to lean forward and whisper into Carvalho's ear so that none of the others could hear.

'You are right. We need to talk alone.'

He clapped his hands, which led to all other conversation dying away. All the monkeys concentrating on him.

'Gentlemen, you may take your masks off.'

They did so, and none of their faces suggested the least kind of exclusive club or anything of the sort. One of them asked with a strong Cuban accent:

'Hey, when do they serve coffee?'

Another went even further and asked as rudely as he could:

'Mamma! What's that black guy up to?'

'Don't start that again! Russia is to blame! ETA is to blame!' yet another chimed in, suddenly indignant. A fourth monkey took Carvalho aside and whispered:

'Did you know that in the Cretaceous period lots of mammals stopped laying eggs and were able to give birth live to their young? Another vital initiative seen in mammals was the variety and efficacy of their teeth, which enabled them not only to tear and grind, to gnaw and grind, but to hold their food in their mouths and process it by means of innovative methods. So the biological bases of liberalism had already been laid.'

A smile flitted across Pérez i Ruidoms' lips.

'Don't you recognise them, Señor Carvalho? Didn't you recoginse the people upstairs either?'

Carvalho was on his guard, but the last thing he expected was for Ruidoms to double up laughing, though the laughter was not real, because he immediately regained his composure and said:

'Almost all of them come from the La Cubana company, they organise street theatre and events.'

Carvalho started to clap, and went on clapping even when he became aware he was the only one doing so. The others had put their masks back on, and were snoring with that strange synchronised effect only the best monkeys can achieve.

Pérez i Ruidoms skirted round the dancing couples, and Carvalho followed him to an office where a TV set was showing CNN to no audience. Pérez i Ruidoms turned down the sound, but left the pictures on. They hung like a landscape of jagged shadows on the wall. He took a bottle of champagne out of a refrigerator disguised as an imposing sideboard, and showed Carvalho the label:

'Roederer Crystal Rosé.'

He opened it himself, carefully judging the foam and then handing Carvalho his glass. He sipped his own with great pleasure, clicking his tongue.

'Mmm, I needed that. What were we saying? Either Region Plus or the murder of the Mata i Delapeu boy. Or both of them, perhaps. What do you know about Region Plus?'

'What somebody wants me to know. I'm caught up in a story full of conflicting information, but whose common purpose is to create a climate of confusion. Maybe they're all actors from La Cubana, or behave as if they were. I think they're telling me what interests them that I should know, and they're leading me towards something, but I don't know what.'

'You're not moving, you're being moved. It's interesting you've realised that much. What they're moving you towards is Region Plus, which is nothing more than an economic process aimed at building up links between Toulouse, Milan and Barcelona. The money will come from setting up a communications infrastructure and from the increase in value of land and industry. The triangle they form is like the New Frontier, Carvalho, and the shot has been fired for the pioneers' wagons to start rolling. I won't deny that I'm interested in the project, which the autonomous government here supported at first, but has now become lukewarm about. Somebody has put it into our premier's head that it will harm the interests of Catalonia because it would establish a specially designed region that could undermine his nationalist dream. Personally, I couldn't give a damn about the Catalan nationalist dream, but I don't want to get involved in anything that might prejudice the good relations I have with our government.'

'But elections are coming up.'

'Just imagine if Prime Minister Pujol lost. That would mean Catalan nationalism became the opposition, and so would become more radical: Region Plus would be demonised, and turn into a crusade for those radicalised nationalists. I prefer injustice to disorder. No. The project needs to advance quickly, so it can be presented as a *fait accompli*. But I'm not the only one worried about this: all my phones are tapped, and all the spies' telescopes are trained on my house or my companies. I know because I do the same with my competitors, and they don't complain. But you, Carvalho, are all over the place. I want you to concentrate on discovering the reasons behind the murder of my son's friend. I'm willing to pay you out of my own pocket, in addition to what you are getting from Delmira.'

'I never take money from two clients for the same case.'

'But you'll accept this.'

He took an envelope out of the nearest drawer and gave it to Carvalho. The detective took it and opened it, then peered intently at the photographs and sheets of paper in his hand. The first photo showed a round face like a grease-ball, with tiny eyes stuck in the middle. The other two were of a man who looked like a gypsy and a woman with marble-white skin whose oval face was topped by frizzy blonde hair. The sheets of paper confirmed their identities: Dalmatius, leader of the Sarajevo shock troops, Mohamed Stepanovich, and Silvia Rossler, both also from Sarajevo. Dalmatius had been hired to kill a particular individual, and had passed the job on to the other two, without knowing who their target was. The report added that Dalmatius was willing to collaborate to resolve the problem, and to hand over the two hitmen. It also gave the address of the safe house where they were hiding. Carvalho studied their faces. The woman was pretty, but had a look of compliant stupidity in her eyes, the face of a dumb, obedient animal. Mohamed had a dagger deep in each eye, and his cruel mouth was half hidden beneath an old-fashioned Slav violinist's pencil moustache. Dalmatius was the most striking of the three. His face was ugly, but disturbing and imposing.

'Does the information interest you? You're approaching the endgame.'

'They could all be actors from La Cubana.'

'You're right: I love *trompe l'oeil*. If you saw my residences, they're all full of fake walls, windows, ceilings, fake arches and steps down into cellars that may or may not exist: sometimes I forget which is which. Would you like to speak to Dalmatius?'

Carvalho nodded.

'Follow me.'

They seemed to be going back the way they had come and aiming for the Mont Pelerin room, but they carried on beyond it until Pérez i Ruidoms came to a halt in front of a mural depicting a hotel bedroom, a bed, a washbasin, and a man sitting on the edge of a bed who had no face, or at least did not look sufficiently interesting to tempt the viewer to see whether he had one or not.

'That's a wonderful copy of a Hopper.'

Pérez i Ruidoms touched the man's face with his finger and the wall dissolved, folding back on itself to reveal a room where the only light came from a spot in the middle of the ceiling, pointed down towards a figure on a chair. When they got closer, Carvalho could see that the figure was handcuffed, that it was Dalmatius, and that someone had done serious damage to his eyebrows and nose. One of his eyelids hung down over a bulging purple cheekbone, and the whole of his swollen face was covered in bruises and skin flayed to the bone. Pérez i Ruidoms walked round and round him, studying him closely.

'Not much longer to go, Dalmatius. Soon you'll either be going home or to hell. Just confirm for my friend here that these two were the ones who killed Mata i Delapeu.'

He gestured for Carvalho to put the photos in front of Dalmatius' face. The tortured head moved slowly up and down three times in agreement. Pérez i Ruidoms was satisfied. He pushed his face into Dalmatius's line of vision.

'Take a good look at me, and register my face in your brain. You do the work you have to do, but stay out of my way. Live in your own sewers, but don't even dream of straying into mine. I can

adopt the same game rules as you, but for every butcher you
employ, I can hire ten.'

Despite the physical beating Dalmatius had taken, he still had
his wits about him. Carvalho could tell he was studying him, trying to place him, and had probably even worked out who he was.
He was the kind of person who in even the most extreme situation
could take things in: Dalmatius knew what to expect from Pérez i
Ruidoms, but was not so sure about Carvalho, and so kept his
bloody eyes on him the whole time as they left the room.

'You can do what you like with the information I gave you. By
now the police will have received a tip-off about where the killers
are holed up.'

'Was it them?'

'They're the ones Dalmatius fingered.'

Without another word, Pérez i Ruidoms left Carvalho's side and
went out into the car park, where a limousine with a chauffeur and
two bodyguards was already waiting for him. Carvalho walked
across to his own car, which was still separate from the others, as if
someone had deliberately wanted to draw attention to the fact that
it was the kind of old beaten-up car a predictable detective like him
would drive. He was so predictable in fact that they had prepared
all this just for him, down to the last detail, like a celebration of
simulation. What if Dalmatius had been a fake too? And the two
scapegoats? According to the report he had read, they were hiding
in an apartment in Poble Sec, on Calle Salvà at the corner with
Parallel Avenue, and the police were on their trail. Carvalho sped
down the highway at what seemed to him like cinematographic
speed, heading for Barcelona and Poble Sec. There was heavy
traffic in both directions: people trying to get out of the centre of
the city, and those trying to get in. He reached Plaza de España
then went down the avenue until he reached Poble Sec metro. He
left his car in a car park near the Condal theatre, less than a block
from where Mohamed and the marble-skinned woman were
located. The police had already arrived on the scene, and a searchlight was trained on a third-floor window of the building. Carvalho
stood behind the crowd of curious onlookers whom the police were
shouting at and pushing away from the security cordon they had
put up around their prey.

'Someone's been killed,' said a little man who was so much a nocturnal animal that his skin was as pale as the moon, his veins as dark as night itself. A volley of shots rang out from inside the building, and the police pushed back the crowd even more forcefully. As Carvalho was struggling to get to the front, two men pushed alongside him.

'Lifante wants to see you.'

Flanked by the two men, Carvalho was taken to the inspector, who was standing staring up at the searchlight beam while at the same time listening to messages coming through an earpiece. He looked Carvalho up and down with polite curiosity, then headed for the apartment block followed by the detective. Nobody tried to stop Carvalho going in. They walked up two flights of stairs, meeting more Rambo-style policemen on the way, and finally reached an apartment where the door hung loose like a dislocated shoulderblade. The police here looked weary, and Lifante made his way into the room, apparently oblivious to Carvalho's presence. The two bodies lay on the living-room floor. In the middle, the woman lay with her legs splayed out from her miniskirt. She had been shot in the mouth, and her frizzy hair stood on end as if it had been petrified. The man looked like a puppet that had collapsed on to itself. There was a puddle of blood behind his back, as if it had trickled out of his arse.

'Resisting arrest?'

'Obviously.'

Lifante shrugged, a gesture aimed solely at Carvalho. He gave orders for nothing to be touched until the investigating magistrate arrived, then, without looking at his impromptu sidekick, said:

'You have a very strange way of guessing at happy endings.'

'I heard the shots.'

'All the way up in Vallvidrera?'

'I happened to be down this way.'

Lifante looked tired and frustrated. He had probably not even eaten, thought Carvalho, and someone was going to pay for it.

'We need to talk, Carvalho. Right now.'

Chapter 3

The café that sold cold *horchata* in the Ronda de Sant Pau was open. In summer this was the only place where you could get the drink made with hazelnuts, although Carvalho preferred the *horchatería* in the Calle Parlament that had been his mother's favourite. Two days before she died, Carvalho had asked her the rhetorical question:

'What would you like me to bring you?'

She postponed her wish to die as soon as possible in order to think this over, then dragged herself back from the remote corner where she kept her last wishes stored, and asked:

'Could I have *horchata* and peaches?'

Neither of them was in season, but for years afterwards Carvalho cursed himself for not rushing out into the street to find some *horchata* and peaches, or a bunch of violets, if she had asked him for them in December. Besides, he could have found *horchata* and peaches if he had really tried, but it was too sad to carry out what may not even have been his mother's real last wish, but something that was her last answer instead. Lifante was so amazed at the hazelnut *horchata* that he managed to fill ten minutes of conversation with it, until the policeman in him resurfaced and he warned Carvalho that loyalty to his client, Señora Mata i Delapeu – which I know all about, Carvalho, we're keeping our eye on you – should not prevent him explaining what he was doing here on the very night the police were closing in on the suspects.

'And now you're going to tell me it was a "hunch", because you, Carvalho, are a slave to your character, and a character like you would say: "I had a hunch".'

'I like you, Lifante. You're an intellectual policeman, you never say "balls", for example. Old Contreras would have leaned over, breathed in my face, and told me he was going to cut my balls off, or that I shouldn't touch his balls. You were going to be a semiotician, weren't you?'

'A semiologist.'

'Something to be proud of.'

'Carvalho, I still want to know what you were doing in the right place at the right time. And in Lluquet i Rovelló? And snooping round the Horta Vatican?'

'The Horta Vatican?'

'That's what I call that centre investigating religious sects set up by services more or less controlled by the Catalan government.'

'So you keep everything under strict surveillance.'

'That's our job.'

'Who against?'

'Not against, on behalf of our citizens.'

'Anyone in particular? Do you have the prototype in some Museum of Mankind or other?'

'Every state has its citizens as their reference point, whether they call it the Common Good or the Community of Interest. But we always mean the ordinary citizen, the common denominator of citizens – of Spanish citizens, that is.'

'In other words, someone exactly like you.'

Lifante's great advantage was that he never got impatient. He sat there sipping his *horchata*, then suddenly burst into tears. But the tears came only from one eye, and he pressed a finger against his nasal cavity.

'This hurts like hell. It's when the cold gets up my nose.'

Carvalho expressed his sympathy, and recalled how it had happened to him several times as well. It took the inspector some time to recover, and as he was about to pick up the thread again, Carvalho decided the best answer might be a question:

'Did those two put up so much resistance you had to kill them both?'

Lifante did not like the question: ample proof, thought Carvalho, that it was not true that there was no such thing as a bad answer, only stupid questions.

'Are you saying we murdered them?'

'You weren't there at the time.'

'So are you saying, then, that my men kill on their own, obeying orders from a power over which I have no control?'

'It happens in all the best police forces. I've seen it at the pictures. Nowadays I always go to the cinemas in the Olympic Village. It's easy, all I have to do is drive down from Vallvidrera on the Ronda de Dalt, turn on the Ronda del Litoral, and in ten minutes I'm on the beach or at the cinema. Have you ever been swimming at the new Barcelona beaches?'

Lifante stared down at his arms as if to confirm their off-white colour, the only colour available to someone cooped up in a badly ventilated office all day. When he looked up again at Carvalho, he wagged a finger in his face. Don't get in too deep, Carvalho. You don't know the half of what's going on here. Leave this kind of thing to the professionals. This is a fight between three or four gangs, and even after what happened here tonight, the Mata i Delapeu case isn't solved. Carvalho listened intently, like a student taking notes from a lesson that was not only useful but masterful. Lifante was increasing the sense of uncertainty he felt all around him. Who was who? And what was what?

'Carvalho, the Spain of autonomous regions is a wonderful invention, but like all wonderful inventions, it depends on the use to which it's put. Look at atomic energy. It's a great discovery, but what has it been used for? An autonomous state could signal the beginning of the end for Spain, or it could mean the possibility of a new, more harmonious country. Besides that, there is serious concern internationally about movements like Stateless Peoples or Nations, because they could become the termite eating away at Europe at a particularly delicate moment in its construction, above all in the construction of a unified military force that our fellow countryman Javier Solana is so anxious to see. How can Europe expect to have a serious deterrent force if it has to use its troops to police subversive movements within its own borders? Do you get my drift? Do you see how complicated everything is?'

'So why is there so much religion mixed up in all this?'

This was the question Lifante had been waiting for, and his satisfaction spread from his smiling eyes to the way he let his plump body sink back into the welcoming arms of his chair.

'Because religion is the opiate of the people.'

He saw at once the mocking look in Carvalho's eyes, and became serious again.

'By that I mean religion which isn't religion, of course. I mean superstitions, sects, all that sort of thing. God-given religions are a different kettle of fish.'

Carvalho was beginning to tire of listening to Lifante, and looked down at his watch. Lifante too seemed to have little desire to go on educating him. They said goodbye, Lifante doing nothing more than raise an eyebrow, which Carvalho did on the other side so that he couldn't be accused of aping him. He bought a litre of *horchata* and went to rescue his car. When he reached Vallvidrera, Charo was awake. It was the middle of the night, and she was wearing an old bathrobe of Carvalho's. Still full though starting to droop, one of her breasts was bare, its purple veins standing out around the timid nipple. Charo covered herself, and looked at Carvalho with sad, sleepy eyes.

'Where did you get to?'

'I went to see a performance the La Cubana company put on. It was in several places. It began in Sant Cugat, and ended in a *horchatería* on Ronda de Sant Pau.'

'*Horchata!* How I'd love some right now!'

Carvalho handed her the bottle, and her face lit up. Carvalho made a resolution always to have a bottle of *horchata* with him. Never again would he disappoint anyone by not having *horchata* to offer them. *Horchata* and peaches. Charo was savouring her drink.

'I forgot to tell you that Quimet is very keen for you to call in at Lluquet i Rovelló tomorrow.'

When Carvalho entered Lluquet i Rovelló he felt once again he was returning to his childhood herbalist. His eyes automatically sought out the shelves lined with jars inscribed with the names of all the medicinal herbs. The good-looking widow was not there, but instead he was attended by a discreet punk with mostly blonde hair apart from the occasional purple strand that denoted her subversive attitude. Carvalho whispered: *De bon matí quan els estels se ponen*, and the girl spoke into a walkie-talkie. A few moments later, Quimet, as smiling and freshly showered as ever, came out from behind a curtain. At the same time, the street door opened and in came the man in the tracksuit. He was sweating as if he had been in a race against himself. He started staring at the porcelain jars as though he were fascinated to know what they contained. Quimet gestured to the assistant to close the street door, pulled down a blind that prevented anyone seeing what was going on inside the shop, and asked Carvalho to put the blindfold on again. In the darkness, Carvalho tried to make out any sounds that might tell him what was going on, but all he felt was an arm guiding him some ten steps forward. When the hood was removed, he found they had gone through the wall lined with porcelain herbal jars. In the room sat a dozen people, who greeted Quimet with great respect. He showed Carvalho to a chair facing the others, who sat there as if paralysed, without so much as blinking. The man in the tracksuit appeared from behind Carvalho and sat next to him in a seat that seemed so used to him it looked more as if he were wearing it than sitting in it. Quimet was even more wrapped up in himself, in his essential fussy neatness, but managed to invite the tracksuit man to speak.

'Listen carefully to him, Caravalho, he'll be telling you basic things about what we'd like you to do for us. His name is Xibert –

that's all you need to know for now. He will give you the background to what we're trying to achieve.'

Xibert had a heavy jaw and muscular shoulders. He looked unenthusiastically across at Carvalho and laid out his stall right from the start.

'Catalan nationalism does not aspire to statehood.'

He paused to see the effect these words had on those present, and Quimet closed his eyes, inviting him to carry on.

'That is the only way I have of explaining why the need for an intelligence service that would serve a Catalan state has never been raised. When it's said of a Catalan politician that he "aspires to statehood", that means the Spanish state. We cannot have an army or a foreign policy, but what is there to prevent us having our own intelligence services? The Basques are sixty years ahead of us. As soon as the Civil War was over they set up an intelligence service that operated in two directions: towards Nazi Germany and towards the United States, in case either of them could help the cause of Basque independence. Aguirre, who was the Basque leader throughout the republic, the war and the period of exile, wasted three weeks in Berlin trying to enlist support from Hitler or any other Nazis he could meet for the cause of Basque independence. And Irala and Aguirre used Galíndez to work on the US State Department in the forties and fifties, and practically right up to the return of democracy in Spain. When Madrid decided to set up the autonomous regions, my bosses sent me to the Basque country, and the Basques had already organised their own police force even before the government in Madrid had authorised one; they also had their own intelligence people operating inside the Spanish state. The two reference points for us here in Catalonia were the Basques, because we had both suffered under the repressive Spanish state, and the Israelis, because they have the most effective intelligence services, and considering the quality of their information and the difficulty of the region they operate in, you could say they are very cost effective. Besides, Israel has always been a reference point because we Catalans see them as a chosen race that has always been persecuted for it, just like us. When I spoke to the Basques I realised they weren't just a handful of nationalist youths as we were, but people with proper military training, some of them former paratroopers from the French

Basque country, others from the OAS, who were willing to bring their knowledge to the Basque national cause. They knew how to tap telephones in both the region and Spain itself, and they were amazed to learn we had not infiltrated the Spanish state apparatus. There was none of that here, and when I told our head of government about it, he began to quake in his boots and told me: Xibert, don't get mixed up in all that stuff. I forbid you to. The Spaniards are so obsessed with us that if they caught us peeping through any keyholes, they'd blow their top. They forgive the Basques everything, Xibert, because they speak Spanish. What do you make of that, Carvalho? Nobody here has a sense of statehood, absolutely nobody. You should have seen his face when I suggested we needed our own intelligence service, a police cadet school, people trained in security matters, an elite force of super-agents trained and ready for anything, and mentioned the need to set up secret funding for all this. And Tarradellas, the premier during the transition to autonomy, was even worse. He said that the only thing the Catalan government was interested in was to be in charge of the Civil Guard and the Spanish police force deployed in Catalonia. All he wanted was for the Civil Guard to salute him – to salute him before they put him in front of a firing squad, I suppose, because the security forces that operated in Catalonia, even the commanders of the autonomous police force, were all supporters of a unified Spain, and take their orders from the Spanish security chiefs. I'll give you an example. When Colonel Tejero attempted his coup in 1981, the head of the autonomous police force in Catalonia telephoned his boss in Madrid from the government palace in Barcelona and asked: What shall I do with these clowns up here? He was referring to all the top representatives of the Catalan people, who were meeting with our prime minister. That was how things used to be, and all we have done since then is create an autonomous police force in part controlled directly by officers loyal to Madrid and CESID, the Spanish state's intelligence bureau, a police cadet school that turns out excellent professionals, a police trade union we can trust, and not much else – apart of course from the design of our police uniforms, which was the work of Toni Miró, our Catalan Armani. The Italians are the only ones who can compete with us as designers, although for some reason they don't dress their police in uniforms designed by Armani, the

Italian Toni Miró. But none of this is much use to us, for obvious reasons. We need an intelligence service that works for strictly nationalist political groups, and in addition another intelligence service linked to the Catalan government, but both of these would give Madrid and beyond them the entire European Union something to think about, because they want to be in charge of any supra-national security network in Europe. All of which explains the need to set up this intelligence service outside the system, even though we answer to the system, and helps explain why some of us are here today.'

Xibert took a deep breath out of politeness, even though he did not appear to need it. Throughout all this long speech, his eyes had been fixed on Carvalho.

'Our autonomous police are not allowed to investigate specifically political cases, or any that go beyond the Catalan region. They have managed to infiltrate the sects, the drugs trade, the far right and institutional corruption, but as far as this last is concerned, they've only caught the small fry, they haven't been able to get far with any high-level stuff. For a while they ran a group called the "mortadelos", who uncovered sex scandals and discredited a few men and women, but they often sold their information to new judicial interests, which meant all that happened was they created a new rich set linked closely to those in power. There were some scandals that led to resignations which hit the news, but the only aim then was to see who would make the most money out of them. But times are changing. Our great leader has been fatally wounded politically, and when he goes we could see the rise of forces than are not exactly anti-Catalan but will not push for our nationhood. They would never consider setting up specifically Catalan intelligence services that are in dialectic tension not only with the Spanish state but also with the other autonomous regions in so far as they represent interests different from our own. Not to mention the incipient power structures that globalisation is creating in Europe, such as Padania – the northern Italian region that sooner or later is bound to break away from Rome and split from the south. And to talk of Padania is to talk of the new configuration of national boundaries in Europe after the collapse of the communist bloc and the break-up of Yugoslavia. Nowhere is safe from having its boundaries redrawn, not even Switzerland. And I haven't even mentioned all the investigation we need to cover the complexities of global economic strategy, or ecological movements, or the attempt to undermine the nation-state that the multinationals are engaged in – something which might benefit us in the short term because it would weaken our main enemy, the Spanish state, but which in the longer term is seeking to destroy or intimidate any attempt to think differently. Can you imagine Catalonia without an intelligence service capable of finding out what the French or the Spaniards intend to do over the question of sharing out our water reserves? They are talking about bringing water from the Rhone to Catalonia, but what kind of dependency would that create? What will happen the day the Spanish state is no longer able to share out water supplies among all the regions bordering the Ebro, despite protests from those stubborn Aragonese?'

Carvalho could think of a lot of funny replies to this long list of questions, but he was aware that Xibert was expecting that in his capacity as a supposedly famous former CIA agent he would chip in with a Socratic or otherwise vital question.

'Fine. If you will allow me, I should like to complete this list of reasons why we need an intelligence service with a consideration of the fact that in this global village of ours – that is, in the era of globalisation – there are bound to be fresh civil wars which are already being hatched.'

Xibert agreed, and conveyed his agreement to Quimet with the same stiff politeness that an educated public employs to convey their approval of a singer's excellence. Carvalho waited for the intensity of the silence to create even greater expectation, then added:

'Do any of you know how many conflicts of this kind there are in the world today?'

Nobody was willing to venture a guess, so Carvalho took the plunge:

'There are about fifty armed conflicts, from Bosnia to Sri Lanka, taking in Algeria, Sudan, the Moluccas and Mexico along the way. Most of them call into question a nation-state, and this kind of fragmentation can only lead to further conflicts.'

Carvalho recapped on what they should all remember from all they had heard. He felt as though he had taken on a new role that he had possibly once performed before. That of the expert leader of a team, outlining the essentials for his acolytes.

'There are a steadily increasing number of reasons and possibilities to start conflicts, some of them armed ones, but the global reaction to help stop or alleviate them is sufficiently slow for the side that which strikes the first blow to be able to get in two or three more.'

They were lapping it up. They had found a new leader.

'Intelligence services are becoming necessary for every power structure, from companies to what is left of the State, from neighbourhood watch to the relations between a regional government and the multinationals. This involves spheres as diverse as the financial, the economic in its widest sense, the strategic sphere including the arms question, ethno–linguistic and other racial differences, and the ecological. However, the cultural bases for a complete intelligence service are the same as they have always been: the determination to defend one's identity and the lack of scruples in achieving one's aims. If you want your own service, either you will have to pay very well, or you will have to rely on patriots who are willing to play dirty, to do anything from killing to prostituting themselves.'

The idea of killing was accepted without a murmur, but the mention of prostitution made them all close their eyes in horror, apart from Xibert, who was beginning to regard Carvalho as almost a Mossad commander.

'For example, in the CIA they teach you to kill and torture using beggars, outcasts from society who nobody will miss.'

At that even Xibert briefly closed his eyes.

'If it's sovereignty you want, you have to learn to torture, unless you can come up with another way of demonstrating it, or if you delegate the right to torture your own prisoners to another state.'

This caused such a commotion that Carvalho decided he had to rein in his irony.

'Which of course would be unthinkable. Unless there is some kind of European-wide agreement by which the function of torturer is handed over to one specific state or community, so that the rest do not have to compromise themselves ethically. Perhaps Turkey, if it finally joins the European Union, could do the torturing and hanging to avoid Germany or Catalonia having to do it. In any case, don't forget that the best torture instructors are the North Americans. They spread the scientific use of torture throughout Latin America in the1960s.'

By now Quimet was looking distinctly alarmed at the direction Carvalho's declarations were taking. So was Carvalho himself, and he was greatly relieved when the other man declared the session closed.

When the two of them were alone, Quimet could not at first find the words he was searching for, but his gestures told Carvalho a reproach was on the way, and it was not long in coming. You were too harsh, he said. Nobody here is going to start torturing or prostituting themselves, not while I'm in charge at least. We do things differently here. How could a nation that's been tortured, murdered and subjected to a systematic process of genocide itself use torture, murder or genocide?

'Some of them were listening very closely.'

'Of course. Some of the best patriots have got a screw missing, they've not got much common sense. And if you mean Xibert, you're wrong. Xibert is a pragmatist. But for example, there was someone who suggested we ought to colour the Catalans to show how different we are from other nations, especially the Spaniards.'

'Come again?'

'Well, more than twenty years ago, during the transition after Franco's death, we were fooling around, and somebody said what a pity it was that we Catalans aren't black, because that would differentiate us more from the Spaniards and the French, the people oppressing us. And a young untenured university lecturer, from a science faculty no less, said: It can be done. Can you believe it? According to that madman, if you add a foodstuff dye to something everyone consumes, such as the water supply, then you can change the pigmentation of their skin.'

'What colour would he have preferred?'

'He said it had to be something really different, not black, or yellow, or copper-coloured.'

'How about mauve with yellow polka dots?'

'Laugh if you like, but it's hard to strike a balance between all or nothing, if you follow me. I've supported Pujol since we were in the

Marian Congregations together. I trust him. He is measured in everything he does, but our cause needs a few more radical people, especially when we're living through a period of normality, like the one just coming to an end. It's just like in football, Carvalho. The fanatics bring the crowds with them, but they have to be kept in check. That's why I asked you to come here. They respect you because to them you represent the heroic days of spying for real, when the cold war was at its height. We need you. You ought to come regularly to the classes we're giving, but before you do I want to make one thing clear: we're not an official service, we have no links to the autonomous police or the government's security adviser. We aim to operate in parallel to them.'

'In the service of what or whom?'

'Of Catalonia.'

'Could you be more precise?'

'We may lose the next elections, or if we do win them it could be with such a fragile majority that we are only in power for a short while. So we have to make sure we have created stable networks for Catalan power that any new majority cannot dismantle, because whatever they say, they are bound to be more in favour of Spain. We don't need an intelligence service now, but we will in the future. So please, make sure you attend the classes. We're happy to pay you, but above all, stay in touch with me. You'll be getting instructions.'

Carvalho set off for Horta and the Catalan Vatican, hoping he might meet Margalida as she was leaving, without having to use the tapped telephone. But the girl did not appear at the normal time for lunch, so he took the report on Lucifer's Witnesses from the car, and walked briskly over to the building as though he were returning it as agreed. There was no security at the door, but he saw the eyes of a closed-circuit TV camera following him down the corridor to the door of the office dedicated to Satan and his spawn. He opened the door wide, as if expecting to find no one in, but Margalida was there, head down on her desk, trying hard to choke back her tears. Carvalho stood waiting at the door until the sobbing had given way to deep sighs, then cleared his throat. Margalida looked up, her face moist and bright red from her eyes to the tip of her nose. At first she was amazed to see Carvalho standing there, then horrified.

'I came to bring the report back.'

'What report?'

'The one on the Lucifer's Witnesses.'

'Nobody asked you to give it back.'

Carvalho shrugged, walked over to the desk under Margalida's hostile gaze, and left the report on her keyboard.

'I didn't want to take the responsibility of keeping something so obviously unfinished. By the way, I met Señor Pérez i Ruidoms. He's a great actor.'

'He's a great son of a bitch.'

The words had escaped her with hatred, fury, with all the violence needed to force their way through tightly clenched teeth. This seemed to suggest something more than a problem with her job, but nonetheless Carvalho asked her whether she had been fired. Margalida rejected the suggestion with all the confidence of someone who knew that nobody and nothing could ever fire her. She even managed a condescending smile.

'You were right, then. Nobody here is what they seem. Perhaps not even Pérez i Ruidoms. An actor. A very rich man. A protective father.'

'If there's one thing he isn't, that's a protective father. He's always been a castrating father.'

Margalida seemed to know what she was talking about. Carvalho pointed a melancholy finger at the report on the desk.

'I'd really like to be present at one of the Lucifer's Witnesses rituals. You must know how I can get to one.'

'The other day, you followed me and saw me meeting up with Anfrúns.'

'For some time now I've been starting to think that everybody is following everybody else.'

'It's only natural I should know Anfrúns. I'm an expert in satanism.'

For a few moments she went on mentally calculating the risks of giving Carvalho what he was asking for, then finally nodded in agreement.

'*Vale, tio, però no et passis de rosca ni de llest o a la primera bajanada, s'ha acabat el bròquil.*'*

---

* OK, but don't try to get round me or to play games, because if there's any funny business, that's it.

It was obvious that, for Margalida, absolute truths could be spoken only in Catalan. After that, the two of them talked about the pleasures of summer, and how bracing their time on the beach had been, but Margalida pulled her blouse down to show him her burnt shoulders, and the sore mark where her bra strap dug into the tender skin. The straps looked very substantial for someone with such young and firm breasts, more like those used by a middle-aged matron than a girl with a face like hers, a maid of Orleans ready to die at the stake of personal and nationalist passions. Carvalho pointed to the four walls, the report, the computer, the eye of the supposedly hidden camera.

'Is this your vocation? Or do you need the work?'

Margalida rummaged around in a backpack and pulled out a packet of San Julián cigars. She offered one to Carvalho, who rejected such an obvious sign of regression in smoking taste, but when he saw her lighting up, asked for one.

'I've changed my mind. A woman should never be left to smoke alone.'

'You're even older than my father: not even he would talk such crap.'

Carvalho repeated his question: did she have an anti-satanist vocation? Or simply a need to work?

'I'm Catalan, and I work for the independence of Catalonia. That means that for now I work here; tomorrow it could be somewhere else. It's in my blood. My grandfather on my father's side was killed by Franco's army; my grandmother had to go into exile with a sick husband and four kids. When she came back, the Fascists in her village accused her of being a separatist, and made her life impossible. Castor oil. They killed her dogs. That was a village in what they call the "heartland of Catalonia", where four Fascists, with the help of the Civil Guard, could keep everyone under control. The Catalan language was banned, and you were in trouble if in your Spanish exams at the Balaguer Institute they detected any hint of a Catalan accent. That was my father's experience. Do you get it, Carvalho? Franco was everywhere, but in Catalonia we had a double dose of him: he was against the Reds and against us as Catalans. And my family were both. Do you get the picture now?'

'Let's call it a vocation, then.'

He felt like giving the girl a secret hug, without her even realising it; not a joyous embrace but one from someone who shared not
so much her ideology as her historical memory and patience.
Instead, he simply shot her a sympathetic smile, and said:

'I'm not a separatist. I don't believe in independence, but I
detest all kinds of dependence. I don't know if you follow me,
Margalida.'

'If my name's too long, call me Marga.'

'With a name like Margalida, you shouldn't let anyone ever call
you Marga. If you were called Margarita, it would be different.
But Margalida is a real name.'

'You like it?'

Her face had lit up.

In the Caritas office for immigrants, Delmira Mata i Delapeu was still called Delmira Rius. She did not use her second surname, Casademont, or even her little copulative, for which Carvalho was extremely grateful. When Delmira came into the room, her arms were full of files, her glasses hung round her neck, and her mind seemed elsewhere – all of which meant it took her a while to breathe the same atmosphere as the detective. At Caritas, she was in charge of the North African children found wandering the streets of Barcelona after getting into Spain illegally, or whose parents were either dead or in prison.

'We have some cases where the parents went to France to find work, and the children don't even know if they're alive or dead.'

Delmira Rius responded to enquiries with all her five senses, as if putting herself to the test as much as anyone else, and this gave Carvalho the chance to confirm in silence the initial good impression he had got of his client, after he had managed to rid himself of his initial misconceptions. She was very busy, or perhaps was just trying to gain time before Carvalho could speak to her and lay bare her grief yet again. Eventually, though, she took as deep a breath as her ageing lungs would permit, and motioned for him to go ahead. He started with what had happened during the fake end-of-summer party – that is, with the latest developments. He took it for granted that her husband would already have received the police report on the deaths of the two people who had killed her son. Delmira was surprised to discover that Carvalho was surprised at her surprise.

'My husband and I don't even speak to offer our condolences. We live in separate houses. In separate countries. I don't want my country to be his. I didn't want it to be my son's either, but I couldn't prevent my husband's country affecting him. That was the land his killers came from. My poor son. He was nothing more than a scapegoat, chosen at random and ruthlessly.'

'To sum up, señora. Officially, the case is closed. Pérez i Ruidoms will send his son to study abroad, and then he'll begin a new life so that one day he can live like his father, be like his father. Satanism isn't in the sects. It's everywhere else. The other day on TV I saw a report in which some men were training a fighting dog to tear to pieces a still-attractive poodle that they must have stolen or snatched in the street. The dog didn't seem particularly interested in biting the poodle's most sensitive areas, so it was a human voice that was urging it on: the neck, now the legs, now its balls. The dog obeyed, and the other one soon lost the strength to yelp in protest – and whenever it tried to escape, the men formed a barrier to stop it doing so. That's where satanism is. The human voice was satanic. The human bodies were satanic.'

'I see or read about scenes like that every day. Except that instead of a poodle, imagine young children, old people and women, all being torn to pieces.'

'Two thousand years of Christian education, a hundred and fifty years of emancipatory rationalism, Marxism, anarchism . . . and what's the result? The Creation was a waste of time, all prophets speak with a forked tongue, and the selection of species has been a failure. The cruellest species won. OK, do we call the case closed?'

'Have you got to the bottom of everything?'

'I'm not even sure that the two who were killed were the real murderers. Whatever the truth, they were shot in an ambush.'

'Who is behind it all?'

'The drama of their two sons was a warning to your husband, Señor Mata i Delapeu, and his great rival Pérez i Ruidoms. Someone killed a Mata i Delapeu and put the blame on to a Pérez i Ruidoms. So someone is trying to frighten them.'

'Trying to frighten my husband? Don't you know who he is?'

'I know he runs everything that Pérez i Ruidoms doesn't, and earns all the money Pérez i Ruidoms hasn't got his hands on, and vice versa. But it's more complicated than that. There may be foreign interests at stake here, which could mean there is a multi-national level of kidnapping and high-level crime involved.'

'Too powerful for you?'

'What about you?'

'All I do is pay. What do you suggest?'

'Could you get me some life insurance? If I die, I'll leave two orphans who are far too old to start retraining.'

'Try to find a company that isn't run by either my husband or Pérez i Ruidoms. If you want to carry on, so do I.'

Carvalho left the Caritas building with a note to an insurance adviser whom Doña Delmira trusted, and headed back to his office determined to get Biscuter to do some more digging.

'I want you to join a sect, Biscuter. How are you getting on with the Cathars?'

'A friend of mine, Blackbottom – you remember him, he was a cook in Lérida jail, like Lausín . . . he's joined a sect too.'

'But you were particularly interested in the Cathars.'

'You have to believe in something, boss.'

'I'd like you to join one that's called either neo–Catharism or Cathar Universe. You sort it out.'

Biscuter went into the kitchen, savouring the word 'Cathar'.

'It sounds good, boss, like something between catgut and catheter.'

Carvalho looked through the timetable of classes Quimet had given him, and over the next few weeks went to most of the courses organised for would-be spies during their August holidays. It was like going back to the CIA school for agents at the end of the1950s, when the idea of underground work was taking over from that of simply collecting preventive intelligence material. The CIA had already overthrown Jacobo Arbenz in Guatemala, and tried to do the same with Sukarno in Indonesia, and was employing all the techniques of 'dirty wars' on the peripheries of the cold war. As a young man, Carvalho had been impressed by the blending of spying and superstition when he heard about the methods used to persuade Filipino peasants not only to reject the communist guerrillas, but to attack them. The CIA spread the word that the guerrillas had brought the *asuang*, vampire-like evil spirits, to the region. To prove it, whenever they captured any *huk* fighters they killed them and made two small holes in their neck to show they had been victims of the mythical vampires. What Carvalho had found hardest was the torture training on living victims, usually tramps who had no relatives. They were used as guinea pigs in the torture sessions in order to train agents, but above all for the Third World military leaders chosen by the CIA to defend Western, Christian civilization against the communist threat. To Carvalho, all that part of his life seemed to have been lived by another person, but now, in this crypt dedicated to the Catalan Theology of Security, he was overwhelmed by a great sense of melancholy at the wilfully frivolous way the teachers behaved like disciples of Baden-Powell, and at the students, divided equally between unemployed people desperate for any kind of work, and true patriots who had given their lives and if need be their deaths to the cause of Catalonia's independence. ·

There were only a few different topics. The History of Catalonia. The New International Order. Intelligence Services, comprising: History, Theory and Practice. The Practice sessions were made up of three seminars: Legislation and Intelligence, Equipment, and Deontology of Intelligence Services. The course leader was a man called Piferrer, who on their first day recommended they all buy black Myrga notebooks and diaries, without explaining why this was so necessary. Carvalho soon noticed that his fourteen male classmates had covered the front and back of their books with stickers of the Catalan flag, Barcelona Football Club, Sharon Stone, the Catalan top model Judit Mascó, while the three women had preferred images of the motorcyclist Alex Crivillé and the footballer Josep Guardiola. One of them had even stuck on a photo of Subcomandante Marcos, the intellectual leader of the Zapatistas.

The History of Catalonia they were taught consisted of the eternal postponement of statehood from the Catholic majesties to Jordi Pujol's government. A lot of emphasis was placed on the nationalist renewal in the 1970s based around the meetings of the stateless nations and the role of CIEMEN, the Escarré International Centre for Ethnic and National Minorities. Out of this centre's philosophy came the proposal for a new international order, which currently involved the Europe of Regions, the brain-child of a French politician, Edgar Faure, and a former Montserrat monk by the name of Aureli Argemí, and backed politically by Jordi Pujol. They proposed the setting-up of a European-wide front of stateless nations, supported by the tiny states born of the new geopolitics created by the fall of the Berlin Wall. They called for an assembly representing European nations that had no state, to include Galicians, Basques, Corsicans, people from Padania and Friuli, nationalists from the High Adige, Bretons, the Welsh, and the people of Occitania. These representatives would develop the agreements reached at the start of the eighties in the Benedictine monastery of Sant Miquel de Cuixà. The classes on the new international order and stateless nations began with the history of the regionalist movement, especially with the struggle for the recognition of regional or minority tongues such as Danish in Germany, Frisian, the Serbian still spoken in parts of eastern Germany, the different varieties of Gaelic, Catalan, the Albanian language spoken in several communities in Italy, Croatian, the language of Friuli, Provençal in the south of France, the Greek still found in the south of Italy and Sicily, Occitan, and Sardinian. Every state contained a non-official language enclave that was usually repressed, and in some cases these languages were the source of a sense of national identity, as in the case of Catalonia or the Basque country in Spain, and to a lesser extent Galicia, because the claims to a separate nation there had been controlled by right-wing pro-Spanish parties, and had become nothing more than regionalism. Summer courses held at the University of Prades or the Cuixà monastery had kept this spirit alive during the last years of Franco, but contrary to expectation, the return of democracy and autonomy in Spain had not given a fresh impetus to the stateless nations' struggle.

'What did those stateless nations want? A state?'

Perhaps because Carvalho asked the question in Spanish, it seemed to him that the ensuing silence was twice as heavy.

'They want sufficient sovereignty to be able to decide whether they want to become states or not. Fifty million Europeans live as repressed or controlled minorities.'

In the handouts they were given, the name of Aureli Argemí frequently appeared. He was the man who from his base at the monastery of Sant Miquel de Cuixà was the driving force behind the movement in the seventies and eighties. Argemí was a strong believer in the role of NGOs in creating both a new order from the bottom up, and a spirit of solidarity. A Europe of small nations would set the benchmark for a new international order. The Spanish government had not directly opposed these new movements, but had done its best to hinder their work, in Spain and at international meetings.

Carvalho's progress in these matters was witnessed by a Charo busily preparing her shop for the holidaymakers returning to the city, but the detective did not reveal anything about these refresher courses to the only client he had left, Delmira, to whom he merely sent occasional reports of the scant progress he had made on her case. So August fell from the calendar, and with the change of month Carvalho decided he had to conclude the Mata i Delapeu affair once and for all. To his surprise, he discovered he was not at all keen to do so, and when he questioned himself sternly about the reasons, he concluded he was missing the fax messages.

When the first series of talks on history and geopolitics was over, the classes turned to the theory and technique of intelligence-gathering. First they were told about how to set up an office for scanning media output and making summaries, as well as how to channel confidential information and to filter it. The phrase 'covert action' exploded in class one day, and Carvalho thought he was in a time warp back in the CIA school where euphemisms were frequently used to mask reality. One thing is an intelligence service that can operate publicly, they were told, and another is the sort that relies on 'covert action'.

'By covert action I mean all those unofficial and occasionally illegal means we use to obtain information or create situations that are favourable to the cause we serve. I do not intend to discuss the ethical implications of this, merely to describe them pragmatically, taking for granted that they are linked to collective goals above and beyond individual ones.'

This statement provoked a lively debate, because one of the youngsters, poisoned by neo–liberal ideas, challenged the idea that there could be collective goals.

'Only individuals can have goals.'

'What is a nationalist struggle, then? Or a social one?'

'I can admit the nationalist goal, if by nation we understand a wish for a common identity held by a large number of individuals, but a social struggle presupposes a privileged collective identity that takes precedence over the person and their individual rights, and I can't accept that.'

The teacher agreed to disagree. Carvalho realised that in fact he was scared of his student. It was as if he had been caught out clinging to an obsolete emotion or argument, and fearful that the thoroughly modern youngster might be in a position to consign him to an old people's home. Two of the female students had no such qualms in standing up to this perverse individualist. They insisted that groups and even classes had rights, especially that of the legitimate self-defence of the oppressed social classes.

'There are no social classes any more,' declared the prophet scornfully, which brought a stinging reply from one of the women:

'What test tube were you born in? The only human beings entitled to be so individualistic are those who are two metres tall, supremely handsome, rich, strong and intelligent . . . and it seems to me you're nowhere near tall, handsome, or intelligent enough, even though you might be rich.'

'I will be one day.'

After that the individualistic spy followed the class with his ears and cheeks burning. He was a novice in neo-liberalism, and had just fought his first battle with NGO feminist militants. Reds are not created or destroyed, they simply transform themselves. There were only a few days of the course left, and so far they had heard nothing about the tools of the intelligence trade, as if it were all a question of sending a fax or going online, but then one morning Piferrer arrived and told them that the time had come for the classes to take a new turn, and that he was relying on their ethical maturity to understand the scope of what was meant by 'covert action'.

'You do, however, need to be informed of all the latest techniques for economic or political espionage.'

No one protested. They were all ethically mature, or otherwise they would not have enrolled for a course on spying and admitted they knew nothing about it. Spying is to a spy what courage is to a military man.

The first teacher of this part of the course turned up with a large suitcase and gave the whole class in a furtive whisper, as though he were a failed accountant surviving by giving classes on economic espionage. His material consisted of either published documents or leaflets, or information provided by rivals. The section on legal investigations ended with 'legitimate interviews for people who work for your competition'. If the boundary was crossed into illegitimate interviews, you were committing either a venal or a deadly sin. Among the former were the observation of the secret production cycles of the target, offering fake employment to their employees to get information, and pretending to enter into negotiations with competitors with a view to discovering what other negotiations they were engaged in. Among the deadly sins were those of employing a specialist to get all the information he could by whatever means, bribing the competition and their employees, placing a plant on their payroll, the use of electronic devices, robbing plans or even resorting to extortion and threats. Carvalho thought he detected a slight sigh when the teacher spoke of extortion and threats as the final means to be employed.

'Nowadays, there is a wide range of equipment that can be used in covert actions of this type. When the class is finished, I'll give you some catalogues and an address where you will be able to purchase a more or less complete kit of audio-electronic devices. If you mention my name, they'll give you a ten per cent discount.'

Without further ado he opened his suitcase and pulled out a telephone.

'This is the father of all espionage.'

How to tap a telephone? Or a fax? The most important thing, he said, was not the phone-tapping itself, but having a receiver whereby you could listen and store recordings. That was the least violent option, because nowadays there was a very advanced technique by which, once the required information had been received, the telephone could be blown up, and the person being spied on along with it. This technique was of course only to be used in cases where there was no further information to be had from the poor headless man. Mobile phones could be tracked from cars or vans adapted to intercept their conversations, and at the end of the course they would all be taken out in one so that they could eavesdrop on conversations in some district of Barcelona or other. Every student had their preference, and Carvalho suspected they all wanted to listen in to their own neighbours; curiosity always begins at home. After the telephone, the tape recorder is the mother of all espionage. Don't forget, the father and mother.

'A great deal of the taming of the workers' movement in Spain was thanks to tape recorders hidden in union meetings. They helped inform the bosses of the workers' negotiating strategy, so they could identify any weak points. Nowadays there is recording equipment which can fit into a ballpoint pen.'

With that he got out a disposable pen that did not even have the dignity of a Biro; something as miserable as that could never have seen a recorder in its life. But beyond these introductory remarks, the teacher proved to be much more professional and competent than his timid gestures had led Carvalho to believe. How to spy in the open air? How to hack into computer archives, or create a guerrilla war of disinformation on the Internet? In answer to each of these questions, he pulled out of his bottomless suitcase a new piece of equipment, which he not only showed his students, but allowed them to hold, so that they could judge for themselves how small anything to do with transferring knowledge could be. Fortunately, the economic espionage industry and its techniques progress so swiftly that scarcely a year goes by without new equipment and counter-equipment appearing:

'Listen carefully, ladies and gentlemen, because this is one of my key points. There is no espionage without counter-espionage. There are no sophisticated telephone-tapping techniques without equally sophisticated techniques to help prevent it. It is just as true in the world of espionage as anywhere else that competition exists and that one thing automatically gives rise to its opposite. And bear in mind that I've been talking to you about a world where the wealth or poverty of individuals or nations are what counts, but you also have to be prepared to get involved in political decisions which affect individuals and nations . . .'

Carvalho did not sign up for the practical lessons because he vaguely remembered what he had learnt more than thirty years before, and because he was waiting to attend the decisive classes on political espionage and hand-to-hand stuff. Even so, he left the class more worried than he had started it, as if he had discovered that life and history were for real even in Barcelona, the absolute capital of an imaginary world called Catalonia, and the relative capital of a relatively autonomous community. He reached his office just in time to beat Biscuter to the fax:

How were your holidays? I kept stumbling in mine, in other words I kept stumbling over myself. Accidents which I can only put down to my impatience over our meeting. Or re-encounter. I was very nervous and got the idea into my head that if I came back earlier I might be able to get to see you sooner. So I tried to get in touch with you. At first I was surprised that your machine wasn't a combined phone/fax/ answering machine, because I got no answer at all (I was even afraid I might be the reason for such a silence), but when I insisted a gentleman (Biscuter, I suppose) answered and told me he hadn't seen you for two days. A few minutes ago I verified that you had switched over to the fax again, so I am sending you this note in the hope that tomorrow you will get in touch with me either by fax or telephone. Whichever you like, just tell me when and where I can see you.

The message was like a signal that summer was over, as if to warn Carvalho he had been putting things off for far too long, so with a mixture of curiosity and exasperation, he called SP Associates. Who should he ask for? Scarlett? Fata Morgana? Scarlett O'Hara?

'Scarlett O'Hara, please.'

'You must have the wrong number.'

'Scarlett O'Hara sends me fax messages from this number. Take a good look round. Perhaps you haven't noticed. Why don't you call out: "Pepe Carvalho is asking for Scarlett O'Hara!"'

'I'm not in the mood for jokes.'

'Some time ago I called this number, said something similar, and someone came on the line.'

'One moment.'

Then he heard the fax cow's voice, but now she sounded like a lean, smart young woman with the crisp tones of an important civil servant in some ministry or other, and that could not be right, because he wanted her to be fat, short and pedantic. The voice was saying:

'At last. So dreams sometimes do come true.'

'Scarlett O'Hara?'

'Rhett Butler?'

'Why not Ashley?'

'I see you've seen the film or read the book.'

'Both, but I could only burn the book.'

'I suspect you're calling to arrange a meeting.'

'What about Can Boadas or the Ideal Club? They're both

perfect places for us to get to know each other better. Or the Café de la Opera if we have to talk.'

'I know you perfectly well, and you know me imperfectly.'

'We'll see. Tomorrow?'

'At seven?'

'In the morning?'

'At that time of day I hate myself. I haven't even fixed my face. I prefer seven in the evening, and at the Café de la Opera. We need to talk.'

Chapter 4

The woman sitting behind a screen in the Café de la Opera waved at him, and she was a complete woman. Carvalho could have come a hundred times into a room where she was sitting, and he would have picked her out a hundred times and looked at her. She was beautiful, too beautiful for him to believe she could be the fax cow, but he went over to her anyway, and they shook hands, studying each other. When Carvalho sat down and had her opposite him like a silent bust, the silhouette of another woman buried deep in his memory tried to impose itself on the one in front of him now. He blinked several times, as if staring at her in this way might help dredge the image up into reality.

'Do you still not remember who I am?'

'I remember you, but I'm not sure where from.'

'My name is Jessica Stuart-Pedrell.'

Now the two images had fused completely. Yes. It was Yes. The daughter of the business tycoon who never managed to reach the Southern Seas. He suddenly saw her, a shadowy adolescent, stroking a little puppy – Bleda, whose death still pierced Carvalho's heart. But that fleeting impression was replaced by another more solid one of the same girl seen from behind, before she turned to face him, in the Stuart-Pedrell mansion. He remembered when he first saw her: her narrow waist accentuated by a red belt that divided her youthful body in two. Jean-clad buttocks rested their tense and rounded youth on a piano stool. Her back was arched with a studied delicacy. A blonde ponytail with a few loose strands of hair, her head thrown back. As she swung round on the stool, Carvalho immediately registered her grey eyes, her skier's complexion, a large soft mouth, cheek-bones of a fashion model, and the arms of a fully formed woman. Her eyebrows were perhaps a little too thick, but they underlined the features of a girl who would not have looked out of place in a 1970s American TV commercial, for the spark of life Coca-Cola can offer, or one for milk: Everybody needs milk.

Carvalho realised she was the same woman twenty years older, and that all her features, modified to fit those of a beautiful woman in her forties, were exactly the same, especially her light grey eyes, her large mouth that no longer looked so soft, and which had the first suspicion of wrinkles at the corners of her lips, her blonde hair that had now taken on a coppery sheen and was cut short to accentuate still further high cheek-bones that would guarantee her a beautiful old age. It was as though this woman fitted into the earlier version, rather than the reverse.

'Mystery solved?'

'That mystery. There are others.'

'Such as?'

'Why now?'

'It took me a long time to realise I needed to see you again. I needed to grow up. In all senses. It's been a long absence, but somehow you were always present, as if you were always accompanying me, in every nook and cranny of my life. Do you remember this note?'

There it was, written by him:

Maybe it *would* be a good idea for you to make this trip – but alone, or with someone other than me. Find a nice boy whom you'd be doing a favour by inviting him along. A sensitive young man with some culture and not much money. You'll find dozens of them at the Faculty of Philosophy and Literature. I'm enclosing the address of a professor friend of mine who'll help you to find one. Don't abandon him, at least until you reach Kathmandu, and be sure to leave him with enough money for a return ticket. Carry on with your journey, and don't come back until tiredness or old age get the better of you. You'll return to find that everyone here has become petty minded, mad or old. Those are the only three ways of surviving in a country than did not make the Industrial Revolution in time.

She watched anxiously as Carvalho took in what he had written, and respected his silence as he tried to gain time and the possibility of an ironic comment, while all he really felt was a huge weight pressing on his chest, as if he had suddenly discovered he was responsible for a disaster, one in which he too had been a victim.

'I did everything you told me to. I went to see your friend Sergio Beser, and told him: Help me find a poor, cultured student who would be willing to come to Kathmandu with me. Sergio said: They'll be queuing up, but then he helped me find one from his home town or close by, not from Morella itself. I bowed to his sense of regional loyalty.'

'Did the student make it to Kathmandu?'

'He's my husband. The father of my two children.'

On the table where his note had been, he now saw a photograph of two boys in their late teens.

'The elder was born in Afghanistan. After Kathmandu we did the Silk Road.'

Carvalho's eyes were asking: Is everything all right? but he said nothing, because Yes's eyes had filled with nostalgia.

'You were right to brush me off. I was a snobby drug addict, I was unbearable.'

No, thought Carvalho, you weren't. Don't believe what you might have seen in my eyes. You were a wonderful girl, generosity itself, a real woman, the golden child I had been longing for ever since I was a boy, but . . .

'What did you think of me the first time you saw me?'

'The first time I saw you I thought: Get a Gary Cooper in your life, girl. You looked as though you were waiting for a Gary Cooper to rescue you, and you had beautiful long legs.'

'You were wrong there: Gary Cooper had gone out of style.'

'I know, but I had to protect myself from the impact you'd made on me, to reduce you to a golden girl on the screen, a Technicolor reality.'

'It's strange, but often when I remember you from twenty years ago, I see that puppy you used to have.'

'Bleda.'

'That's right, Bleda. What became of her?'

'They killed her.'

Both of them closed their eyes as though mourning the dog's death right in front of them, and somehow it was true, Bleda had just been killed again. Carvalho could sense the cardboard feel of the puppy's fur when he found her with her throat slit, and recall how he buried her in the garden up in Vallvidrera. Her remains were still there, and he still occasionally paused at the spot and said her name in the way one names an absence, in the way one remembers the most terrible injustices, the biological ones.

'What about your mother?'

'Older and even more unbearable. She and my husband administer what's left of my father's affairs. I've dedicated myself to culture, to reading everything I hadn't read when I met you and was so scandalised that you burnt books. I work a bit at SP Associates in public relations, I love that sort of thing. That's where I send you your faxes from.'

So SP Associates was Stuart-Pedrell Associates. Carvalho caught himself staring at her again: her eyes were red, from the contact lenses perhaps, although from where he was sitting he couldn't tell whether she wore them or not.

'Conjunctivitis. I've got conjunctivitis,' she said, precluding any further debate on the subject. All of a sudden there flashed through Carvalho's mind a scene of him in bed with Yes – no, two scenes, one of them an ordinary one, and the other he erased as quickly as he could, so that she would not see it as she studied him so closely, still with a smile on her face, still with her eyes moist. Carvalho's heart was aching with joy. He ordered a whisky, then another and another. Everything that came from Yes's lips seemed wonderful, and then he remembered a bolero and started to hum it. She took it up, and sang out loud the words that expressed the euphoria he found so hard to suppress:

'"Then bells of celebration ring out in this heart of mine".'

He watched her lips mouth the whole song:

> *Only once in our lives do we give our soul*
> *In sweet, complete surrender*
> *And the moment that this miracle*
> *Turns into the wonder of love*
> *Then bells of celebration*
> *Ring out in this heart of mine.*

'Who is the best spy these days?'

The students' silence only served to increase the teacher's sense of anticipation. He rushed to answer his own question before anyone else could spoil it:

'The spy satellite. A satellite can pick up conversations and track people's movements, but it is used basically for large gatherings – although that doesn't stop it being employed to intercept a vast number of one-to-one conversations. Despite this, however, man is still essential as an intelligence-gatherer for what is known as "covert action". And today's agent can count on a sophisticated array of equipment to help him: which of course has given rise to an equally sophisticated array of devices to detect any such equipment being used. It's a constant game of give-and-take, and you should all be familiar with the most basic elements. To start at the beginning, you need to know how to listen from a distance, to see from a distance, to attack, if necessary, from a distance too. If we take the idea of listening from a distance, there are different ways of doing so: using cables, magnetic suction devices, optic fibres, lasers or the atmosphere. In other words, everything from telephone clamps to microphones or zoom mikes. We may have an extraordinary range of gadgets at our disposal, but the people using them need to be properly trained, because don't forget that it's the human ear which does the listening, and the human eye which does the watching, so we have to know how to do everything from tapping a telephone line to hacking into a computer system, from analysing the contents of the target's waste-paper baskets to being able to disguise yourself so that you exist right next to him without arousing the slightest suspicion. This involves a process of mimesis that requires a lot of thought. We have to learn to disguise ourselves without appearing to have done so. We have to spy without arousing suspicion: which means we should do all we can to avoid looking suspicious. Above all, don't wear a trench-coat if you're going to spy on someone.'

Some of the students were copying all this down. Their teacher had the gift of stating the obvious, although sometimes he lightened up and showed them spy thriller films. Then they would all sit and discuss them, like in a cinema club. Carvalho was impressed by *The Conversation*, especially the opening sequence where spies are listening in on a young couple taking pity on some old tramps.

'To prove to you how important the human element is in all this, I'm going to ask you to do a practical exercise. Each of you will have a specific objective. You are to find out the information, and bring back the results.'

The teacher assigned them their tasks: one had to head for the Barcelona assembly to find out what the Socialists' strategy was concerning the high-speed train, another had to discover–without of course being discovered himself–to what extent Spanish state security forces had infiltrated the Catalan autonomous police. Carvalho was given the job of uncovering what preparations were being made for the next meeting of Stateless Nations: where it was to be held, and what the agenda was. The students trooped out disguised as themselves, thinking over all they had learned, and with strict instructions that they could use only use their four senses, and no other tools.

'Remember, before Picasso became Picasso, he had to show that he could draw a cat.'

Where did he start his drawing? Carvalho took advantage of the deserted classroom to chat to the teacher about how all the patterns of espionage had changed, and how the nature of what was being spied on had made this change necessary. For example, in the sixties I was keeping an eye on how young people were becoming more and more radical, but now that I am investigating agents from the stateless nations, I'll have to adopt a very different attitude. The teacher could not agree more.

'Above all, remember that this is no routine meeting, part of the usual round of diplomacy, so it could well be kept a secret, and not aired openly.'

'So it might not even be held in Catalonia.'

'Obviously. It'll most likely take place somewhere in Padania, because they could be the driving force behind the movement in Europe in the coming years.'

'What is the link between Padania and Region Plus?'

'Politics can create strange bedfellows. In fact Bossi's Padania isn't a strictly nationalist movement. Its aims are economic, so the idea of Region Plus does not bother them. But it could be a catastrophe for Catalan or Basque nationalism.'

If they had carried on talking, the teacher would have told him everything, but Carvalho was beginning to like the idea of going back to the ABC of spying, without gadgets or disguise. So he went to Lluquet i Rovelló, where the good-looking widow greeted him with great satisfaction when she heard him say: *De bon matí quan els estels es ponen*, and when he added that he needed urgently to get in touch with Xibert before he left for Italy. The widow was sorry the trip had caused so many problems, because everything was being done at top speed, and it was going to be no easy matter to reach Grinzane Cavour in time.

'But there are still a few days left, aren't there, Señora . . . you didn't say what your name was.'

'Madrona, Madrona Campalans. More than a few anyway, it's not until the start of December.'

She showed him into a small room behind the counter, and soon came back carrying a hood.

'Oi que es posarà la caputxeta? Oi que serà un bon minyó?'*

Carvalho was delighted to put it on, and to allow himself to be led by the widow's still-firm arm, and even more delighted when his forearm brushed against the outline of her breast in a springy bra. When she took the hood off, he was in the room where they had held the previous meeting, and the man in the tracksuit was studying him intently.

'What can I do for you?'

'I wanted to talk about your trip to Italy for the Stateless Nations' meeting.'

'How do you know I'm going to Italy, and for that reason?'

Carvalho feigned astonishment.

'Is the meeting in Padania meant to be a secret?'

Xibert was furious at this, and started to pace up and down the

---

* You'll put the hood on, won't you? You'll be a good boy?

confined space in the hidden room. He let out a stream of curses. Who had slipped up on the security procedures? This will never be a state, Carvalho, no one thinks in terms of a state. Carvalho agreed, there was no sense that this was a state, but perhaps meetings such as the one at Grinzana Cavour could help create it little by little. By now Xibert was more sad than angry, as if his pride were wounded.

'Do you know what I think, Carvalho? Sometimes I think I'm the only one who takes these things seriously. Since Franco's death politics is full of johnny-come-latelies who have no idea what it's like to be arrested even for an hour, or to have been on the wrong end of a police beating. It's the same with our nationalists. They've all signed up for this because Catalan nationalists have won in parliament, but the day they lose, it'll be *ciao*, Catalonia.'

'But perhaps the meeting will achieve something. The setting-up of a network of intelligence agencies among the Stateless Nations, for exmaple.'

Xibert looked at him admiringly.

'Your brain works inductively and deductively, Carvalho. That's exactly what the meeting is about.'

I'm so happy . . .

The chemist says my conjunctivitis comes from too much light. He said it seriously, gravely even, while I was trying hard not to burst out laughing. It seems so strange that my 'bedazzlement' could be cured by an eyewash. I'm giving it a try.

I foresee – or rather I can sniff out – problems, now that in addition to being a flawless myth I find you are a warm, accessible, gentle, disturbing, perturbing, singular, surprising man. So to the weight implied by the constant tyranny of the myth (the gods are never satisfied with all the sacrifices and offerings they receive) I have to add the yoke, the oppression of such an interesting and attractive man.

One last thing. If you ever want to call me, do it because you want to. I'm not such a self-centred person that I care nothing for expressions of interest as to my emotional well-being – I truly appreciate your kind-heartedness – but from now on, if we are going to have some sort of a relationship, it has to be something we both want, although of course we don't have to want the same thing.

I'm happy, happy, happy. You can play whatever music you like, I'm feeling extra generous today. Of all the misfortunes that afflict mankind, the very worst is being conscious of so much and being able to control so little. Our consciousness does not stop us committing sins, but it does prevent us enjoying them.

A single word you spoke that heavenly night placed me between my past and my future like a ship between the deep blue seas and the skies. I am Yes, and the secret of happiness is not always to do what you want, but always to want what you do.

Probably what I was least expecting were your hands. I remembered them exactly. It's strange that they're the same hands you had as a child, because they still look like a child's hands. I saw how you had attacked the nails with your teeth, and when we shook hands to say goodbye, I could feel how warm and soft they are. They're the same hands you use to draw the outlines of murderers or thieves before you uncover them; the same hands you use to experiment on cooking sauces with mushrooms. Merlin? They're disciplined hands that never once crossed the diagonal, slanting, oblique space where he sat. Diametrically opposed to you. All the complicated nonsense of your strange personality can be explained just by looking at your hands, although I never realised it when I was only Yes, the pretty, or perhaps only good, daughter of the tycoon Stuart-Pedrell.

Your character is the result of a constant addition. You don't seem to have left anything behind: you're not like other people who have to leave one thing to become another. It seems to me you don't abandon the past, you don't resist the present, and you are open to anything the future may hold.

You take on History, you make it, and you wait for whatever it may throw at you.

I love the way you ask things. You do it in the most open way, and you skirted round the questions you didn't ask (lots of them) so perfectly that I immediately saw what you wanted to know and what you didn't. That's because you're a detective. A perturbing detective.

They say that one of life's greatest pleasures is to put limits on yourself. After thinking about it a little – a very little – I came to the sage conclusion that if there is going to be any private territory or any other kind of boundary between us, it's not me who is going to insist on it.

So then, la–di–da to all that; it would have been nice if you had called me last week, but seeing I wasn't so lucky, I'm not going to add to my misfortunes the anxiety it would cause me by trying to stop writing or calling you.

Whenever Carvalho felt depressed so frequently in one day, he usually tried to work out why, and usually succeeded in discovering the deep-seated or immediate reason for it. Now he was depressed because he heard bells of celebration in his heart and was constantly hoping that the fax would start up, as a way of rekindling their relationship. Yes's face kept appearing all around him, as though some parapsychological force had helped it materialise in a corner of his office, on the piece of paper he lifted to his eyes, on the edge of the tray on which Biscuter had served him a strawberries gazpacho.

'Yes, strawberries, boss. It's a recipe by la Ruscadella, that girl from Sant Pol who's such a good cook. I made myself a piece of bread with tomato, salt and oil on it as usual, except I used strawberry instead.'

Yes was in the strawberry that Biscuter was trying to rub on his piece of bread, and Carvalho had to stop himself protesting, as if afraid that Yes was suffering an indignity. He was annoyed at this new dependence of his, especially of his thoughts, because he found himself imagining she could read what he was thinking, and even caught himself talking out loud to her so that she could hear him. But so as not to surrender completely, he denied himself the pleasure of calling her. It also distressed him that every time he had Yes in his thoughts it meant he was neglecting Charo. She had phoned three times to remind him of her presence, the last using Quimet as an excuse: they're expecting you. They haven't been able to get in touch with you. And a message from Margalida. All she said was: Satan! and left a mobile number. When he thought of her, it was of their swims together at the end of summer, and he imagined her wading out of the water again as soon as the first warm days of spring arrived and the two of them could regain their lost country of the sea. Although October was drawing to a close, Carvalho had no sense of time passing, not even of the change of seasons, even though in recent years he had become much more aware of them, as though he were counting each one, and calculating how many more he had left. This time, it was as though everything around him was flat, and the only three-dimensional reality was the tunnel that Yes's call would travel down, and through which he would rush to meet her. Margalida arranged to see him in the Café Velódromo in Calle Muntaner, one of the few places still resisting the pickaxe of oblivion, where the billiard tables and waiters were as he or his nostalgia remembered them always to have been. Margalida came in wearing biker's gear, a helmet in one hand and her hair gathered in a compact bunch over one of her breasts.

'Come with me, if you don't mind riding pillion.'

'That's all I've been doing recently.'

They rode down Calle Muntaner to Plaza de la Garduña, then walked as far as the garden of the old Santa Cruz hospital. Margalida sat on a bench and waited for Carvalho to do the same. She scanned the horizon, taking in the Gothic architecture and the gardens where old people and a knot of out-of-work immigrants were the only people visible, then seemed to relax.

'Don't be so sure. They could be watching and listening to us through telescopes.'

'I've taken precautions, and my mobile isn't bugged. We don't have much time. You never told me what happened when you went to that end-of-summer party.'

'I got to know Señor Pérez i Ruidoms.'

'That's what I mean: what do you think of his son?'

'Nothing. That he's innocent, like the vast majority of mankind.'

'Far more innocent than you might think.'

Carvalho again detected an unusual interest on her part in the Pérez i Ruidoms boy.

'Albert and I have been friends since we were kids. We studied in the same schools right up to university, and you could say there was something between us until he went crazy over this sect idea, and became determined to try everything, absolutely everything.

He was a victim of his father, just like Alexandre Mata i Delapeu was, and will continue to be, if we don't do something.'

'What have I got to do with it?'

'You have to talk to him. His father has got him locked up and is planning his whole future for him, but we have to save him from that.'

What or who was driving Margalida to act this way? To Carvalho she seemed like a girl who was madly in love and desperate to save someone who probably did not want to be saved.

'You ought to talk to him. You'd not only be doing him a favour, but yourself too. I don't know if you realise just what you've got into. Have you ever asked yourself why you are where you are?'

'There's a whole lot of reasons. Let's say that some of them are spontaneous and positive, others are more calculated. What I'd like to know is where the calculation begins and why.'

'Don't forget that as far as I'm concerned that shark Pérez i Ruidoms is behind everything.'

She was staring at him with wide-open eyes, as though this were the most convincing proof of her sincerity.

'And you, did you get into this because of that boy, Albert?'

'Yes.'

'And so far, you've managed to fool everyone?'

'No. Some day I'll explain, but I need to be more sure I can trust you. If you don't object, I'll arrange a meeting with Albert, but I can't tell you when. Don't be surprised if you have to wait several weeks. At the moment I don't even know where they're keeping him.'

It was not a fax, but the voice of Yes herself which poured like a soothing balm into his lonely ear. She suggested they meet in a bar called El Zigurat, and Carvalho arrived hoping they could get beyond the stage of being talking heads and go out into the street together, stroll along together, so that he could feel all of Yes's body next to him, so the two of them could inhabit their own space, a space just for them created by the simple fact of walking along side by side. But Yes sat steadfastly at her table, content with passive seduction, and talked endlessly about her husband, Mauricio. She mentioned him as if they both knew him well, as if she did not realise that Carvalho could only see him as an intruder in a space reserved for just the two of them. Or perhaps she was doing it on purpose, like pin-up girls who hide their breasts behind books when they already have their arms folded across their chests. And as well as the formidable Mauricio, so understanding and so wise, indispensable right-hand man of the Stuart-Pedrell widow, who trusted him much more than she did her own daughter, there were the two sons, marvels of beauty, diligent study and filial love. In other words, they were the complete opposite of Yes herself when Carvalho had first met her: floating, scatter-brained, directionless, childishly drug-addicted to the point where she made lines of coke even on the hand mirrors in the luxury English-tiled bathrooms of the Stuart-Pedrell mansion. Do you understand what a perfect world I live in? How can you think for a minute I'm going to destroy that harmony, or that you have any right to do so? Were these rhetorical questions, or did she really expect some sort of answer from Carvalho? Things couldn't be that perfect if you felt the need to find me again, and tell me I'm the man of your life.

After the Zigurat, Yes changed the decor and suggested the Hemiciclo, another bar where they sat like talking heads, although if they arrived early enough he could sit beside her and admire her beautiful, decanted profile, the sparkle of her rounded features, the controlled gestures of an actress completely in charge of her own code of signs. The woman with a score of ten, they would have said a few years ago, when there was still some historical and biological hope left in the world.

'We could go to the cinema together some day.'

Twenty years after they had made love in Carvalho's bed, the idea of going to the cinema together was almost a transgression, and it helped bring back into Carvalho's mind the image he had been rejecting, the one where he had been on the point of sodomising Yes, but didn't do so because he thought it was simply to prove his power over her, a kind of social humiliation, to fuck a girl from a rich family up the arse. Just recalling it hurt him in some part or other of his body, the part where guilt is stored, and yet even so, when she walked in front of him, he could not help looking down at her backside, to see whether any memories of that bright object of his desire stirred within him. Whenever they said goodbye, Carvalho promised himself he would end it, but found that the only distance he could bear was to wait for her to take the initiative, and it took her an agonisingly long time to send for him again . . . the explanation for the delay was always work, social engagements or family matters, the mere mention of which tormented Carvalho, and left him mortified when it turned into a complete description of a dimension of her life he was not part of. Whereas she seemed capable of getting on with her real life, with this added slight transgression of recovering a myth of her youth, Carvalho found it impossible to deal with everyday existence. He was neglecting Delmira, the son's widow, he kept his distance from Charo, and he could barely keep up with Biscuter's discoveries in the world of sects, even though he noticed a huge increase in the number of books that the little head damaged at birth by forceps bent over and studied: *The Phenomenon of Fundamentalist Sects, A New Dictionary of Sects and Satanism, The Sects among Us, Magie et Sorcellerie en Europe, Atlas of the Cathar World, Destructive Sects, The True Face of the Cathars, the Catalan Templars, Guide to the Cathars, The Secret Legacy of the Cathars, A Dictionary of Religions,* as well as several books by the chief local expert, who thrived despite suffering the indignity of being called Pepe

Rodríguez. Biscuter said he was fascinated above all by the positive potential of satanism.

'The Cathars didn't exactly see Satan as a positive force, but that's what interests me, boss. If the world our official God created is such a mess, why not see Satan as a necessary rebel?'

Carvalho promised they would talk about it all one day, but that day never arrived. Nor did the one when he was due to talk to Quimet about reaping the rewards of the spying course he had passed with distinction after he had presented what was regarded as excellent research into the Stateless Nation movement. He was waiting to be able to enrol for the higher level, where students were given training in the use of weapons and attack and self-defence classes. These were run by a Colonel Migueloa, a French Basque who was an ex-OAS commando and who happened to live in Barcelona because he had a daughter married to a Swiss philologist, expert in the use of *salar** in the spoken language of Majorca and the Ampurdán. But there were very few places on these courses, and they had to be held in secret, given the fact that they took place outside the usual security networks so that the CESID or the autonomous police did not get wind of them. He missed Yes so much he lost track of time, and distance became a repugnant sticky mess that made him feel bad about being where he was without having her there. So he imagined that she was with him in everything he did, and caught himself talking to her about everything that affected him, from buying half a dozen pairs of socks to choosing cods' heads in la Boqueria market or the purchase of a pan to make *tempura* in. This consisted of a flat tin tube about twenty centimetres high, which was plunged into boiling oil with a hole at the top into which the mixture to be fried evenly was poured. He ordered it from a traditional ironmonger's at the back of the market, opposite the Turia restaurant, where he often went to eat freshly cooked market produce at prices designed to help a near-pensioner spend what little he had left. Carvalho had discovered another interesting restaurant in Plaza Real one day when he went looking for a taxidermist's shop he remembered and found it no longer stocked stuffed birds but sardine tarts, terrines of foiegras with quince cooked in port, rice with clams, or vegetable

---

* The use of *sa* in place of the definite article.

'brick'. The restaurant was called El Taxidermista and was run by a woman who appeared constantly amazed that Plaza Real was like a dress rehearsal for globalisation, together with her mother, Nieves by name, who spoke as though she had just left Madrid in 1936, the 'capital of glory'. Nieves was a lifelong Republican, through all the post-war years, and all the transition to democracy, as she confessed to him when she cooked him a special dish of *arròs amb fesols i naps.** Perhaps he would take Yes to El Taxidermista one day.

Yes wasn't convinced by his tin tube. Where are you going to put it? It's the sort of thing you buy and then never use. You'll see, I'm going to use it tonight. He cut some vegetables into strips, sprinkled flour over them, added water, an egg, and peeled prawns. He heated oil on the stove until it was boiling, plunged the tube into it and then poured two tablespoonfuls of his mixture into the top. When it started to solidify, he removed the mould and the frying blob of food swam in the oil until it was ready for turning. The *tempura* was wonderful with soy sauce, or with horseradish and ginger. See, o faithless woman? Yes tried a piece and approved with that enthusiastic look only she could give, a look of astonishment that kind-hearted rich people like her could put on, and poor companions like Charo really feel. Then the enchantment wore off, and in his lonely Vallvidrera dining room the lack of Yes's presence was even greater than the space her absolute presence had filled.

Carvalho was jolted out of his self-absorption *à deux* by Delmira. In no uncertain terms, she demanded an explanation, insisting she did not want to die without knowing exactly what had happened to her son.

'I'm waiting for a meeting with Albert Pérez i Ruidoms, but it's not easy. He could clear up a lot of things for us.'

'Why isn't it easy? Isn't he free to come and go?'

'His father has got him hidden away.'

Delmira burst into floods of tears, while Carvalho shut his eyes and did all he could to let the sofa swallow him up.

'Why are men so cruel? Or perhaps a better question would be: why is man so cruel?'

'It's true.'

---

* Rice with beans and turnips.

'Read this.'

Delmira handed him a piece of paper. Carvalho read:

Dear Delmi.

Since the death of our boy I've been giving a lot of thought to the life we share, and it doesn't make sense, although I also can't see how we could separate legally in view of the complexity of our joint interests and holdings, not to mention inheritance problems, because I'm sure you have favourites whom you want to inherit on your side of the family, whereas it is possible I may want to start another family and have children who might compensate for the loss of our child. My enemies have wounded me in my most vulnerable spot, and I need to regain my strength to strike back. For the moment, I am off on a long journey; I'll return when my need for flight is exhausted. Try to understand me, as I understand you.

'Could you find out who he is going with?'

'Does he have a travel agency he uses regularly?'

'Avionjet. He always deals with Señorita Fina.'

It was the least he could do faced with the twofold widowing, the twofold virginity of someone like Delmira, who could offer herself the luxury of travelling wherever she liked, but possibly not that of forming a new family and having children.

It seemed as though half of Barcelona was in the Avionjet office arranging trips for the end of the year, century and millennium, and Carvalho overheard the most exotic ideas for a getaway.

'Taking into account where the sun will rise in the year 2000, where do you recommend so that we can be the first to see it?'

He asked for Señorita Fina and was directed to the rear end of a computer that was considerably more curvaceous than the girl operating it. Fina was so thin he could hardly see her beyond the machine.

'Señor Mata i Delapeu wants to go through his itinerary, and asked me to get you to confirm the details.'

'Shall I fax it to him?'

'No, give it to me so I'll be able to check it with him.'

Fina poked a corner of her face round the computer, just enough to be able to fix one eye on Carvalho, as though she were so narrow that only one eye could fit her features.

'I've never seen you before.'

'Señor Mata i Delapeu wants all this to be kept strictly confidential.'

She gave him the file on the trip that Madrona Campalans Martínez and Joan Mata i Delapeu were planning to make to the Seychelles.

'That's the first stage, after that there's the option to fly to Sri Lanka and the Maldives or to take a cruise from Penang to Bali.'

'If you'll just give me a second, I'll see what Señor Mata i Delapeu told me, and confirm.'

He took a notebook with addresses scrawled in it out of his pocket, consulted it with a stern look, then said condescendingly:

'Yes, that seems all right.'

'All right?'

'Yes, all right.'

'Do you want me to send him a fax to confirm?'

'That won't be necessary.'

The name Madrona Campalans rang a distant bell in his memory, and made him smile. To make sure, he paid a visit to Lluquet i Rovelló, and when he saw the assistant, asked straight out:

'Señora Campalans?'

'Yes, Madrona Campalans, but how do you know my maiden name?'

'A good-looking widow like you immediately becomes single again.'

He invented a need to see Xibert. The man in the tracksuit was not there, so Carvalho insisted they find him. Then he went to meet Delmira, and told her the details of her husband's trip.

'Do you know the woman? Is she the typical young whore? A bimbo, as they call them nowadays?'

'No, she's a widow. A widow spy. She's going for what she can get out of him.'

'Money?'

'Information.'

It took several meetings for them to overcome twenty years' distance: on the one hand, Carvalho was trying to preserve his own space, as if he were offering Yes the possibility of building a new one after two decades of solitude; on the other, she kept insisting on her daily life, her husband and children, as though they were the ever-present border guards at her meetings with him. Mauricio, the sensitive youth she had taken with her to Kathmandu, had turned out to be an extraordinary businessman. And her two sons were beyond compare as students, sportsmen, and in their concern for the world and its problems. They belonged to NGOS, just as their grandfather was no doubt a member too – of Tycoons without Frontiers, thought Carvalho, then took himself to task for his sarcasm, because Stuart-Pedrell had been one of the last and only generation of business tycoons with a conscience. It was as if Yes had never been that young woman who had snorted drugs up every orifice of her body, and even made lines of coke for breakfast. Now she was a woman with a perfectly balanced existence, filled by her husband and sons. She wanted Carvalho to take her back to the city of his childhood, as if she wanted to possess him right from the beginning. When they visited what had once been the Barrio Chino or Distrito V or Raval as it was now known, she was as sad as he was when he described how the bulldozers had torn down his childhood cinemas, his childhood schools, his childhood neighbours – who had been replaced by another wave of immigrants from a much more distant south: Korean, Latin American or Pakistani children who played football in the white shade of an ultra-modern museum of art that backed on to the former Casa de la Caridad.

Perhaps she was offering him this interest in his past to compensate for rubbing his nose in her daily life. By the tenth time she had told him about Mauricio and her two boys, Carvalho felt existentially offended, and mentally sent her packing. Either she was doing her best to protect a part of her life he had never wanted to invade anyway, or she was building her own security zone around herself. This meant that not only did he have to talk about the near-ghostly land of his childhood, but about his strange 'family' as well. Yes had adopted Biscuter. He seemed almost like a portable treasure. I'd love to take him home with me, she said. On the other hand, she made no attempt to hide her distaste for Charo, as if she had the right to protest about a rival Carvalho might be involved with, whereas he was supposed to regard it as perfectly normal that she should have her Mauricio and two marvellous sons still clinging to her apron strings – what an Oedipus complex they must have. Although she was capable of suddenly making an imaginative leap and saying things like:

'You and I are lovers, aren't we? It's as if we were anyway.'

'We hide as if we were lovers. I don't suppose you tell your husband we are still seeing each other.'

'I wouldn't have a problem telling him,' she said tartly, as if the matter needed no further discussion. But Carvalho was irritated at all this talk of a perfect, intelligent and understanding husband, all this stuff about her boy wonders. To him, they felt like three intruders in a magic kingdom where only he and Yes should be allowed to enter.

'But you haven't told him.'

'Let's just say I didn't want to cause any "social panic".'

She started laughing, more and more effusively, until her forehead brushed against Carvalho's shoulder. This jerked the detective out of the situation of being two friends living in Barcelona playing at being platonic lovers, and he felt suddenly ridiculous. Twenty years earlier they had gone to bed together, and now probably she, and definitely he, wanted to repeat the experience.

'No, we're not lovers. Lovers don't have limits. They don't hide behind tables in cafés. They don't talk about husbands or children or parents because they build a world of their own, for however long it lasts: five minutes, an hour, a whole lifetime. Lovers have a different language apart from kilometres of fax paper. If I kissed you right here, you'd die. You'd faint.'

'Try me,' she said, offering her face to him defiantly. Carvalho took her head in his hands and drew her towards him. He could see the terror in her eyes until she closed her lids as she felt the tip of his tongue pushing between her lips, searching out the most secret corners of her mouth. When they moved apart, her eyes were still closed, and she heaved a deep sigh. Then she fell back in her seat, and looked across the gulf separating them as though in a state of shock.

'You kissed me.'

'I remember.'

'In other words, we're lovers now.'

'Only very superficially.'

'You mean we have to go to bed together to be lovers?'

'Something like that.'

'But I can't lead a double life. I can't have sex with you during the day and then go to bed at night with Mauricio.'

'I can understand that. We've reached a stage of sexual inhibitions. Twenty years ago, what you just said would have seemed ridiculous to you.'

She leaned forward and laid her hand on his arm.

'But what I would do is run away with you. For ever. Never forget, you're the man of my life.'

Yes had vanished. Before him, Carvalho could see only an abyss beckoning. His chest hurt.

'At my age, that for ever would only be a very short time. What about your wonderful husband, your marvellous children? They would never forgive you. All your ecosystem would be destroyed.'

'I wouldn't care, so long as you knew why I'd done it. All or nothing.'

So it was down to him. She had put the responsibility on to him, and was gazing at him with a mixture of fear and pride on her face. Please don't reject me, she was begging him, but from his lips came words more like a fax message than a declaration of undying love. Age had made the distance too great: he could not destroy his own ecosystem because that would mean destroying Charo and Biscuter and their worlds; and above all, he could not be responsible for destroying her world. Can you imagine a life without the people who depend on you? What kind of a sense of guilt would that give you?

'Whose sense of guilt are you talking about? Mine? I'm so in love with you that I don't have any sense of guilt. What I don't want is two lives in two beds. I only want one life and one bed. With you. Your life. But only one bed.'

You don't answer my calls or my fax messages. Don't you have any more landscapes of memory to show me?

You want me to leave you in peace. The most wonderful stories would love to have such a happy ending, with no dead bodies and no tears; an elegant riposte – more like a headed goal – that punctured every bubble of possible continuity.

You said you don't want to risk destroying my ecosystem. Each and every one of your laudable reasons, as irreproachable as they were irresistible, helped your cause. Even I – the mistress of improvisation- was unable to evade or blunt such a thrust. You positioned yourself perfectly, calculated the distance exactly, chose your moment well, and executed the move with great precision. This ignorant but humble woman could only admit defeat in a stunned, bewildered silence.

It's very important to be right, and you are right, utterly right . . . but that's all. At my age – about 540 years old – I'm not interested in being right. I've paid homage to that idea for far too long; by now I've reached the conclusion that passion isn't the most important thing: it's the only important thing. Besides which, I can't understand how anyone can claim, at this stage of the game, to bargain with their emotions by bothering about such prosaic matters as problems that upset our timetables or our habits, or having a husband and children . . .; when the gods offer us something so rare as hope, it's supremely arrogant, if not unforgivable, to reject it.

Someone like you who I imagine is a slave to the aesthetic sense must be facing a dilemma. What I mean is that it must be very hard for you to pass up a spectacle such as me; almost as hard as giving up your way of life, your comfort and your moral peace and quiet. I forgot to tell you that in the final close-up, just before I bowed my head and left, I kissed your forehead, cheeks and lips with my eyes, as quickly as I could. I don't like to bother people. None of this implies I'm trying to destroy an idol: I can accept his feet of clay (should he have them) because my faith is unshakeable: it's survived the passage of the years, and all the passing fashions.

I admit I was wrong to suggest an 'adventure', not just because of how ambiguous that word is, but because I kept our re-encounter from Mauricio. I don't know why I did, there was no need for it: I must have let myself be influenced by the atmosphere that was being created around us. Now to top it all WE HAVE RECEIVED AN ANONYMOUS LETTER. It could be that I'm surrounded by people who don't exactly like me: after all, I'm the boss, and nobody likes the boss. Anyway, I'm sure my need to talk so compulsively about you will soon pass.

Another thing: I think the perfume shop or whatever it is that Charo is setting up now she is back from Andorra (isn't it strange how whores always manage to turn life to their advantage?) ought to be called 'In Essence' or 'Essentials' . . . you deserve to have someone like her return 'with silver threads among the gold', but ready to transform everything that was once so sordid in her life into something transparent, and positive. Her new shop will enable her to turn her former clients into new customers, and make their partners clients too. Pepe Carvalho will finally become a client like all the others: will that be revenge? Anyway, you'll all be clients, but at least the business is honest, socially acceptable, smart and chic.

I've been stupid, blind, and a real nuisance. It's fairly obvious that you don't need me at all. You answer when I call or write, but your actions are just reflex ones. I had thought I could get to know you, have some fun and games, and not hurt anyone in doing so; to praise you a million times and offer you the occasional entertaining date does not seem that harmful. I felt that making our relationship real (we always talk a lot in my dreams) was too attractive an idea to pass up, and it seemed quite innocent.

When the anonymous letter arrived I felt I had nothing to

hide, so I told Mauricio everything, EVERYTHING. I could do that because in fact nothing has happened. I can accept and even control all kinds of romances: they're nothing more than passing fancies, distractions, and so don't destabilise anything. They're nothing more than inconsequential skirmishes, practice sessions, which often do not go beyond verbal jousting. Now and then I have had admirers, who are known about and accepted by my family without any great trauma – in fact, my husband and sons are flattered that anyone in our circle should show such an interest in me. They talk of 'my victims' or 'that new victim of yours' and of how happy it makes me to claim yet more scalps. They say I am ruthless, scatter-brained, an incurable flirt, and they 'scold' me, but without malice. All three of them are aware that none of this means anything to me, that it's simple gymnastics and that in any case it is never me who provokes this kind of situation. So on the one hand I'm flattered, while on the other I find it a burden.

Apparently it was far-sighted of me to sign some of these faxes 'Alice through the looking-glass', because that's where I am now. It's rather an uncomfortable position to be in, but I'm sure I'll sort out all these problems, and will try not to be too much of a bother to you. At the same time, I hope you will not 'bother' me either (I'm sure you understand what I mean), because I will not allow any of this to disturb the balance of either my own or my family's emotions. My apologies, and my best wishes.

ALICE

Perhaps it was better this way. If he thought of his re-encounter with Yes as an accidental adventure, as something his mind and spirit would come to consider unreal, as if it had gone from magic to mirage all in one, or as if he had lived the fantasy of Fritz Lang's *Woman in the Window.* The days went by and there were no new messages, until suddenly:

> *Morose magical mask*
> *Astonished, aghast, alarmed.*
> *Necromancer, new Nibelung,*
> *Ulysses urging utopias.*
> *Exact expectation ever*
> *Libertine lunatic language.*

Too short to be serious. Carvalho stayed close to the fax to see whether there would be any more, but two, then three hours went by, with Biscuter coming in and out without a word, off to buy the food, then into the kitchenette to prepare it, a Mediterranean soufflé, boss, tuna with capers, there's nothing like Mediterranean food, boss. He had time to eat the soufflé accompanied by a properly chilled *albariño* wine from Galicia, muttering all the while his contempt for those who drink champagne, sparkling or any other white wines at any warmer temperature. There was also time to leave the office with Biscuter, who was determined he should go along to the Jesuit cultural centre on Calle Caspe, where there was to be a lecture on the Cathars he might find interesting, given by someone called Guifré González. Title of the lecture: 'From Opus Dei to the Cathars'. Guifré González sounded like one of those characters who are always introduced by saying they need no introduction. Perhaps he had heard him on the radio or at some literary gathering, or vaguely taken in an interview with him. The room was full, and Biscuter had reserved them two seats directly behind Margalida the Comely, the Maid of Vallès, who turned round to smile at them. Behind the platform the back wall was ready for the projection of a film or video. Carvalho glanced round the hall and could see the man in the tracksuit, the young neo-liberal from the spy classes, and Anfrúns, surrounded by a gaggle of young men and women who hung on his every word, whisper or protest. The same corrupter of youth as ever. Three men appeared on the platform: Francesc Marc Alvaro, Guifré González, and a Jesuit, who presented Francesc Marc Alvaro as one of the most brilliant and balanced of the new generation of intellectuals. When Francesc Marc Alvaro got up to speak, he launched into an ironic paean of praise (the only civilised way to praise someone) of Guifré González, who he said could be considered the most important mind in Catalonia, one of the best-stocked brains in all Europe. How could you stock a brain without reducing the empty space available? Alvaro asked himself to conclude his brief but brilliant introduction, leaving his audience wondering whether perhaps Guifré's brain was somehow stuffed to overflowing. The lecturer, now known as Guifré González, was the fake priest and fake uncle of Neus, who in reality was called Margalida. No longer dressed in either cassock or tropical shirt, he looked every inch a member of the intellectual celebrity circus. After thanking the Jesuits for their liberal attitude in inviting him, he began by describing the crisis of modernity in the Catholic Church and the difficult years of struggle ahead, especially in the territory of Catalonia, where the Church had so far proved itself incapable of embracing ecclesiastic autonomy, and ran the risk of alienating its followers, who demanded from religion the right to be different. The Catholic Church in Rome was staking everything on Opus Dei as its new defensive force, one that could help connect it to the strategy of acquiring temporal power thanks to material power, and vice versa, but Opus Dei had not taken the necessary steps to ensure it was in tune with the new globalised world order based on identifiable nations. What was to be done? Perhaps the moment had come to leave the Catholic Church on its downward path to obsolescence, since it had chosen to take this 'path' together with Opus Dei, and to look instead for a religion specifically designed for the territory of Catalonia. And in order to avoid disastrous schisms, perhaps it would make more sense to delve into their collective memory for some religious stratum which in the past had tried to offer a new form of spirituality. For this reason, the new Europe of the twenty-first century should consider what Catharism had once been. It was a religion of solidarity yet fundamentalist at the same time. It was part of the ancient, modern, eternal desire to return to the primitive, humanist Christianity of the people, which after the institutionalisation of the Church under Constantine had set Europe ablaze from Bulgaria to Toulouse, from Koblenz to the region of North Catalonia in the twelfth and thirteenth centuries. At that moment the lights went down in the hall, and projected on to the back wall was a map showing the extent of Cathar beliefs in the twelfth, thirteenth and fourteenth centuries, sometimes confused with the Albigensians or the Vaudois, although this was nonsense because Catharism was apparently finally crushed in 1321 when Belibastre, the last known Cathar 'perfect', was burnt at the stake in Vila-Roja, Termenes. In addition, Guifré went on, warming to his subject, there are people who argue that the Cathars wanted to set up the principality of Septimania, and others still, like Javaloys, who claim that the Jews were behind this idea, and that the king of France and the pope made common cause against these schismatic, politically incorrect heretics. Although scattered, the Cathars still clung to their faith, and many of them came to live in southern Catalonia, where they hid their past in order to avoid more repression, but they did leave traces. Guifré González went on to prophesy a new religious spirit based not on some kind of religious genetic engineering, but on the reappearance of a religion recreated out of its ruins, as though it had just been waiting for a new sensibility to appear. The objective and subjective conditions for this resurgence now existed.

'Poverty, solidarity, a sense of commitment in the face of the savage capitalism that has grown up thanks to the connivance of all kinds of power groups.' The Cathar religion had touched part of northern Catalonia and people or regions in the southern part too. Structurally denied nations such as the territory of Catalonia could use it both as a religion and as the defining principle for a spiritual territory based on a desire for freedom opposed to the pressure to create new territories based solely on economic arguments. We should not forget that in their day, the Cathars were known as the *bonshommes*, because they at least aspired to goodness and charity, as is shown in the fundamental study of them by Jordi Ventura i Subirats. What about the here and now? We need a mystical belief controlled by non-religious thinking in order to defend ourselves against the dictatorship of economic forces which is threatening Catalonia. The idea of a Catalan nation could evaporate if the economic power of Spain and the multinationals, helped by the *botiflers* or renegade Catalans, succeed in destroying it as a unified imaginative space, and put a triangle of economic interests in its place.

Margalida applauded with unbridled enthusiasm. She whistled and hooted as though Guifré González were a rock star and not her uncle – her fake uncle. Anfrúns meanwhile was orchestrating the response of his flock, keeping one eye on Carvalho's lack of reaction. When questions from the audience were invited, Anfrúns stood up to speak.

'My dear Guifré, I find your proposal to create a new pan-Catalan Catharism controlled by a lay and possibly even atheist entity very appealing. But if we really are faced with a threat from overwhelming economic forces, what is to prevent those who are busy scheming to create an alternative to the idea of Catalonia from simply adopting neo-Catharism as a religion for the Region Plus triangle? Because although you did not mention it by name when you talked of the threat from economic power, you were referring to Region Plus. Just look at the territory shown on your map as being where the Cathars operated.'

'It's not a triangle,' protested González, and Alvaro and the Jesuit backed him up. The Jesuit went further:

'It's more like a squashed oblong.'

Anfrúns lost his patience.

'What does it matter whether they are triangles or oblongs?'

Guifré returned to the attack:

'What is needed is a new spirituality, guided by a non-religious entity, so that a new humanism can prosper, after the failure of the attempts to create one based on the strictly rational arguments of the Enlightenment or Marxism.'

Anfrúns stood on tiptoe and began to pray out loud:

Our Father who art in Heaven, hallowed be thy name. Thy kingdom come, thy will be done, on earth as it is in Heaven. Give us each day our suprasubstantial bread, and forgive us our trespasses, as we forgive those who trespass against us. Lead us not into temptation, but deliver us from evil. For thine is the kingdom, the power and the glory, for ever and ever.

The audience seemed split between those who were horrified at the prayer, and those who listened intently. As soon as they had settled down again, Anfrúns whirled round to face the public, and spoke directly to them rather than to the three men up on the platform.

'I have just recited the Cathar version of the Lord's prayer for you. I agree it is a religion which before our loss of sovereignty formed a buried spiritual layer for many Catalans. But beware of Cathar Manichaeism. The Devil created the human body, God the spirit. And listen to the end of the prayer: "thine is the kingdom, the power and the glory". This does not mean a tangible kingdom, but rather an assembly of spirits, even though through his sacrifice Jesus delivered us from evil. Jesus Christ redeemed the kingdom and offered it to God the Father, but we Catalans have to give that kingdom a geography. As far as power goes, we have seen it undermined and destroyed by all kinds of weaknesses, but now we Catalans must turn those weaknesses into strengths. As for glory! In a psalm, the Lord says: "Awake, my glory, Awake the harp and zither": the kingdom, the power and the glory represent the spirit, the life and the soul of each individual. How can these individual characteristics become part of the collective assembly of a people?'

He was throwing down a direct challenge to Guifré González, and he accepted it:

'I don't see Catharism as a symbolist revelation born out of a sense of apocalyptic catastrophe. I see it as an ethics of rebellion and participation with a religious slant, an ethics perfectly suited to the cause of a popular Catalan identity, free of all collusion or the kind of petit-bourgeois servitude and tepid nationalist ideas promoted by that shopkeeper Jordi Pujol Soley. I sincerely hope he is defeated in the upcoming elections, so that we can enter into an era of post-nationalism. But beware: those who call for post-nationalism should not be confused. There is a beginning to every end, and we have to finish with the necessary but shameworthy nationalism that Pujol or the PNV in the Basque country represent. Only then can the era of post-nationalism usher in a new nationalism.'

This speech was greeted with whistles and applause in equal measure. Contrary to what Carvalho had been expecting, Anfrúns looked very pleased with himself as he sank back into his seat. Then, when everyone was making their way out of the hall, the leader of Lucifer's Witnesses came up behind Carvalho and whispered to him:

'You've just had the opportunity to see Manelic in his element.'

To underline his words, he nodded towards Guifré González, who was still talking to Alvaro and the Jesuit. Then, excusing himself, he left Carvalho and led his flock off to Satan's green pastures. Margalida muttered that Carvalho would soon 'be hearing from us', and repeated the plural 'us' to make sure he had got the message. The detective decided to pass by his office before he went home to Vallvidrera. As soon as he entered, he saw there was another fax message from Yes spewing out of the machine like a long white tongue, and Biscuter had gone on from the Cathars to another of his evening classes, possibly English, another lecture on globalisation, or voluntary work for the Zapatistas in Chiapas.

My foul temper has affected everyone, and I've done it deliberately so that all the people around me suffer too. It's a nasty thing to do, though I would have justified it to myself if it had been any use. I'm frustrated, irritated, perplexed, dismayed . . . furious.

My rage is arbitrary, out of all proportion, and it's gnawing away at me.

No one is to blame for my bad mood. On the contrary, I must have been a pain to you, chasing you, cornering you, forcing you to make gestures and confessions you would never have made on your own account. Despite all that, I am not only dissatisfied but angry that you don't feel the same, with the same intensity as me. The fact is that I adored you so much I thought I could demand the same from you; when I realised the distance between us, I could have slapped you. It was not until much later that I saw how far you felt obliged to do as I asked. It was me who boarded your ship (sailing without any set course, not peacefully, unhappily, but with a horizon in view) without being invited, assaulting you and calling for – demanding – all your attention and devotion.

I don't think it's wrong of me to say that I was also confused by a certain degree of (logical) vanity on your part, the desire to prolong the pleasant sensation of being adored. Adding the spice of the difference in our ages, which must have seemed flattering to you (but the gap is closing by the minute, I can feel myself growing older all the time), and throwing in the attractiveness of my good looks (let me at least take some pride in my outward appearance) I can see why it was I came to believe that your gestures and attentiveness to me were born of a need to share deeper emotions. My stomach is a 'nest of vipers' whenever I meet you; my most important aim is not to worry about Mauricio's concerns.

You have such a need for affection that you can never get enough. And you have the added problem of being so (wonderfully) generous that you feel obliged to respond to (to thank?) anyone who loves you. But behaving like that always leads to a mess you can hardly ever resolve. You force yourself to keep up an act of reciprocating the signs of affection you are given; that way you hope to repay the other person and at the same time to help them go on loving you. And since we're talking about love and affection, it seems appropriate to mention that you set up a dynamics of 'the fatal embrace' – in other words, you deceive yourself, you lie to yourself. I wouldn't be surprised that when you feel (I know you do feel) tyrannised by your Charos and your Biscuters you explode, only to almost immediately try to patch things up with fresh demonstrations of your affection, and their inevitable repercussions. You have my admiration, my affection, my respect. You've restored my hopes, my dreams, my fantasies, and my doubts, all my doubts. I'd be so glad if that brought you any happiness, but: I owe you nowt, and you owe me nowt.

I'm in a state of grace. You were the catalyst, but as such, once the chemical reaction has started, I don't need you at all.

And you must take me out of your list of acknowledgements.

ABSENCE

Absent magic mask
Betrayed aghast alarmed.
Stylite, new Nibelung,
Exact expectation, libertine lunatic language.
Nullify it, you and me
Catch my voice in the desert.
Excuse my pain, it's of this world.

Yes, absence. And from another desert A SECOND ANONYMOUS LETTER HAS ARRIVED. I think I know who is behind them: a poor wretch I once took into my confidence (don't ask me why) and told something about our relationship. He's part of my husband's world; to be precise he's his lawyer.

I got a temporary safe conduct, between three o'clock and half past three of a tormented, stormy morning, and played your voice again – it sounded like someone reciting a psalm or a spell, like a muezzin calling/ordering the faithful to their pagan prayers. It was so dark, and with all the flashes of lightning it was like *Night on Bare Mountain*. I realised you had been alone without me, just as I was alone without you. Throughout all this endless weekend, punctuated by strange phone calls which I took to be frustrated or suggestive attempts by you to call me, I furnished my solitude with the weight of my family. I tried to rediscover my affection for them, to be there for them, to reply honestly to questions like: 'But apart from growing . . . what's happening to you?'. I can't find the way to be honest without harming them; the truth hurts. I doubt if anyone could give up imagining or expressing the kind of emotions I feel, but I can try. Nor do I know how anyone can look a loved one in the face and cause them irreparable harm; I have no idea how to convince myself of the (comfortable?) illusion that I am sparing them. Then all at once I forget these problems and find myself somewhere in paradise, in a shared session of one unending kiss; those marvellous kisses you give me – crushing, astonishing, disturbing: antepenultimate, and if that word doesn't exist, it does now. So there I am on cloud nine, but at once I come crashing down to the world around me, a world I've built step-by-step, hopefully, lovingly, devotedly. It's as though I am sabotaging myself, kidnapping myself, it's pure terrorism.

I'm not surprised that old people have the faces they do; in my case, I fear the worst.

Carvalho did not respond to Yes's fax, because Fuster rang his bell in the nick of time, bearing gifts of *rancio* wine and Villores truffles that were from before the '99 harvest and the start of the new millennium. And along with the truffles they were soon engaged in the inevitable discussion of why white Spanish truffles could not compare with the Italian ones. Fuster, who came from a family of truffle hunters and was therefore a born truffle expert, lamented the fact that the Spanish ones were like perfumed potatoes, whereas a *tartufo bianco* from Alba was a wonder of nature.

'A truffle auction in Morella is something to behold, and the way the peasants keep the truffle areas secret as though they were gold mines is proof that the theory of value is based on the rarity of the commodity. Truffles have a symbolic, saturnalian value. But you wanted to talk to me about religion.'

Carvalho offered him the choice of three new whiskies he had found in the vintner's on Calle Agullers. Fuster preferred a Linkwood, while Carvalho opted for a vintage Springbank, as always. Fuster liked lighter whiskies, he said.

'I don't know too much about it, but the ones you prefer taste like cognac or Armagnac to me.'

Carvalho recounted his explorations in the world of religions, and how surprised he was at their close links to nationalist claims. Fuster raised his eyes to the heavens and exclaimed: 'Mother, Land and God! The Virgin Mary as the link between God and Earth, with the priests acting as pandars to every nationalist movement. They think the idea of nationhood makes existence sacred, draws it closer to the essential truths, and in the end the number of chosen people is equal to the number of priests willing to support their candidates. Internationalism has always been atheist.'

'What about ecumenism?'

'That's something else. That's Catholic imperialism, but it's fading away now. Catholicism isn't growing. It's lost its usefulness now there are no more huge landowners, and roads and TV have appeared. It hasn't even prepared its faithful for the struggle for material hegemony the way Protestantism has.'

Carvalho was of the opinion that Catholicism was a religion for primitive capitalists and the rentier class, which meant it was bound to be in trouble at a time when interest rates were falling. Besides which, with rationalism in the ascendancy, the mysteries of Catholicism were in crisis – all the Christian mysteries were, but in particular those offered by the Catholic Church.

'I don't like talking that way, because it makes me seem like a typical anti-clerical ranter, and it's not that. Or is it?'

Fuster countered with:

'What about the new Christian solidarity movements? Liberation theology?'

'That sounds to me like Marxism for the God brigade. The most modern thing I've found in Catholicism is Opus Dei – just imagine, it's Christianity with a cheap dose of business Manichaeism *à la* Dale Carnegie thrown in. A *Reader's Digest* Christianity. I'd love the old rites to make a comeback. Religion without theatre is worthless, it's nothing.'

It took another two whiskies for Carvalho to give Fuster a brief summary of the situation – his financial situation. Fuster pondered the problem and replied:

'Forget about all this religion stuff and listen to Charo. I'm your accountant, so I know what I'm talking about. To put it bluntly, you don't have a cent for your old age. A real job, with proper benefits, would mean you had a pension. Finish the case with the widow. Give her a coherent final report, and don't get into any deeper waters.'

'But whether I like it or not, the link does exist. Something dark and complex is going on here, and I suspect that even if I didn't want to get involved, there are others who would push me in anyway. But why?'

Fuster could not provide the answer, nor could Carvalho's pillow. The next morning he confirmed that good whisky does not produce hangovers, and left home determined to follow Fuster's advice. As soon as he got to his office, he began to write a report for Delmira:

> I have reached the point in my investigations where I feel compelled to inform you that my work is at an end, because no new evidence is forthcoming. A desire to implicate the financier Pérez i Ruidoms in a scandal leads X to hire gunmen to kill your son, given the fact that he is linked on every level with the Pérez i Ruidoms boy. At first the murder appears to have been one of frustrated passion, until someone, let's call them Z, reveals the true motive and suggests it is all a mercenary crime thought up by a pressure group opposed to Pérez i Ruidoms, although it could not have been the Mata i Delapeu group because that is headed by the father of the victim, and this does not appear to be a confused Greek or Jewish tragedy, the sacrifice of Isaac, for example. The way the police were led to the hired killers also seems suspicious, as was the way they were gunned down at the moment of arrest, although as an eyewitness to the police assault I suspect not even Inspector Lifante was pulling the strings that led to their elimination. Following your suggestion, I tried to clear up two mysteries: who were X and Z? X had to be the man who had planned the killing, and Z the one who revealed the true motives behind it. I have no means at my disposal to clear up those mysteries . . .

When he reached this point, Carvalho stopped. No, it wasn't true. He could go farther, but for the first time he was unsure of himself. He was frightened of going too far, of getting in too deep. That kind of idea had always stimulated rather than inhibited him. Until now. The anguish of feeling anguished. The fear of feeling afraid. He crumpled the piece of paper into a ball and threw it into the waste-paper basket, but a moment later, he changed his mind, fished it out, and stuffed it in his pocket.

All at once the fax started chattering again:

> You cruel, coarse, rough, savage, ferocious barbarian. You compartmentalise your heart and your brain methodically and strategically, you sweep away anything that is not strictly useful to you with a wave of the hand; and you cynically

rejoice in it. You have the nerve, the effrontery and the inso-
lence to think you have found the magic formula. And the fact
is you've succeeded, your plan is perfect in every detail except
that you're left without a heart to enjoy it.

You do not feel or suffer from love, desire, or need . . . you
simply deploy, employ those feelings, you set them to work
for you like investments in industry, and while you are distributing and manipulating them, you are busily making them
wither away as emotions. It is not so much the straitjacket of
your education that has caused the huge gap between your
gestures and what you say you feel; your (rare) gestures are
perfectly attuned to what you feel (almost nothing). You're
too intelligent not to realise that there's something wrong in
the equation; you're incapable of understanding that the
charm of the unnecessary is necessary.

Ah! But those kisses, all those kisses you've probably
decided I've had my quota of: give me them all, soft, wet,
slow, powerful, blue, and . . . counted; as the song says, what
I want you to do is *bésame mucho*. As I sit here writing to you
on my own personal computer, nearly drunk and in a night
more night than any other I have known, two songs are flying
round my brain: the bossa nova in your eyes, from 'Bossa
Nova', and 'Somos'. I can't get organised, I don't know how
to; I feel completely useless for everything and everyone; my
legs refuse to obey me, they creak like a rusty old bike, and yet
I have to get out of here and run however I can, the memory
of you shows me a path that I sometimes think I know, or at
least am getting to know . . . and there I was thinking I could
invent caresses on the harp of your veins . . . and had invented
new kisses.

You don't reply, but I have your voice. I have just been talking to you, your voice impresses me so much, it's as though
you know what I'm going to say. It's serious: I love you, I love
you, I love you. I'm not playing games with you, I don't want
to play games with anybody, I don't want to be a public men-
ace, and I know one day I'll be completely on my own.

I have other very strange physical sensations, I won't
describe them to you because I don't think you're old enough
to understand.

You who know everything, couldn't you send me that wonderful instruction manual you use? I know you're not indifferent to me, that you like me a lot.

It's something to know that I can at least have some effect on your hormones, and that talking to me is something you enjoy and look forward to, that you remember me. But it's an unequal relationship. I need you so much. When you left after my ultimatum about two beds, I followed you and saw you go down the staircase to the car park, so then I posted myself (what an expression!) on guard on a corner to watch you drive out. The car sped away, or rather I moved away from it, and I was left bemused, alone, ridiculous. I don't know if you've ever felt such a boundless passion as the one I feel for you, I imagine you have, but although you also met obstacles and had to sort out dependencies, I'm sure you took all your scruples, all your loyalties and your nobility, bundled them up, and tossed them at the moon.

Then when the 'episode' was over, you decided you had been right to conclude there was no point in disturbing the family peace; from that moment on you don't feel affected, no matter how often it happens: you simply pick up the manual and follow the instructions without a care in the world. Mauricio is extraordinary, there's no one like him: even being so much in love with you I can recognise how superior he is. I ought to be completely sincere with him, and the only proper way I have of being that, it seems to me, is to share the loneliness and sadness I am going to cause him; in other words, to be equally lonely and sad myself. I've already told you that nobody should be ashamed of their feelings, they don't ask to be born.

I'm sorry, Mr Troglodyte Bear, you must be exhausted and uncomfortable; all you wanted was a light-hearted, inconsequential bit of fun, so this must be the last thing you need. If it's any consolation, I'll just say that there must be dozens of pretty women you can set on the right path in life, although it's not possible to send them to Kathmandu any more.

Chapter 5

When the elections came in Catalonia, the moderate nationalists won again, but by such a small margin that the sense of the end of an era would not go away. On the contrary, while socialists and former communists were busy preparing for early elections, the different nationalist groups were preparing for the fight to be anointed as Pujol's true inheritors. And life went on, with seasonal mushrooms beckoning to Carvalho as he plodded enthusiastically around La Boqueria market. This year there were masses of the *ous de reig*, aptly named Caesar's mushroom, which Carvalho considered the queen of all mushrooms, as against the mycological patriotism of those who defended the *rovelló* or lactarius as the metaphysical national mushroom, the claustrophobic clitoric preference for the morel, or the cosmopolites who supported the cepe. He tore up various faxes from Yes without reading them, hoping that by so doing he would somehow create a desire not to see her again, but was delighted when Margalida called him. She appeared on her motorbike, and again demanded he ride pillion. This time he did not want to freeze, so she stuffed folded newspapers (the Catalan edition of *El Periódico*) inside his jacket. Nor did he want to be waving his arms around in the air while she insulted taxi-drivers, so he wrapped his arms round her and clung to her back. She not only zigzagged between cars, but kept a sharp lookout in her rear-view mirror to see whether they were being followed, and suddenly turned down the strangest streets, heading first for Hospitalet, and then beyond that towards the sea, until they were finally out of the city and in among the last fields between it and the airport, all that remained of a scant nostalgia for the countryside. The fruit and the rubbish dumps of the Prat, with their carts and draught horses, were both part of Carvalho's childhood, the memory of which had recently been competing in his mind with premonitions of old age. Here the roads were no longer asphalted, and the bike headed for an isolated farmhouse with a water wheel in the midst of a clump of palm trees, close to the River Llobregat. Margalida came to a halt in front of the crumbling house. They got off, she unzipped her leather jacket, took a torch out of her backpack, and strode to the front door. The beam of light went beyond musty-smelling rooms and pointed them towards a staircase. They descended the stairs until they came to a locked door. Margalida tapped out some sort of code on it, and the door was opened by a young man who looked like a Hindu prince in exile, a likeness increased by the fact that he was wearing a white djellaba that covered him from head to toe, and made him look like an alabaster statue gliding rather than walking across the carpet of the only room that appeared inhabitable as well as inhabited, with a stereo, furniture and bar. Albert Pérez i Ruidoms came to a halt in the exact centre of the room, and sat on folded legs as though he were about to start yoga exercises. He seemed to have been in a trance, and only slowly became aware he was with others. Margalida watched him respectfully, Carvalho with the fascination he always felt when he saw theatricality applied to daily life. Albert's silence was an open invitation to them to talk, but Carvalho was in no mood to be the curtain-raiser, or one of Socrates' disciples asking leading questions.

'Albert, Señor Carvalho is on our side. What he wants is an explanation from you about what happened, especially poor Alexandre's death.'

Alberto deigned to address Carvalho.

'I suppose you are aware of the Enlightenment concept of the death of God first posited by Immanuel Kant.'

'The only lights I'm aware of are the ones in my electricity bill.'

Albert was so taken aback by this that Margalida had to rush in and explain:

'Señor Carvalho has a great sense of humour.'

Albert closed his eyes to show his utter contempt for any kind of humour whatsoever.

'Well, we needn't go back as far as Kant, but in my view all totalitarian unitary systems, whether they are revolutionary or right-wing capitalist ones, are part of the failure of rationalism. Irrationality is not the negation of the human capacity for

understanding, but a universe full of possibilities which rationalism denies. I am not Satan. The Satan we know has been created as
part of the Christian affirmation of God, and never existed. Satan
is another way of seeing, and as we can tell from the Earth, life and
history, Satan is the light of negation. Lucifer's Witnesses were
trying to assert this different way of seeing.'

'*Were* trying to? The sect still exists. Anfrúns is their leader
now.'

'Satan can also have his Judases, and Anfrúns is one of them.
Anfrúns is a puppet, his strings pulled by my father.'

Carvalho looked across at Margalida to see whether she agreed,
but she was lost in contemplation of Satan, as if she had already
reached the beatific eternity of the underworld, and all her happiness was to be found in an infinite contemplation of an infinite
Satan. Albert went on:

'Ever since I was fifteen I've been searching for alternatives to
everything my father represents, just as poor Alexandre did. He at
least had the advantage of having a sensitive, intelligent mother,
not like mine. Every time I dropped out of my father's world, he
came and took over the space I had found, because that meant he
took me back as well. I thought that Lucifer's Witnesses was so far
away it was in another galaxy from him, and he would never reach
it. I was wrong.'

His speech was interrupted by a noise outside they could not
possibly ignore. Startled, Margalida rushed over to a window at
ground level to try to make out what was going on in the already
dark world outside.

'It's them!'

Albert scrambled to his feet and stood there paralysed, but
Margalida shook him out of his stupor.

'*Surt per la cava i agafa la meva moto. Nosaltres ja ens espavi-
larem.*'*

Margalida had boundless confidence in herself or in Carvalho,
but the detective had no time to set her straight, because Albert's
hasty exit was immediately followed by the entry of four shaven-
headed thugs armed with iron bars, shouting warnings that occasionally became intelligible:

* Get out through the basement and take my bike. We'll be all right.

'We'll cut your balls off, you bastards!'

Margalida's reaction took them all by surprise. She sprayed two of them in the face, then whirled round and kicked a third man right in his crotch. Carvalho realised it was up to him to deal with the fourth, and launched himself head-first at him, hoping to prevent him getting any distance away. But the man did, and the detective fell forward on his knees, receiving a smart kick to the ribs for his pains. He turned to get to his feet again, just in time to see Margalida like a wild beast with all claws bared as she seized hold of the fourth man's top half, eyes and groin included – her nails gouging his eyes, feet flailing at his groin. The two men blinded by the spray had left to seek the supposed balm of fresh air, and Carvalho arrived just in time to give two kicks to the head to the man Margalida had left doubled over. She, meanwhile, was treating the fourth man to a display of karate kicks that came from her soul, her body, and from a cold, murderous rage. The two men outside had started a car, and she could not prevent the others running out after them. One of them shouted:

'He's got away on a motorbike!'

Margalida ran out too, but by the time she got outside their car was already lurching along the track in pursuit of the tiny rear light of Albert's bike. Furious, she turned back to Carvalho:

'Your pistol! Why didn't you get it out?'

'I hardly ever carry one.'

'Some private eye you are! You have to have a gun for this kind of thing. Now they're going to catch Albert.'

She felt like crying, and did not hold back her tears. Carvalho resisted the temptation to touch her to console her, even with his fingertips. Margalida went back inside the house and collapsed on the floor. Carvalho stood beside her. She stared around at the walls, the decor, the wasted home comforts.

'It took me weeks to get this place prepared so he could hide here from his father. The farmhouse used to belong to my grandparents, and it was more or less abandoned. And now . . .'

'Who were they?'

'Thugs his father hires. He has lots to choose from. Sometimes he uses Dalmatius and his gang, at others he prefers skinheads. There are agencies for that sort of thing.'

'What sense does what Albert said about Anfrúns have?'

'Is it that difficult to work out? The almighty Pérez i Ruidoms used Anfrúns to infiltrate the world of sects.'

'What about Alexandre Mata i Delapeu's murder?'

'Albert's convinced his father was behind it.'

'We have to get out of here. Have you got a mobile? We should call someone to come and fetch us.'

'I wouldn't risk it. They may have a listening van near by. Let's walk to an inn that still exists round here.'

They followed the track the motorbike and its pursuers had taken in the direction of a lighted group of houses. Suddenly Margalida saw something and broke into a run. When Carvalho caught up with her, he saw a motorbike on its side, and heard her say:

'They caught him. He's back in his father's claws.'

Yes persisted in her line of lyrical reproaches, leaving Carvalho no other line of defence than silence. Yes was too much for either his pessimism or his optimism.

You can take consolation in the fact that the stars will never be indifferent to your return. So Antares, Altair, Rigel and Aldebaran have told me. Apparently, the most important aspect of my present situation is that I have moved from the stage of tactics to that of strategy. Tactics are employed when one has a lot to lose; strategy is what one turns to when all is lost.

I'll never be able to build anything with you, but despite that I'm going to do all I can to stay as part of you much longer than you can imagine. You have never known what to do with this story of ours; you're too scared to believe in it and so you try to reduce it, boil it down like a consommé. I'm not going to let you get so used to me that you remember all my birthmarks, or any other skin blemish I may have. I don't want to wake up and find myself in your attic with all the other broken and discarded toys. You want to create a pleasurable situation, one you can smile your way through: you think gestures can replace feelings, like those personal tips in newspapers which say that if you deliberately frown you're bound to end up in a bad mood, or if you smile enough, you must be happy.

At the same time, deep down inside, you want to prove yet again that it was all a mirage, and that for this journey you won't be needing saddlebags. You already know enough about me to change the impression you had from twenty years ago, and I know you aren't entirely unattracted to me. That's a lot more than I could have imagined, but a lot less than what I want now.

I'm leaving, and that's that.

I'm going to scuttle this boat that was meant to take us to our brave new world. I was stupid to build it, thinking it might save you from having to live in a skyscraper in Manhattan and would take you . . . under a bridge on the Isle of Extravagance. Yes, it's laughable, I know. Just when you realise there are still a lot of surprising things about me for you to find out; and even more, when you're still interested in doing so. When you're searching for, or inventing, points in common between us. When the sprinkling of hope I've given you makes you start to sing to yourself. When you still think I'm a strange combination somewhere between black and white, a particular perfume, a remembered gesture, the question: 'Do you know what?'. When listening to a bolero, like this one, still stirs your soul:

> *Wait, the boat of forgetting has not yet sailed*
> *Let's not allow all we lived to be wrecked*

Admit it, my strategy's perfect. You'll get over it, of course, but you won't have completely destroyed me, in your memory I'll be intact. Every bolero you hear will remind you of me, and boleros have always been the shortest distance between two human beings. You'll be with me just as you always have been, and nothing and nobody will be able to rob me of the glory of knowing you were not just a dream.

Neither of us has much time left. I was always aware of this, and have always lived as if I were going to die the next day. It's the most sincere, honest and truthful way of living, for oneself and for others: neither I nor anyone else should waste time on my behalf. I've accepted the consequences, assumed all the risks; I have always acted as quickly as possible in everything and with everybody. I've been accused of being too hasty, apparently because I prefer not to know why I am doing something than to know why I'm doing it; people say this choice isn't very intelligent . . . it can't be true, they tell me. Who tells me so? My husband has guessed everything: his eyes tell me so, and so does my mother's mouth.

She never stops scolding me for being so crazy. She tells me you are her age. Tells me what can you expect from a man that age. My mother has had the absurd idea of talking to you, of persuading you to leave me alone, as though you were still in your right mind whereas I had lost mine completely. I haven't been able to dissuade her, so expect the worst.

I may not be perfect, but I am true to myself. Anyone who gets involved with me knows this is the guaranteed real-life original, I'm not a signed photo of some moment frozen in time. I have no reason to reproach her, even now everything she says and does is proof that she can't accept she is losing me, from the false assumption that I once saw her as a mother. One of these days she'll realise that it is not up to her or to me.

I'm increasingly enchanted by the idea of having a picnic together.

The letter from the Stuart-Pedrell widow arrived like a summons to pay a fine. His first reaction was to tear it up, and write a few lines in reply recommending that she should put her daughter into a nun's reform school or make sure she met her every day outside work and took her straight home. But Carvalho was also attracted by the idea of playing the role of an ageing vampire about to sink his teeth into the tender white neck of a rich heiress, but stopping off first to discuss her future with an over-protective mother. Yes was not involved in this particular game; it was all about testing the widow's flesh and neurons. So he accepted the invitation, not to enter into the argument about whether his relationship with Yes made any sense, but out of a curiosity to see whether he would still recognise a woman who he seemed to remember had reminded him of Jeanne Moreau. Forty years had gone by altogether, but fortunately only twenty since his last conversation with the Stuart-Pedrell widow. He recalled the merry widow's invitation on that occasion: Have you ever been to the Southern Seas? Would you like to come with me? I want to go on a trip there. At that time, she reminded him of Jeanne Moreau, and seemed to him dangerously older than him, just as Jeanne Moreau herself did, with those patriotic lines round her eyes and her out-of-body lips, one body inside another, the most provocative of all her many attractions. But he said no, he didn't want to travel to the Southern Seas with her, even if it was all expenses paid.

The house was still everything one could expect from the heights of Pedralbes, the extensive gardens were still among the most beautiful he had ever seen; the only thing that had changed was the all-purpose butler, who had given way to several Asiatic servants, proof that globalisation helped keep down the wages of domestic staff. It was not so much that the widow had aged badly;

she had simply aged. The telltale signs were the taut skin, evidence of a facelift that had left her with a doll's cheeks and narrow slits for eyes, and the way her plump lips had given way to a slit encased in collagen; the mouth was as dramatic as the dull eyes. She had never been kind or gentle, and still wasn't:

'Do you know why I called you here?'

'Because of some crime in the family or the family business? There are no tycoons left who have a sense of guilt like they did in your husband's day. Back in 1978 they thought they ought to apologise for having supported Franco. Now they've recovered their morale. The world is theirs.'

'Just as I thought; you're as disagreeable as ever. I won't waste your time, then. Twenty years ago I suggested you leave my daughter in peace.'

'You were more subtle. You told me Yes was looking for a father to replace the one she had lost, and I agreed. I told you almost word for word that I hadn't reached the age when pederasty could be disguised by a desire for youth, or vice versa. What you didn't know was that I had already got your daughter off my back by sending her to Kathmandu.'

The widow pointed a finger at him that was as dagger-like as her look.

'So you're the one who got her mixed up in all that madness? What are you trying to do now? Destroy her marriage, the family, our business? Her husband knows everything. He's distraught. You've reached the age now when you could be a vampire and think young blood might rejuvenate you.'

'Your daughter is a woman of over forty. And no, I don't think I'm a vampire any more, but I do know I'm a lot older than her, and that I am growing less young by the day, but I don't like the word "old", and I don't like absolute commitments.'

'How much?'

The widow had moved towards the same piece of furniture from which she had taken the cheque book to pay him to investigate her husband's murder. Carvalho turned his back on her and, as he left the room, spat out:

'You're a complete idiot.'

Down in the garden, he walked over to a hedge and while a Filipino servant looked on with politely disguised astonishment undid his flies and started to piss against a myrtle bush. Out of the corner of his eye he could see the widow was watching him from behind a shutter up on the first floor. A huge range of appetising purchases awaited him: a picnic basket from Vinçon, complete with champagne glasses, caviar, blinis, and marinaded salmon; French champagne from Seamon's, where he also splashed out on a bottle of Gevrey Chambertin, an excellent wine for adulterous picnics. He was hoping Yes would bring the more substantial part of the *atrezzo*, and was not disappointed: she appeared with a tartan blanket, silver cutlery, crystal goblets, a tablecloth for Western movie-style picnics, and a complete collection of sweet desserts. In addition, she brought herself, radiant as if in anticipation of a battle finally about to begin. She was beautiful and guilty.

'Aren't you worried that the strange spy who's sending you the anonymous letters might see us?'

'It must be a disappointed admirer. I have thousands of them.'

Carvalho concluded that the letters had never really existed. Of all the possible choices, Carvalho had rejected anywhere close to the city, and instead headed out along the highway towards the Sant Llorenç national park. This was the closest thing to the Far West in Catalonia, with red rocks and Mediterranean vegetation, and standing like a portal to the Vallès and down to Bages. As though acting the part of a couple hiding from themselves, they left the car parked on the edge of the wood, then looked for a clearing protected by trees and carpeted with pine needles and dead leaves. It was Yes who spread out the blanket and the tablecloth and converted the clearing into a forbidden bedroom and dining room. It was Yes who clinked glasses and sought out his lips, who surrendered to him as though she were knocking on his chest for him to welcome her to the darkness inside that she was so afraid of; Yes who took him like someone covering the shortest distance between two points, without allowing herself any time to feel embarrassment, shame, or remorse, simply giving herself to him completely and irremediably. She was no longer the sparkling, innocent golden girl, or the mythomaniac who for twenty years had nurtured her obsession with the first man she had ever slept with, not counting the tender adolescents who taught her to sniff coke and took her virginity between two highs. Now she was a woman with no past and no name, a strange fruit sprawled on her tartan blanket in the middle of a wood. Her face revealed her doubts as to what she was doing there or whether she had been victorious, as she lay there, one breast exposed, the other covered, her lower half naked, and her eyes searching desperately for Carvalho's own eyes, if not his lips, to send her a message of love. Carvalho studied her partial nudity, the slender ivory or purple glimpses of her smooth body, the slits which rubbing and the cold had turned into bruised wounds, the delicate lilac of her sex, as surprising as Jeanne Moreau's mouth and which stupidly reminded him of Yes's mother. Carvalho closed his eyes to drive away the association, then wrapped her in the blanket, as though trying to protect her and give her back her lost identity. He hugged her bundled-up body, rocked her gently, and was on the point of saying I love you like someone launching themselves into the void, until he was silenced by the thought that he could already make out the outline of the victim's body at the bottom of that abyss. Her body. When Yes finally managed to push her tousled head out of the blanket, her face was so happy that Carvalho was afraid he had gone too far. He stood up, lit a Rey del Mundo cigar, and stood looking down a ravine that ran up the hill towards them. He pretended he was interested in the slow movement of cars and trucks down on the distant highway, part of a universe that had nothing at all to do with the one he and Yes inhabited. He began to sing under his breath: *Only once in our lives do we give our soul/ In sweet, complete surrender/ and the moment that this miracle/ turns into the wonder of love/then bells of celebration/ ring out in this heart of mine.*

Her arms snaked round him from behind.

'What are you thinking? What were you humming?'

'I was thinking of a film I saw on TV the other day.'

'A thriller?'

'No, more or less a love story. It was called *Nelly et Monsieur Arnaud.*'

'What an odd title.'

'Nelly is a young girl, and Arnaud an older man. She helps him type up a manuscript, and he falls in love with her, while she feels attracted to him. But they are both aware their love is impossible because of the difference in their ages, their worlds, the codes they live by.'

'Does it have a sad ending?'

'That depends on how you look at it. They separate, but are haunted by the thought that perhaps they never told each other what they wanted to hear.'

I finally got to see *Nelly et Monsieur Arnaud*, it was really good, though disturbing and with some surprising coincidences. He is intense, impenetrable, programmed and calculating, as dominated by dreams as he is by habits. He is worldly, distinguished, wise but frail, because he finds he has to be a coward (or rather, prudent), just like you. And she needs to make her dream and reality coincide at whatever cost. She makes things happen at once, just as she has imagined they ought to be. She is painstaking but attractive, wise too, but strong, because she has no other option but to be wise, just like me.

The film creates a balance: he is growing old and as well as being a man (which is still a privilege) is comfortably well off. She is young, and in addition to being a woman (which is still a handicap) she has no money. That's not our situation. Or are you terrified that I am relatively rich, whereas you are completely poor?

Nelly and Monsieur Arnaud are what they are; if you are prudent you will be prudent whatever the circumstances: if you are young because you lack confidence, elderly because you are out of it, well off because you're afraid of losing it, not so well off because you could have even less. But it's the same for someone who's daring: if you're young, your lack of experience leads you into dangerous situations; if you're older because you think you have to live what's left of your life to the full, if you're well off because that will make everything easier, if you don't have anything, because there's very little to lose.

The two last scenes show the only thing they have in common, which is that they are both wise, are both alone, and

know that there was a moment when they could see themselves reflected in each other's eyes. I'm not distributing roles
underhandedly, and I'm not criticising you. I already knew
what you were like, and your personality seduced me. It still
does. You're the man of my life. Yes, I know, and now what?
That's easy, you'll carry on alone as you always have, but this
time with no corpse to strangle. For a while you'll feel solitude welling up inside you like a waltz, the same one I can
hear now. What a strange affair this is becoming. I am completely at a loss, I can't find any kind of equation which fits
this situation, much less one that resolves it. What most
worries me is not the fact that I can't find any rational arguments to dispel so many mysteries (although that does worry
me a lot): what's worst is this feeling of emptiness, this endless and previously unknown sense of sadness that has
become my constant shadow. I'm going to fill my diary with
activities, duties, commitments, to pour my glass so full it
overflows so much that either it helps me see clearly that
there's only one thing worse than being with you, and that's
being without you, or to give life the chance to distract my
attention, to soothe my soul, to silence this frustration – I
don't know how or with what, but whatever it takes.

You can't imagine how brave I have to be to tell you in all
sincerity: I love you! while at the same time renouncing all
possibility of making my dreams come true. No, you cannot
remotely imagine it! I won't ask you to share in the description of fear and solitude I get from reading novels by people
who have known what fear and solitude really are.

But what you could share is . . . I don't know, you could say
something that would console me, would help me feel held,
perhaps even loved, as I did on the day of the picnic (I know,
that's too much to ask . . . desired, then? That will do as well);
anyway . . . don't worry, I'll sort it out on my own. For once
in my life I'm sorry I don't arouse pity, which apparently is
the sign that you are in love with a real flesh-and-blood
woman. Nor, even though the postman always rings twice,
have I ever received a (divine) letter that would raise me to
the altar: that would be even more than a token of love, it

would be a formal declaration. Falling in love with you is the most solitary thing I've ever done.

And soon it will be Christmas, then the end of the year, the end of the century, the end of the millennium.

Happy holidays!

This last letter was still in his memory's eye when Yes, the one and only Yes, appeared in his garden up at Vallvidrera. After twenty years, he had found her again, with a smile on her lips that spoke of a secret conversation with herself. Between the first kiss, the first attempted words cut off by another kiss, followed by the long-delayed complete nudity in a bed, it was only a matter of minutes, but those minutes seemed much longer than any normal ones. She was the one who took the initiative, intent on proving to herself what she was capable of. Afterwards, she lay, thoughtful but still smiling, staring up at the ceiling and occasionally at Carvalho, who preferred not to think, but above all felt grateful.

'It would be wonderful. All or nothing. Can you imagine what that all would be like? Do you remember the descriptions of paradise? All our needs would be fulfilled, all we would have to do would be to contemplate God. Day after day, for ever. You and me. What more could we want?'

The look on Yes's face was as warm as her body kneeling up under the sheets. She stroked the back of his head while she talked and imagined the future she was creating in her mind as if it were already there with them in the room.

'We'll make a clean break. I'm ready to leave everything. Right now. Ask me to do it now. Today. It's ten past seven. I'll phone home and tell them: I'm not coming back. I would do it! Shall I? No, don't fool me again; don't send me off to Kathmandu with someone else.'

'That Kathmandu no longer exists. It probably never did.'

'All or nothing, José.'

He was José, he recognised himself in a name used only by his mother throughout too short a period of knowing each other. She never called him Pepe. José. Always José! The clothed mother.

José. José! Now here was the naked mother suckling a man already more than responsible for his face and the decades under his belt. An image from the end of *The Grapes of Wrath* flashed through his mind, the one where the young mother offers her milk-filled breasts to a poor starving old man. All or nothing. For however many years he had left, he could start a new life from morning till night, obliged to deceive himself to get through the moments of terror, those when the mirror showed him how decrepit he was, or when the doctors had him at bay, the wounded stag, and all there was left was the final blow, the final 'I'm sorry'. Too much self-deception to forget his state of health, a catastrophe waiting to happen, just ready to pounce and finish him off; too much to be able to conjure up the polite formulas with which to cross the icy deserts of a destroyed family: Mamma has gone off with an old lecher and now they want us to spend Christmas together. Christmas together with two boys savagely and balefully mauled. And Yes would have to be content with having only Carvalho and Biscuter for company, and perhaps Fuster too, but definitely not Charo, who he would probably never see again. A small corner of paradise for so much eternity, because perhaps not even the transports of joy would bring on Carvalho's death, perhaps on the contrary they would help him live longer until he became an unbearable lover, even though she still might bear him. The two things that shrivel up most horribly are a person's sex and their charisma. Old people's charisma shrivels up so much that they either become horrific to themselves or invisible to everybody else. And don't tell me love conquers all, and that we would be happy just living in our own world, as we live in our own self – literature has made a woman of you, Yes, and now you know what to say, but you don't own the words. Words always own us, Yes. One morning, after maybe three months, a year, or two at most, you'd do your profit-and-loss account and calculate whether or not I had managed to replace nothing with a threatened all. You'd discover you were living with a man without any pension or retirement plans, with no profession and no savings, someone who cannot get it up when the moment comes, and who sooner or later is going to need a tube to be able to urinate without disturbing anyone else. When that day comes, his silences will seem to you stupid rather than mysterious, and you won't sip his dribbly words with the straw of slow pleasure, you'll clean them from your ears like a sticky goo that doesn't allow you to hear what you want to hear. If I had lots and lots of money, Yes, I would buy myself an enormous mansion and we could surround ourselves with armies of servants who could help me grow old without being a burden to you. I would even have lifts from my bedside to the indoor swimming pool, where masseurs would stimulate my ghastly blood. I'd have a wheelchair fitted with the most intelligent electronic chips so it could feed me my pap with the patience of the condemned of the earth who have to look after rich old people, and would wipe my arse when I no longer had control over my sphincter, all the while playing some famous but catchy tune, something from Brahms, for example – the leitmotif from *Aimez-vous Brahms?* perhaps. How many old men covered in shit have you seen, Yes? After a while, when I was truly gaga, I'd let you have a discreet young lover, something like an incestuous grandson. I remember how in the cinema of the seventies, when avant-garde directors were seeing how far they could go exploring the limits of behaviour, this kind of problem was common: with lots of counterpoint, context and silence. I could play the role of John Gielgud in *Providence*, the most lucid of old men dying of rectal cancer, but still drinking the best white wines and still attracting women thanks to his ability to remember and to associate those memories with life, as though that were living and not just scattering the crumbs of dead memory for the birds who are the greediest, or coldest, or most in need of listening to you. But once I'm finished as a private detective, I won't even have the possibility of making ends meet.

'Have you got nothing to say? Didn't you like my dream?'

'I never thought that contemplating God for all eternity was even a tolerable idea.'

Yes pummelled first the sheets, then Carvalho's chest.

'Can't you even say something to commit yourself now? You never say anything anyone can believe in.'

Carvalho could feel the anxiety building up, and with it the saliva building up in his mouth. All he could find to say was:

'I love you.'

But he refused the embrace that would have meant their apotheosis, and instead got up and went into the bathroom to look in the mirror at a generous imbecile who had just saved the girl in the film from herself, at the price of condemning himself not to live another life. Perhaps that was why he pretended not to realise Yes was asking him for a kiss when he dropped her at the taxi rank, and turned his head the other way to study a traffic problem only he could see.

Before he had left home and completed a morning he might even have described as happy, he had gone to his library, found an old edition of *The Grapes of Wrath* and burnt it in the fireplace, unable to stop himself sneaking an occasional glance at Yes's magnificent breasts as he did so.

The abrupt change in his behaviour needed a constant drip feed to keep him unaware of it, and this tranfusion came from the profuse fax messages from Yes and the no less urgent reminders from Charo that she still existed, while Biscuter suffered in silence from his aggressive indifference towards anything that was not the reams of faxes accusing him of being a coward, or of passionate songs trying to renew a dance that had scarcely begun again. Yes was a great lover of songs.

> *Bossa nova in your eyes.*
> *Bossa nova in your words.*
> *Bossa nova in your arms.*
> . . .
> *That way maybe you'll remember me*
> *More and more each day.*

This syncopated, lazy tune that I sing to myself in a gypsy rhythm is my soul's safety valve, geyser or fumarole. Whenever the pressure inside builds up and I feel like I'm going to explode, then it's: *Bossa nova in your eyes, bossa.* It may be that everything I've lived amounts to nothing – do you remember, it was you who said that: nothing has ever happened to you? – whether true or not, it must all have been useless, because it's of no use to me now. And yet . . . I know everything. Does Charo, the one who lives and reigns in your heart, know that much? No matter, I know it, and with no ulterior motive (I think) I can tell you that you have all my sympathy.

Don't be sad, even though the only song that comes to mind right now is:

What dark nights for prison
the locks are crying
the heart beats.

Don't be sad, because being sad only makes you look more handsome, Mr Troglodyte Bear.

Sometimes Yes tried typographic experiments in her poems:

Astounded amphibian
buffeted by a sea
of geometric gestures
common, uneven, unappealable.
Azure, azure, azure gestures
stairs, strides, stretches of a crossing.

On other occasions, she heaped reproaches on him, which he felt as kisses.

You are the only person capable of telling the rosary of your soul in silence; of collecting taxes; of lashing out shyly and slyly; of being Aristotelian and precise; muzzled and cruel; a clueless and clawless caresser. Above all, a survivor. What a great idea it was to call you the Troglodyte Bear: omnivorous, solitary, hibernating animal who avoids trouble, licker of honey, warm and fierce, above all fierce. The wolf! the wolf! the wolf! No doubt about it, work days are the real thing, days off are simply a way of procrastinating, fake promises of the supposed eight day in the week.

As an adolescent or half-adult you looked for that eighth day guided by the melancholy of a magnificent drunk Polish writer, Marek Hasklo (whom not even Wojtyla or the CIA could rehabilitate). Perhaps that eighth day is nothing more than an afternoon, an encounter, a painful absence, a moment that becomes the flower petal pressed between the paper walls of the mansion that is memory. That novel. Memory.

Alone facing the year 2000, a mountain of seconds we have to make meaningful before time decides how long we have, what our mortgage of history is to be.

The year 2000 is not the eighth day of the week either, or so the premonitory entrails of the aforementioned Troglodyte

Bear foretell. Happy Year 2000! At the risk of being unfair to all those around me, on Twelfth Night I'd like to receive the most unexpected, extraordinary, overwhleming present: you for me, all for me, all mine, mine, mine. You're the complete hedonist, carefully choosing from (sifting through) the sack of pleasure to decide what, who, when, how, where. You're like a property owner who rents his houses to the highest bidder, but has problems with a few squatters . . . one of them is particularly unruly, she even dares to stretch out on a couch in your living room when you have guests, you find her like a fly in your soup, she really goes too far: but you'll get over it! Tell me, what would become of you if I didn't love you so much?

It's true, what would become of you, Pepe Carvalho, if Yes didn't love you so much, if Charo didn't love you so much, if Biscuter didn't depend so much on you. But above all it was Yes's love which revitalised him to such an extent that he had to cling to his immense fear of failure and of looking ridiculous to resist it.

Do you know something? I so terribly want to see you.

I've been thinking we could discuss two or three things – anything – to begin with. I imagine that at this moment you're humming a tune to yourself – is it something you do often? – and if so, I'd like to think that at least you're choosing more romantic music now.

When I was a little girl they taught me that a question mark meant the question needed a reply. Reply to my first question, then to the one that follows. I know we'll never live together, but we could write something together: what about a love song? However much you try, you'll never find your way home. I understand and you understand what I mean.

I suspect you feel you're being forced to say you're somehow in love with me, and that worries me. Let me explain: to you I'm not the driving force behind all your thoughts, dreams and hopes . . . I'm something as positive as all of that (I'm not making any value judgements here) but different: I'm someone new, flattering, refreshing, perhaps even lively and pretty. The way you talk of me reminds of that old saying: 'Women have to be in love to fuck. Men, if necessary, have to fall in love to fuck . . .'

I am revising all I thought and did in my life as a couple, and adding the damage I've done not just to myself, but unintentionally to others. It may be that because I'm leaving my skin in the process, I don't feel guilty about it, but I do at every moment know I am responsible. I made Mauricio into something more than a husband. I've been doing so ever since he took me seriously when I made him that rotten invitation to come to Kathmandu.

How was I to imagine all this; what was it that seduced me so; how can it be I miss someone so much when I've never had them; how come I know their fears, their (in my opinion) wonderful hopes and illusions, which are both childish and fleeting (in his opinion). To me, he is a complex and contrary being.

PS: You should remember that homing pigeons only do just that; they fly home.

You were very generous when, standing in front of my mirror, I tried on nightdresses, pyjamas, tunics, Greek gowns, kimonos, djellabas, and other dresses just to please you. You simply agreed with everything I tried on and took off, and eventually chose a smart pyjama with a bold pattern on it, cut like a man's. You buttoned me up right to the top.

Do you realise you are here with me in every moment of my life? I even see your face as I'm tearing up lettuce leaves – don't be angry, what I mean is you are everything I want to touch, you're everywhere I want to be. Those brief moments I snatch or hide have become the high point of my day; all the rest of the time, I drag my feet back to my other reality (I have to drag my feet to pull them away from you); then when I'm with Mauricio and the boys I spoil them as though I had just come back from a long journey and am trying to make up for being away, although it quickly becomes obvious that no sooner have I arrived than I'm leaving again.

He would never find his way home. Perhaps Yes was designing the house that could make a couple of them, the one they had built in the woods or during the evening they had spent together in a bed that remembered them. Or perhaps she was talking about everyday reality, the complicated everyday reality of being a private detective, someone on the borderline, a voyeur who should never allow himself to become the object under surveillance. Or perhaps not finding his way home was a bigger, more essential curse, like the telltale tiny signs that announce the final disaster.

For the moment he decided to go on refusing to reply to Yes's faxes, and to pick up the phone the next time Charo called.

Charo's voice sounded tearful.

'Where did you get to? Nobody could tell me where you were. It was as if the earth had swallowed you up. Pepe, my love. They're after Quimet! He's at his wits'end! You know: the phones.'

What did Carvalho know about the phones? That they were being tapped. Nothing else to do then but turn on the radio, with its news programmes repeated incessantly from six in the morning. In this case it was the Catalan stations which reported what had happened in more detail. Evidence had been uncovered which suggested that Joaquim Rigalt i Mataplana had been illegally financing political parties and organising parallel networks of dubious origin. It was obvious that the fight for power in the post-Pujol era was getting dirty, and, according to the news, Premier Pujol had declared that Rigalt i Mataplana had no administrative function in the autonomous government, but had been a personal friend for more than fifty years, and that this friendship was more important than any temporary difficulty, which should not in any case have repercussions on Catalan political life. Rigalt i Mataplana, he insisted, held no official position. Carvalho was ignorant about the procedures for getting rid of someone in this way, until mid-morning he received a call from Inspector Lifante in his office. He was asked to come to police headquarters, but if he could not remember the way, some officers would take him there. Carvalho preferred to walk, and was pleased to note that his blood pressure did not rise as he climbed the headquarter steps, now that there was less risk of him being handcuffed or maltreated as soon as he stepped inside. Lifante was coming and going in the offices, and left Carvalho to stew in his own juice until he was ready for him. Then the inspector disappeared into his own cubbyhole, and soon afterwards Carvalho saw a waiter go past with a glass of red vermouth, a soda siphon and a dish of olives on a tray, and enter the inspector's room. He calculated that this meant he would have to wait however long it took to eat a dozen olives, but had no idea of the inspector's eating habits. He might well be one of those obsessives who chewed each olive or grain of rice thirty-four times before swallowing. There must have been something to that, because it was another hour before the door opened and Lifante himself asked him to come in. The glass and the dish stood empty on the table.

'There's a smell of vermouth. I love vermouth with soda and olives.'

'I've just had one.'

'The smell is lingering.'

'I'll get them to bring you one up right away.'

'I'd love it with a portion of anchovies as well.'

Unperturbed, Lifante placed the order by telephone, and Carvalho was at his mercy.

'That's a good start, Carvalho. Let's see if we can keep it that way. Come on, explain it all to me.'

'You want me to start with Adam and Eve? I never believed in that apple story. Unless it's a metaphor for the need to kill to survive – in other words, the origin of the justification for cookery, and in particular for nouvelle cuisine.'

'You're not going to get your vermouth.'

'Worse things have happened to me.'

'Do you know where the information that has sunk Rigalt i Mataplana came from? From the case of those Slavs who murdered Mata i Delapeu. No, not from our search of the apartment they were holed up in, but from further investigations. All of a sudden we found ourselves in possession of documents that linked Rigalt i Mataplana to the payment of commissions to the ruling party in the Generalitat, and indirectly to the financing of illegal nationalist groups. What do you know about any of that?'

'Aren't you impressed by this sudden desire to have everything out in the open?'

'I'm not stupid, Carvalho. I know when I'm being given things on a silver platter.'

'So why did you let the news about Rigalt out so quickly?'

Lifante banged the desk with his fist, got to his feet, and roared at Carvalho from on high.

'Don't insult my intelligence! Who is it that controls the information that gets out? Nobody knows who gave the news first thing this morning to all the radio stations in the city. I found out about Rigalt when we were following up on the clues that had led us to the Yugoslav hitmen. Let's just say that in an archive we discovered in an information service, we suddenly came across a whole dossier on Rigalt i Mataplana. Just like that. So we began to draw our own conclusions. You turned up on the night of the siege of the Yugoslavs, your name was mentioned in twenty reports on Rigalt's movements, your girl, Charo, is his protegée. As I said, I'm not stupid, Carvalho! I want to know who is pulling the strings. Who is moving you, Carvalho?'

Carvalho shrugged. We don't move, we are moved. Where had he heard that before? At some point in the days when he believed in culture, and especially in Beckett: 'This isn't moving, this is being moved.'

'Who does this crime benefit? Would you like me to pull on that string? Perhaps it's closer to you than you realise, Lifante. I'm like a duck on Everest when it comes to all this nationalist stuff, but I use my deductive and inductive powers. If Rigalt i Mataplana goes, that leaves Pujol all the more exposed, and there are important events coming up.'

'You mean the meeting of intelligence chiefs from the Stateless Nations? The meeting of Nations without a State or States without a Nation or whatever crap it is will not be happening, I can assure you.'

Lifante had given him a glimpse of some of his cards, but only half of them.

'There are too many meetings in this city,' mused Carvalho. 'I was afraid of that. They built that huge auditorium for the Olympic Games, and now they've got nothing to fill it with.'

'Carvalho, neither the meeting of the intelligence chiefs of the Stateless Nations nor the one about Region Plus was going to be held in Barcelona.'

'What I am sure of is that the Spanish, French, Italian, British and German governments were well aware of all this. They are keeping a close eye on all the peoples chosen by God but denied a state. Has it ever occurred to you, Lifante, that God might have chosen them precisely not to have a state? God works in mysterious ways. Perhaps you're merely being fed information from CESID, in other words from the Madrid government's intelligence services. When it comes down to it, you're only a marginal police force.'

'I'm not rising to that. I serve only one country and one state.'

Lifante raised his forefinger to show his impatience, but Carvalho was rather enjoying himself.

'I'm being manipulated too, but so far I've no idea by whom or for what reason.'

The moment had come to find out, so as soon as he was free of Lifante, he called Charo to ask her to arrange an interview with Quimet. Impossible. He insisted, and Charo finally gave way. Come to my shop, but above all don't go and buy those herbs we were talking about. They're no good. She repeated it before hanging up: don't even think of buying those herbs I mentioned. In other words, he was not to go near Lluquet i Rovelló. He walked down to the Olympic Village, prepared to wander around until the time for his meeting. His presence seemed to have aroused an unusual amount of curiosity, as though four or five people had confused him with Julio Iglesias or Sharon Stone. Followed by his very obvious followers, Carvalho made his way to the quays of Port Nou, where he pretended to be examining the second-hand boats for sale. As he was gazing at an old yacht flying an unidentifiable flag, he felt a pressure against his back and a voice in his ear telling him:

'Get on board without doing anything silly.'

What could be sillier than climbing on board a yacht in the month of November?

Mr Big was the fat man sitting in the swivel-chair of the supposed captain of the boat. Carvalho deduced he was Yugoslav or something similar because he spoke exactly like all the pre-Yugoslavs, Yugoslavs or post-Yugoslavs who had come to train Spanish football clubs. He made no secret of the fact that he was called Dalmatius, and Carvalho had to swallow the surprise that this Dalmatius was not the one he had seen being tortured in Can Borau. They looked alike, but this one seemed determined to impress his guest, and his four assistants looked as if they had just come out of the shower at some football stadium or other. Why did all young Yugoslavs look like soccer or basketball players? Carvalho did not have time to answer his own question, because he could feel Dalmatius's dark eyes burning into him out of a greasy white ball his best friends might have deigned to call a face. He was the only one present who did not look like a Yugoslav soccer player, much less a basketball player, and yet he definitely was not the Dalmatius that Pérez i Ruidoms had shown him in his private torture chamber. Yet another *trompe l'oeil*.

'I'm going to make you a gift, my friend. A warning in return for you telling me who you work for.'

'You go first.'

'You can go straight to the bottom of the port with your stomach slit and filled with stones, or you can burn to death up in your Vallvidrera house with one of the girls you usually entertain there. You choose which one you prefer: Rigalt i Mataplana's little whore, or Jessica Stuart-Pedrell. Or this can simply be a warning, if you help us complete the picture. Who do you work for?'

'For myself. I'm a private detective.'

'A private detective!'

Dalmatius' scorn invited the others to laugh. They laughed.

'A private detective! You've been seeing too many films!'

They were all still laughing, so Carvalho decided they must be ill-informed.

'None of you are from here, so perhaps you don't know me. I'm a private detective of some renown, probably the best known in Barcelona. In fact, the two most typical figures from the city are an albino monkey known as Snowflake and me, Pepe Carvalho.'

Someone punched him on the back of his neck, and he fell on to his knees. He tried to fight back and almost succeeded: he sprang back to his feet and head-butted the first human shape he could make out. It was as if his brain had come into contact with a jawbone, and this caused Carvalho an intense intellectual pain, as though he were about to lose consciousness. He spun round and flung a punch at the next shape coming towards him, but missed. His fist connected only with air, but the two he received were better aimed, one to the liver, the other to his ear. Carvalho tried to spin round again on one leg to lash out at whatever he could come into contact with, but someone kicked out the knee he was standing on, and he found himself on his knees waiting for the inevitable beating. He fell flat and then rolled against the legs of one of his attackers, knocking him to the floor as well. In the confusion of bodies he managed to stand up and run to the stairs up to the deck. One of his eyes was pouring blood, and he did not want to use the other to see whether he was being followed or not, but as he reached the doorway and the hope of freedom, he could not help noticing it was filled by yet another Yugoslav basketball player. He was immensely tall, and had some sort of spike in his hand. Carvalho halted, lifted his hands in the air, and went back down to where Dalmatius and his crew were waiting for him, tense but calm.

'A private detective!' the fat man growled yet again. 'A private, dead fool, that's what you are, a dead fool. I'll warn you one more time: leave things as they are, and call the Mata i Delapeu case closed. You've caught me on a good day, but remember treachery has to be paid for, and sometimes with death. There is always somebody willing to kill, especially in squalid times like these.'

No one was blocking the gangway now, so Carvalho made his way on deck, trying to smile with the half of his face that was not covered in blood from his split eyebrow. The tallest of the Yugoslavs gave him a towel so that he could wipe the blood away before he got to the quayside, and Carvalho kept it pressed against the wound until he reached Charo's shop. She was with clients, and motioned for him to go into the back of the shop and wait for her. When she came in and saw what had happened, she stifled an urge to cry out, and instead went of in search of gauze, plasters and some fizzy water.

'Clean it and put some plaster on it, but I'll have to go to hospital so they can stitch it up.'

Charo called a taxi and sat silently crying as they sped to the accident department at Peracamps. What harm have we done anyone, Pepe? All that stuff about Quimet this morning. I'd hardly opened my eyes when I heard all about it. What's going to become of you?'

'And you.'

'The shop is in my name.'

Charo had recovered her composure to pronounce these soothing words, but then lapsed back into despairing mode. And Quimet could have done the same for you, Pepe.

'I need to see him. Urgently. Wherever he can manage.'

Charo opened her bag and took out a folded piece of paper. As they were getting out of the taxi, she slipped it into Carvalho's hand. Carvalho glanced at it as they started queuing to see someone in Peracamps, which he still thought of as the dispensary of his childhood. Once his cut had been stitched up, he escaped from Charo, who was clinging on to him trying to extract a promise.

'We should spend Christmas together.'

'Celebrating Christmas is the last thing I feel like doing.'

'Well, Christmas Eve at least. Are we all going to spend it alone in our own homes? For seven years in Andorra I was all alone, Pepe, because Quimet had to be with his family.'

'Yes, Christmas Eve, perhaps. But I want to sleep the other two days while the greater part of humanity is making a fool of itself.'

He left Charo hopeful, glanced a second time at the address on the bit of paper, and walked off down the avenue the bulldozers had ripped into the bowels of the Barrio Chino, the bowels of the country of his childhood. Soon not a stone of it would be left standing. Some verses tucked away in the memory of his days in prison rose to his lips. The Modelo jail. Record requests on the loudspeakers. Yves Montand. *Loin très loin de Brest, dont il ne reste rien.*

The fact that Quimet had chosen to hide in a social assistance office in Raval proved that, despite all the changes to Barcelona, the district was still beyond the pale. It was here that the fallen angel felt safe, exiled from his world, exiled from the kingdom, the power and the glory. And the guardian angel of his refuge was a girl who could have been Margalida's twin sister, equally ready to volunteer for any task, to answer the call . . . *de bon matí quan els estels es ponen, hem de sortir per guanyar el pic gegant* . . .*. A patriotic girl scout who would protect Rigalt, and like all the other young people working there was aware she was protecting more than just a job. Rigalt was at the far end of a corridor, in a windowless room ventilated by a small fan on the exterior wall. Quimet did not look like a fallen angel: on the contrary, he was exultant, as if he had been freed from an unsuspected weight. He embraced Carvalho as though he had found another survivor from the shipwreck. Where on earth did you get to? We were all very worried about you. You didn't even stop by to pick up your diploma. In response Carvalho merely shrugged resignedly, as if to say: That's life, sometimes we run into each other, sometimes we don't. When the detective continued to say nothing, waiting for the illustrious personage (as some of the newspapers were calling him) to explain what it was all about, Quimet thought intently for a moment about how to begin his speech. You have a right to know everything. What happened to your face? Was it Dalmatius? Things have got out of control. If Dalmatius is acting on his own account, that means things are out of control, and I'm afraid Madrid has got involved. Since it appeared that Carvalho did not

* In the morning when the stars are fading, we have to leave to climb the giant peak . . .

understand who Madrid might be, or at least the Madrid who had got involved in all this, Quimet went on:

'I mean the central government, through CESID. A large part of CESID's work consists of investigating what their strategists call "potential civil wars", in other words the possible spread of the independence movements that exist in the Basque region and Catalonia. I tried to warn people we were going too fast, and that if we did not stick to a very careful timetable we would be crushed almost before we got started. But then uncontrollable forces were unleashed around me, and worse still, there were moles we never suspected. Moles who were acting as agents provocateurs. Mata i Delapeu's murder set the ball rolling. There's a twin strategy that the Madrid government is employing, with the backing of other European states. They want to do two things: destabilise the plans of the Catalan autonomous government, and undermine the Region Plus project. In order to win over the Catalan capitalists attracted to the idea, they demanded we outlaw the most radical nationalist groups, and above all that we dismantle the weak intelligence network we were trying to set up. We had planned a meeting for the intelligence services of the Stateless Nations, and then all of a sudden there were a number of strange coincidences. Several of the supposed participants have been arrested and accused of activities against different states, and I have been linked to all this dirty business. I can't leave the country.'

'What part do I play in all this?'

'That's a personal affair. Charo had mentioned you to me.'

'And?'

'You were part of what we called "the worst-case scenario". As an outsider, a professional who was neither Catalan nor a nationalist in the strict sense of the word, if we brought you into the construction of the intelligence network and things went wrong, you would be the one to pay. Don't worry, Carvalho, I had a soft landing prepared. You wouldn't have suffered much. But the shooting of those two who had supposedly killed Mata i Delapeu set the alarm bells ringing. Someone was bringing things to a head. Pérez i Ruidoms was bringing things to a head.'

'You mean the father?'

'He is the one in the best position to set up Region Plus.'

'So he has his son's lover killed in order to implicate his own son?'

'Everyone else is as amazed at the idea as you are.'

'That makes Pérez i Ruidoms the mole.'

'No. He's a ruthless tycoon with no nationalist sentiments. He's playing to win, and he's got strong political backing from Madrid. It's a mutual aid society. Pérez i Ruidoms is not the mole. That wouldn't make sense.'

'So who is it, then?'

Quimet waited three full minutes for Carvalho to draw his own conclusion, and when the detective still said nothing but kept staring blankly at him, he sighed and elaborated:

'Anfrúns. It could be Jordi Anfrúns. Pérez i Ruidoms uses him, but Anfrúns uses all of us.'

As Carvalho turned away, he heard Quimet's voice behind him:

'Whatever happens to me, the others are still counting on you.'

'I'm sorry you won't get to travel to Italy. There's a really interesting castle at Grizane Cavour, and the wines are good.'

He did not turn round, to avoid disrupting the look of consternation on Quimet's face.

We live in a democracy. Someone rings on your doorbell at four in the morning. Therefore, according to political analysts, it must be the milkman. But Carvalho suddenly remembers he doesn't drink milk, except to use it to make béchamel sauce or for hot chocolate. So it cannot be the milkman. His gun is hidden somewhere or other he cannot be bothered to recall, so despite the bitingly cold winter wind up in Vallvidrera he goes out on to the balcony. Looking down, he sees Margalida and with her, draped and hooded in an enormous coat, what appears to be a tall man. When he opens the door he finds his intuition was correct, and standing there is the young Prince Pérez in exile, unless he has adopted both his father's names and is now the once and future Pérez i Ruidoms.

'Can we stay here until daybreak?'

'That's only three or four hours.'

'Perhaps a bit longer than that, then.'

They made their way in, obviously relieved to be in a warm house again, and came to a halt in front of the remains of the fire in the hearth, holding their palms out to it as though invoking the spirit of its ashes. They sat down while Carvalho prepared them an emergency coffee in the kitchen. He asked whether they were hungry, and when he got no reply, took out a cheesecake made from feta left over from Greek salads he had never got round to eating, and raisins. When they saw him appear with coffee and cakes, Margalida's eyes beamed with gratitude, but the young man still looked suspicious, especially as far as the cheesecake was concerned.

'Are you a satanist or a vegan?'

'Why do you ask?'

'Because you're staring at the cheesecake as if it were about to offend your most macrobiotic convictions. I can never tell my yin from my yang, but it's nothing more than an innocent cake made from fresh Greek cheese and a few raisins.'

'I'm not a vegan, but I have my own ideas when it comes to food.'

'If you're a satanist, you must like it well done, barbecued or roasted.'

'Not even the pope believes in hellfires and brimstone.'

'That's because this pope doesn't trust anyone. He doesn't even trust condoms.'

They drank and ate, the holy man nibbling with obvious distaste. Carvalho brought them up to date with what was going on. They told him they had nowhere to hide, otherwise they would not have bothered him. This disturbed him, because his house was not exactly a safe spot, and at any minute could be invaded by post-Yugoslav killers sent by NATO, or skinheads out on a day trip. Margalida took off her leather jacket, revealing her splendid breasts under a tight-fitting jersey, and the butt of a revolver tucked into her belt. This was meant to reassure Carvalho, who asked:

'Do you still think I should keep my gun with me too?'

'Yes.'

Carvalho went into the bathroom, rummaged around among all the empty boxes in the cabinet, and managed to slide back the wall panel. He put his hand into the hidden cavity, and drew out a cloth bundle that contained his Luger. He went back into the living room and showed it to Margalida. She could not contain her scorn.

'I didn't know you had a museum up here. That belongs in an antique shop.'

'It fires. And straight. What are your plans?'

Albert had escaped from his father's men and they wanted to get out of Spain. They had a contact who could get them across the border at Port Bou. That was where there were fewest controls, but if they suspected Pérez i Ruidoms' men were anywhere in the vicinity, they knew someone who could take them by boat from Port Bou to the French coast. Margalida could not use her network, first because this was a personal matter, and second because Pérez i Ruidoms had infiltrated it at every level.

'He's acting together with CESID, and the other main European police forces involved in all this. Albert has discovered

some hair-raising things, Carvalho. On the one hand, they're trying to set up Region Plus, and on the other they have a terrifying
guerrilla strategy: they have groups who could bring everything
crashing down.'

'Here in Spain?'

Albert took over:

'One of the groups working for my father is called Templars
2000. They have the capacity to start guerrilla activity along the
border between Catalonia and Aragon, using the pretext of the
conflict over the waters of the River Ebro. They calculate that this
outbreak of violence would lead to the intervention of the Spanish
army, and we'd be facing a new Balkans war. Supply routes for
arms trafficking have already been set up – and don't forget, that's
how the problems started in Yugoslavia.'

'Is your father really mixed up in this? Are you sure he didn't
hire the La Cubana company to put on a show for you?'

'No, for the moment he's not directly involved. All he's done is
listen to them, and to ask an occasional favour from them. Nobody
knows who these Templars really are. They don't seem to be anything to do with Catalonia, and I wouldn't be surprised if they
weren't a destabilising group from some secret service or other.'

'If it weren't for the fact that you haven't the faintest idea who
Fu Manchu is, I'd say you think like him when you dream up these
ideas about your father.'

'He's not dreaming up anything.'

Margalida said this so forcefully that Carvalho had to take seriously the threat of a second battle of the Ebro.

'And if not the Ebro, it could be anywhere else. These conflicts
are there, under the surface, just waiting to break out. The world
is in such a bad way . . .'

Then Satan launched into a speech that started by ridiculing
Paul Claudel for having argued that only evil takes an effort,
because it flies in the face of reality. Wrong, and wrong again.
Reality is evil, and all the nonsense the bourgeoisie talks about
satanism is only helped by those satanists who fool around slitting
the throats of chickens and lambs.

'Satanism is a spiritual force that can become a physical one. It
works like homoeopathy – for example, in the realm of sexuality it
can lead us to absolute virility through homosexuality, and women

to absolute femininity in the same way. Jean Genet, "Saint Genet", saw this clearly, but I refuse to accept that as André Gide says I am serving the "lord of darkness". Satan is not a dark force, he is the light of negation: the original Hebrew word means "someone who accuses in court". God is lord of this world, and Satan is the negator of the idea that his creation is good. Satan is our critical intelligence, the culture of resistance.'

Prince Pérez i Ruidoms' tone became even more high flown:

'Modern-day satanism sees Satan as representing indulgence against abstinence, existence against spiritualist distortions, knowledge against hypocritical self-delusion, kindness towards the weak and arrogance towards the powerful, rightful revenge rather than any namby-pamby turning of the other cheek, a sense of responsibility for those who stand up to psychic vampirism. It represents the truth of man as animal, an animal more dangerous than any that go round on four legs, because his so-called "intellectual-divine" development has made him the fiercest of all creatures. Satan represents fruitful doubt, and the only thing that can be held against him is the fact that he has been the Church's main supporter, because it's thanks to him it has managed to survive all these hundreds of years. We satanists are united by the need to negate everything that institutionalised religions defend.'

Except for the references to homosexuality, Margalida had taken all this in with a devotion bordering on ecstasy.

'Why run away?' Carvalho wanted to know. 'Stay and become your father's crown prince, the possible future king of Region Plus, or any other designer nation.'

'What about my soul?'

These were strange times indeed if Satan was worried about losing his soul, and socialists were busy perpetuating capitalism, but they were still young and had their whole lives before them to toughen their hides in learning about death. He put them in a room with two beds, and entrusted them to Saint Genet's protection, unless Margalida's powerful attributes did not somehow reverse Albert's heterosexual amnesia. That was their problem; Carvalho's was simply to get to sleep again, and to try to push their escape plan out of his mind. That's their problem, he told himself over and over, they're playing at escaping because they're too old to play at doctors and nurses, and I'm too far gone to be playing mummies and daddies. But there was no way he could sleep, and he eventually found himself studying a road map, tracing the escape route Margalida had mentioned, and then in the kitchen staring at the open fridge, with the vague idea that he should be doing something more than just worrying himself silly. Cooking, for example: and at that time of the morning he could think of nothing better than a seafood tartare, a recipe he had been turning over in his mind since the previous morning, a sort of adaptation of the oyster tartare that Jean-Louis Neichel had invented, but without the oysters. Instead, he had fresh clams, sea urchins, prawns, a jar of unspectacular Russian caviar, and some hake macerated in virgin olive oil, salt and green pepper. He cut open the sea urchins, removed their eggs and chopped them together with the clams and prawns, then added a combination of capers, fennel, shallots, gherkins. He had no seaweed or sea-grass, so the recipe could only be an approximation. He sprinkled oil and lemon on the mixture, spread it on the fish, stuffed in into the empty sea urchin shells, and topped them off with a spoonful of caviar. He opened a bottle of white Preludi wine, and placed the sea urchins, the wine, glasses, toast and butter on a tray. When he succeeded in waking up Albert and Margalida and she saw all this exotic display in front of her, she had to stop herself reaching instinctively under the pillow for her gun.

Margalida and Albert were so amazed at how much they had liked the sea urchins stuffed with themselves, among other things, that they spent the whole first part of the journey reflecting on the error of having spent their whole lives, however short, with gastronomic horizons limited in her case to bread and tomato and *butifarra amb seques**, and in his to supposedly healthy foods. The ways of becoming less alienated are strange, and as he drove along Carvalho enjoyed first their silence faced with these new, transcendental truths, and then, from Llançà onwards, also enjoyed the spectacle of the last stretch of the Costa Brava before the French border, with its small bays and the beauty of its dark greens, greys and blues.

'We arranged to meet them at the Walter Benjamin Memorial. It's by the Port Bou cemetery, on a lovely cliff overlooking the sea.'

Carvalho recalled how moved he had been as an impressionable young Red to learn how Benjamin had committed suicide in Port Bou. A Jew fleeing Hitler's Germany, he had been refused entry into Spain by the Franco regime, and with the Nazis on his heels had killed himself in a public toilet. 'The task of the materialist historian is to save the past for the present,' Benjamin had said or written somewhere: a phrase lost in the void at a time when past and future were both denied. No one was guilty in the past, and the future was nothing more than a present consumed day by day. I'm getting philosophical, thought Carvalho, even though lately I've been eating and making love as I haven't done in years.

'Can I come with you, or do I have to stay a safe distance away?'

'You ought to come. There's a surprise for you.'

'What do you two know about Benjamin?'

---

* Sausage and beans.

'An unconvincing or unconvinced Marxist: you choose' was Satan's scornful judgement. Margalida had vaguely heard of his suicide, and someone had told her that Benjamin was an expert on photography or had written about it. Perhaps in a lecture given by a photographer called Fontcuberta.

'Do you know who Benjamin was?'

'I used to.'

'Have you forgotten?'

'Probably not, but I don't need to remember. I don't need to remember any of the lives I've lived which shed no light on the one I'm living now. Benjamin was part of my ecosystem forty years ago. Now he wouldn't even be any use to help me up a slope. Sometimes, though, phrases of his that once meant something come back to me, such as: "suicide is a heroic passion". When I read that for the first time I was very disturbed, because I thought that suicide was the opposite of revolutionary: how can someone fighting to change society think of suicide as a heroic passion? Nowadays I realise he was right. Suicide is a heroic passion. The only heroic individual passion that hurts only ourselves. All the other heroic passions are dangerous, and the ones that whole groups of people feel are the worst of all.'

A man was waiting for them, framed in the entrance to a tunnel tilted towards the sea. Seeing him out of context, it took Carvalho a few seconds to recognise him in the photo album of his memory. It was Guifré González, alias Manelic, alias Margalida's fake uncle, the prophetic angel of the Cathars. Margalida jumped out of the car first to go and meet him. The other two watched as she started to explain, while Manelic listened with a stern frown, glancing occasionally at both Carvalho and Albert. Margalida was insisting on something, but he kept shaking his head.

'I told her he wouldn't do it.'

'Do what?'

'Manelic didn't know who was coming. Margalida didn't tell him because she thought he wouldn't take me. Why would he want to help Pérez i Ruidoms' son?'

Carvalho got out of the car and marched up to the other two. He confronted Margalida and said sharply:

'You promised me it would only take a few minutes. I can't wait any longer.'

She was so surprised by his reaction that tears welled up in her eyes.

'What's wrong? Don't the Cathars want to help her?'

Guifré looked at Carvalho inquisitively, but stayed calm even when he started jabbing him in the chest.

'Some acts of solidarity are more important than the names people have, my friend. There's a right to work, and a right to escape. His father's hitmen are after him, and all of us stand to lose if they catch up with us.'

At this, Carvalho took out his gun and loaded it.

'Gunshots in Port Bou will make the front page.'

'I haven't said I won't help, but something like this cannot be based on false information, and Neus here did not tell me who was involved. Besides, my network has no reason to get mixed up in personal problems.'

'You're right. But you're up against the boy's father, and he's a shark. The best thing for you is to have the son on your side, not only because he's the Devil incarnate, but because he knows everything his father is up to, and he could be useful to you. Besides, one day he'll inherit his father's wealth, give up satanism, and could even embrace Cathar nationalism. He could shower you with gold.'

Deep in Guifré's eyes, Carvalho could see him asking himself: And what has all this got to do with you? but Manelic nodded and whispered an 'OK' that sent Margalida running towards the car to tell Albert.

'Go down into the port and ask for Eugeni de la Marqueta. It'll be better by sea.'

He stayed motionless next to the memorial as if he were part of it, so it was Carvalho who had to take the two youngsters down to the quayside. Margalida found Eugeni, a man floating in the sea of his own blubber, and he hid them in a shed to wait for nightfall. Carvalho said goodbye to Satan with a meaningful look, realising he was not someone you could shake hands with, still less embrace. He did, though, permit Margalida to fold him in her arms and kiss him on both cheeks, but kept his mouth well away from her just in case she tried to stick that big juicy tongue of hers into it again.

'You do realise who you're dealing with, don't you?'

'He's very intelligent, but very silly. He needs me.'

'He needs you now. Tomorrow it'll be his father he needs again.

I know that kind of rebel. When I was your age, we had rich Maoists who always ended up safely back at their father's home. Now they're satanists, but the same thing will happen.'

Margalida seemed to have no words or arguments to offer in response, so Carvalho walked back to where he had left his car. Manelic was waiting for him.

'Everything OK?'

'Yes.'

'Are you heading back to Barcelona? Would you mind taking me?'

'How did you get here?'

'Eugeni brought me.'

They got in and drove in silence along the twists and turns of the coast road until they reached Lançà and the road to Figueres where the highway began. Seems like old times, when people went into hiding, doesn't it? said Manelic, and Carvalho agreed. Manelic kept glancing down at his watch. What time do you think we'll arrive? After we get on to the highway it should take us about an hour. That's very tight, Manelic said. It would be really, really good if you could reach the Princesa Sofia Hotel before eight-thirty. Then he sat looking out at the countryside with an almost proprietorial air.

'Do you realise, Carvalho, that from time immemorial Catalonia has had hidden layers of religiosity and occultism? In the same way that the landscape conceals hidden rivers underneath, wherever there's a Christian settlement now, there was once a pagan place, and before that a magic one. It's as though the earth itself insists on which spots are to be dedicated to worshipping the gods. That's obvious where we are now: the Cathars were here, and that means the occult too. Did you know that in Sant Pere de Roda monastery there used to be a temple they think was dedicated to Venus Urania or Aphrodite? In other words, it's always been sacred.'

Guifré went on to complain about the shallowness of the present, and the way the links between the magical and real worlds had been lost. But we have to take things as we find them, which means that anything that is different has to stay hidden, Carvalho. Political correctness rules, and whatever doesn't fit has to go underground.

'Where you being serious when you suggested we should resuscitate Catharism?'

'It's not a question of resuscitating it like a mummy, but of adapting a concept of primitive Christianity to a new situation. Liberation theology is too internationalist in the Marxist sense of the term, but there are traces of Cathar settlements in both north and south Catalonia, right up to the fourteenth century there were Cathars in the Empordà, and even the noblewoman Guillermina de Moncada was one. Europe's superstructure may be coordinated, but underneath the different nations increasingly lack coordination, and the cracks are growing wider by the day. Have you noticed how many frontiers have changed in the past ten years? Can you predict where it's going to happen next? Could you please drop me on Calle Diagonal, outside the Princesa Sofia?'

'Are you going to a Cathar meeting?'

'If we get there in time, I'll still be able to see the Barcelona match. It starts at nine. Does that seem too frivolous to you?'

'Barcelona Football Club frivolous? In the days when I was a communist there was a guy who brought his transistor to all our clandestine meetings just so he could follow the games. I remember one particularly memorable occasion when we were debating whether we should abandon the hypothesis of the armed struggle or not. All of a sudden I realised Barça had scored, because the man's face lit up like a beacon.'

'Those were the days. I know I shouldn't watch the game because I hate to see what the team has become now. It used to be the symbolic unarmed might of Catalonia, now nobody has any idea what it represents. It's nothing more than real estate! That president Núñez came to the club twenty years ago with the same idea as Franco – to make sure it was nothing more than a football club, that it wasn't any kind of political symbol. And he's succeeded, thanks to that sinister Dutchman he brought in as manager. All he's done is contract foreigners and push out the fantastic home-grown players Cruyff had been developing. It's all wrong, Carvalho, but then again perhaps we need to wean ourselves from our emotional dependency on Barça. Lots of people think that just by being a member of the club they've paid their dues to Catalan nationalism. They don't want to hear about anything else. But that's too easy, Carvalho, far too easy. There's no history without suffering, we cannot take charge of our own history without suffering. I'm not talking about independence. I'm talking about taking charge of our own history. I reckon that Van Gaal fellow, that Dutchman in charge of Barça now, is going to leave Guardiola on the bench. What do you make of that? He's leaving the player who most symbolises Catalonia on the bench, and filling the team with Dutchmen.'

'What I don't understand, Manelic, is how you are all trying to build Cathar nationalism when you've already got Barça nationalism. What religious cults do you think they celebrated on the spot where they've built the new stadium?'

Guifré was taken aback at first, but then immediately became interested in the possibility.

'I'd have to look into it, but the stadium was built right by the Les Corts cemetery, and wherever there's a cemetery that means there's magnetic magic too.'

Chapter 6

Carvalho had decided to keep his gun with him, but it did not occur to him to use it when he saw that his house was full of post-Yugoslav basketball players. There was nothing worse than killing people at home, and anyway, they were so tall he would never be able to dispose of their bodies. Besides, they had been very polite. They had not insulted him, or even hit him. They had not pushed him or breathed in his face. All they had done was give him a message telling him he was to come to Can Borau, only a few kilometres from his place. But when he said he would just like to make a phone call, the most self-assured of the post-Yugoslavs tore out the phone line without moving a muscle of his face. Carvalho was invited to go down to a car waiting for him outside the gate. It was a very expensive Japanese limousine, with the kind of luxury detail designed to make people forget they came on to the market years after Rolls-Royce. It looked like a car bound in leather inside and out. Sunk in the back seat, he saw there was a drinks cabinet and asked for a dry martini. The others ignored him. The car went down round the bends towards Sant Bugat, turned off towards Can Borau, and came to a halt in front of the house that was as remote and isolated as before, but less illuminated. It could have been an SOS Racism shelter, he thought as the door was opened by a maid like a wind rose – the most apt simile for her kind of Maghrebian beauty – and the post-Yugoslavs kept a respectful distance while a Chinese waiter served him the dry martini he had ordered in the car.

'Did you use Martini or Noilly Prat?'

The waiter knew only how to speak Chinese and to imitate Japanese ceremonial gestures, two talents that had enabled him to get where he was today. It was obvious the dry martini had been made with Martini, and far too much of it. Carvalho tried to explain to one of the post-Yugoslavs that there should be just enough vermouth to wet the ice for it to perfume the gin and change its aroma. None of them was listening: perhaps they were nostalgic for the Balkans, regretting how little chance they had any more to enjoy killing each other while the great powers looked on and commiserated. Then the butler who had been there on the day of the fake end-of-summer party appeared. He asked Carvalho to follow him to the cellar where he had been present at the staged meeting of Mont Pelerin. Pérez i Ruidoms was in the same chair as before, but this time only Anfrúns was with him, looking nervous and pacing the room like a caged animal. He paused in his prowling when Carvalho came to a halt in the centre of the cellar opposite the chair where his host was waiting for him in a pose halfway between Rodin's *Thinker* and the engraving of Goethe lost in thought. Pérez i Ruidoms took a silver tablet case out of his pocket, flicked it open and chose two pills. He took them with a sip of water from a glass perched on one of the wide arms of his chair. He stared straight at Carvalho and spoke in an even tone.

'What you did in helping my son to escape with that girl was more like stupidity than a provocation. You had been warned. We had everything under control, but now it's all a mess again. We've been talking to your friend Anfrúns here, I believe you go way back. It would be very useful if you could help us find where those two youngsters have got to. We would discover them eventually, of course, but in the meantime their little escapade could be fatal. There are a lot of people who would like to do me harm. Remember the murder of Alexandre Mata i Delapeu. Who were they trying to hurt then? My son? On one level, yes, but ultimately it was me they were aiming at.'

Anfrúns was now leaning back against the wall, listening intently.

'Do you know where I took them?'

'To the border at Port Bou. We had everything in place to intercept them, but they didn't cross into France. They didn't go across the mountains. Or along the coast. Tell us what happened.'

'I can't help you much. All I did was leave them at the memorial to Walter Benjamin, a Jewish writer who committed suicide there in 1940, I think. They say he did it out of passion.'

'There are lots of ways to commit suicide, Carvalho. You know

I could easily convert you into an invisible galactic particle until resurrection day.'

Carvalho sighed with disgust.

'Don't tell me you've gone and joined a religious sect too.'

'All sects are religious. OK, Carvalho, I have to get on board my private jet to take me to the island of Lanzarote. I want to see in the new millennium surrounded by the leaders of Mont Pelerin in a house I had excavated from the cliffs facing the best of all oceans in the world. Do you know which one I mean?'

'If you're going to Lanzarote, you must mean the Atlantic.'

'Ten out of ten for geography! I'm sure you must know where my son is, then. To judge by the network that helped him escape, he has to be somewhere in the south of France, in one of those neo–Cathar enclaves they are trying to set up. But I can't wait any longer.'

Pérez i Ruidoms stood up and pointed to Anfrúns.

'I'll leave you to him.'

As he walked past Carvalho, he made to shake his hand. When Carvalho responded, he gripped his fingers and hissed at him:

'Don't try to be too clever, you bastard. I was brought up on the streets, and my name was simply Pérez until I got enough money to add the "i Ruidoms". I couldn't give a shit for the Mata i Delapeus, they're nothing but a bunch of daddy's boys. I made myself what I am, and nobody is going to take any of it from me. I'm not a rich kid like Mata i Delapeu. I didn't start changing my underwear every day until I was thirty. And at home we didn't have a shower.'

This seemed to him a good point at which to drop Carvalho's hand and leave the stage. Anfrúns appeared to find this all quite funny, and stood there with one hand on his chin, the other stroking his ponytail.

'I can sympathise with your boss. I didn't have a shower at home either, and I didn't change my underwear every day until recently. I even have to admit I still don't change my underpants quite that often. Socks are different. I couldn't bear to wear the same pair more than two days running.'

He could not get Anfrúns to join in the conversation, so he decided to shut up. The other man studied him, waiting for the weight of silence to loosen Carvalho's tongue. But the detective was as fed up with staying silent as he was of talking, so he headed for the exit.

'Without my permission, you'll never get out of here. Do you remember what Pérez i Ruidoms told you? You've touched his most precious possession – his own son, in whom he is well pleased.'

'Forget the Bible for once, Anfrúns.'

'But there are lines in the Bible, or in the New Testament, which are priceless. Besides, has it occurred to you that this farmhouse isn't innocent, but could be seen as a castle in heaven or in hell? Do you know the Breton traditions, the Arthurian legend, the myth of the Holy Grail? Don't you think this house could be the white island where the lord of lords lives, the owner of the world, King Arthur, Prester John, Fu Manchu, Dr No, Pérez i Ruidoms? If you like, I'll show you the bloody lance that Perceval or Parsifal sees when he reaches the castle in heaven or hell. I could be annoyed with you. In fact, I could be extremely violent. But I'll give you twenty-four hours to think it over and to give you proof of all you could lose if you don't do as we ask. Tomorrow at ten in the chapel of the Colonia Güell. That's when I'll show you the bloody lance. Now get out of here.'

'You're not expecting me to walk back, are you?'

'They'll take you.'

The car was where it had been left. Carvalho was tense during the whole drive, and kept his hand on his chest as near as possible to his gun, but the giants dropped him right in front of his house, and one of them even opened the gate for him. As soon as he was back in his lair, Carvalho searched for the note he had started to write weeks earlier as a final report for the Mata i Delapeu widow. This time he finished it:

I consider my job done, because nothing will lead me to any fresh evidence. At first I thought that a desire to implicate the financier Pérez i Ruidoms in a scandal led X to hire gunmen to kill your son, because of the links at all levels that he had with Pérez i Ruidom's son. The murder appeared to be one of frustrated passion, until someone, let's call them Z, revealed the true motive, and suggested it was a mercenary crime thought up by a pressure group opposed to Pérez i Ruidoms,

although it could not have been the Mata i Delapeu group
because that is headed by the father of the victim, and this
does not appear to be a confused Greek or Jewish tragedy, the
sacrifice of Isaac, for example. The way the police were led to
the hired killers also seems suspicious, as was the way they
were gunned down at the moment of arrest, although as an
eyewitness to the police assault I suspect that not even
Inspector Lifante was pulling the strings that led to their
elimination. Following your suggestion, I tried to clear up
two mysteries: who were X and Z? X had to be the man who
had planned the killing, and Z the one who revealed the true
motives behind it. The means at my disposal for clearing up
those mysteries have prospered. I can tell you that it was
Pérez i Ruidoms himself who hatched the plot to kill
Alexandre, even if at the beginning his own son Albert was
the prime suspect. Why did he do it? It was part of a dissua-
sive strategy against your husband. A lot of money and power
are at stake. I am writing this brief summary of my conclusions, which I will follow up with a more detailed explanation,
just in case anything should happen to me over the next few
hours, and you decide to take my place in order to discover
the reasons behind my misfortunes. Whatever happens, you
are free to act as you see fit on this report, which I am sending you in confidence.

He had some difficulty getting to the Colonia Güell, where Anfrúns was waiting for him inside the chapel with its columns twisted as though the church were about to collapse – either a metaphor for a shaky faith, or perhaps the monstrous architect had wanted to symbolise quite the opposite, that even twisted columns can support temples. Anfrúns was standing with his back to the altar, smiling as he stared towards the entrance, elbows resting on one of the benches. He did not move when Carvalho walked in as carefully as someone who, if not exactly walking on eggshells, was treading on the crumbs of all those consecrated, consumed communion wafers. From a corner of the short nave came the voices of the priest and a young couple who were of one mind about the service for their coming wedding. Anfrúns invited Carvalho to follow him out of the church and up a tortuous staircase to the roof. When they arrived, he folded his arms and encouraged Carvalho to speak.

'Don't tell me you know everything. Ask me questions.'

'There's no need. Everything leads me to you: the death of Mata i Delapeu, Mont Pelerin, Region Plus, Quimet's defenestration. But would you like to finish the puzzle for me? Just for a second. Then we can scramble it all again.'

Anfrúns lifted his arms still higher on his chest, at the same time raising his head. He stared wide-eyed at Carvalho. Then all at once he relaxed, and ran his fingers through his greying ponytail. It was held in place with a twist of lead of the kind Carvalho had not seen since his childhood, when his mother used to curl her hair with rollers and pins.

'Why should I help you?'

'Out of a sense of pride. If a devil isn't proud, he's nothing.'

'You're starting from the supposition that I'm the Devil rather than God. What's the difference between them? If I am the Devil, I stole the light and left humanity in darkness. Who is more of a god, the one governing in darkness, or the one who has the light? The one who cannot guarantee that good will triumph, or the one who can at least throw light on evil?'

'You were much easier to understand when you were a Marxist. Now you're the pope of a designer religion, do you believe in God, or any other gods?'

'The pope? Why not God himself? I insist: only those of us who do not believe in God can acquire a certain level of divinity, a functional level, of course. Not to believe in God is a supreme human conquest, but it's being sold us as a limitation. If you don't believe in God, it's because you don't believe in yourself. Do you see how it's been turned inside out? How can someone who isn't human, who doesn't know how to live, possibly be a Christian? The agony of the non-believer is seen as a negation of self rather than as a heroic struggle with the abyss of being unable to find an answer to the question of a final cause. Some people prefer to live on the edge of that abyss than to tell themselves nonsense all the time, or to behave like Ernesto Cardenal and all those lefty mystics who search for God in selflessness and works of charity, following the example of St Bonaventura when he said: "Charity makes us divine." St Bonaventura claims that our conscience is the herald of God, and is the proof that God exists. But I would say that religious education builds a conscience in us because God exists, and that it's only when you free yourself from that religiously instrumental conscience that you can see clearly. And since I can see clearly, Carvalho, I could be a god, a major or a minor one. At the moment, a minor one, but at the head of a sect that is perfectly positioned within the ecosystem of power. I'm building Lucifer's Witnesses just as Manelic is building his pan-Catalan neo-Catharism. We're both part of a bureaucratic department working in tandem: we can even employ the same secretary, the ravishing Neus or Margalida. And since I am God, I realise that both religion and nationalism are placebos, and that sooner or later religions will be sold in pharmacies and nationalisms in the Corte Inglés department stores.'

'But you're part and parcel of a nationalist movement.'

'No, post-nationalist, although we're taking along nationalists like Manelic for the ride. In this globalised world, denied nationalisms are merely the starting point for their own self-destruction. We have to be bold enough to build alternative neo-nationalisms which can be metabolised into globalisation: that is what Region Plus is all about. Nations built on sentiment are an obstacle, Carvalho, that's why we have to create them and destroy them at the same time.'

'But nationalists in Catalonia or Padania or Occitania know that Region Plus is nothing more than a manoeuvre by the intelligence services of the European Union precisely to scupper Basque, Catalan or Paduan separatism.'

'That's right, and I accept that because it suits me to do so. Don't you understand what's at stake here, Carvalho? I am Lucifer and Manelic is St Michael the Archangel, but we both work in the same office, even though Manelic is too stupid to realise it. A new modernity is being built, which implies a new synthesis between God and Satan. Just think about the key concepts of the Theology of Security: controlling drugs trafficking, controlling religious sects, controlling the far right and the new anarchistic far left.'

'What about artificial wars? And arms trafficking?'

'Don't be a fool, Carvalho. Do you want to destroy the arms industry? That would be like doing without oil. The economic catastrophe would be so great that then we really would find ourselves in a new Middle Ages, complete with post-industrial warriors and all kinds of cannibals. Doesn't that make your head spin?'

'I'm holding on to it with both hands. All this began when I tried to discover who had killed a boy from a good family who was playing at being the Devil, or at least a demon. Now I learn he was the victim of a new modernity being built by mafias.'

'When the state goes under, who else is left but the mafias? All power is born of spurious origins, whether it's created by mercenaries or the mafia. Don't waste time thinking about that. Think of yourself. Quimet has got you into a mess of his own making, and you don't know quite what your role is, but you can imagine. Quimet is someone who is faithful to the autonomous government, and if he allows all these radical games, intelligence services and international networks, it's because he thinks that way he can keep everything under control, so that when he meets the Catalan prime minister he can say: Yes, they're playing their little games but don't worry, Jordi, it's all under control. And to a certain extent he's right, so long as the power structures remain as they are. But sooner or later things will change, and when they do there are bound to be more deep-seated conflicts in which new elements will come into play which are way beyond Quimet's control. How can anyone claim to be serious in the twenty-first century with a name like Quimet? Even so, he had to be got rid of. He won't play any role in politics for the next millennium at least. That will leave Manelic and me face to face. He as the leader of a patriotic front that I have nothing to do with. I'm playing for higher stakes: I want power, the power to make and break. For once in my life I want to win. For once I'm on the side of the winners, I'm sure of it. And I need you to be with me and the forces I represent.'

'What are they?'

'International economic forces. Pérez i Ruidoms, who is my master and my slave and vice versa. They are the subversive power that the politicians cannot control. Satan. The owner of the castle in hell.'

He was laughing out loud, and obviously expected Carvalho to question his satanism so that he could give him a demonstration of it, but Carvalho just looked at him as though he were reciting the soliloquy from *Hamlet* or the baritone solo from the zarzuela *Los Gavilanes*.

'You're not convinced? Have you got me down for ever as an obsessive, harmless sociologist? Do you want me to show you the bloody lance?'

He dipped his hand into his pocket and pulled out an envelope, which he gave Carvalho. The detective held it as though weighing it, then finally realised it was not sealed, and reached inside to take out a set of photographs. There was enough light for him to be able to make out himself naked, Yes naked, in his bed, in the wood during their adulterous picnic.

'There are worse.'

Anfrúns' voice sounded a warning. Carvalho handed him back the package and shrugged.

'I'm an orphan, so I don't have any parents to upset. I'm not married, therefore I can't upset my wife. I've already got a poor reputation, so you can't make it any worse.'

'But what about her? Is Jessica Stuart-Pedrell an orphan? Is her husband going to like these photos? Are her children? Have you any idea how long we've been keeping an eye on you two? Hasn't Yes – we know that's what you call her – hasn't Yes told you about the anonymous letters she's been getting?'

Carvalho punched Anfrúns in the eye nearest to him and tried to get him in a headlock in an attempt to squash his head or at least banish him from his sight. It was a stupid, childish move that got him nowhere except a handful of greasy ponytail. Anfrúns dodged and kicked Carvalho on the hip, then quickly pulled out his gun and placed the barrel against the detective's nose.

'Take it easy. This is just a warning. You can't be an outsider. There's no room in this brave new world of ours for outsiders.'

Even though I'm crying,
Even though I'm dying,
Do you know why, my love?

I'm longing to stroke you, to stroke you for hours, to give you all my kisses, soft ones, light ones, then others that are rough and passionate, intense, long kisses . . . but above all, lots and lots of them. Do you know what? I can't get enough of you.

Nothing I've ever written was meant to question you in any way. You've always said very clearly that you have your own life and want to keep it that way; it doesn't really matter how you defend it, I'm not here to judge you, I know you have your reasons, and among them is the special, immense and . . . convenient love (which doesn't necessarily make it despicable, and I assure you that on this occasion at least I'm not being ironic) you have for yourself, or for the imaginary image you have of yourself, because I doubt whether Charo, your Charo, is what stands between us.

Yes, with each passing day I realise more and more I am going to end up alone.

Biscuter had insisted on preparing the first course from a recipe he had found in *Sobremesa* magazine: duck *foie gras* with winter vegetables and yogurt with fermented grape juice. It was the specialty of a young chef whose name could only be Basque: Bixente Arrieta.

'How old is this chef?'

'He's twenty-six, and he is chef at the Guggenheim Museum in Bilbao.'

'People at that age don't know how to eat, let alone cook.'

'Don't be such a racist, boss; you're a biological racist.'

He showed Carvalho the magazine in which he had found the recipe, with an article on the newest wave of Spanish chefs. Arrieta was there, along with a group of others Carvalho dismissed as beardless youths. Charo had promised to bring the *turrones* for dessert, and Carvalho was in charge of the main course, a boneless *carré* of lamb stuffed with Spanish ham and cooked over the embers, garnished with slices of sautéd potatoes perfumed with slices of white truffle. Biscuter listed the ingredients of his masterpiece, pointing to each of them with one of his roly-poly fingers.

'First you cook the *foie* slowly in duck fat for ten minutes, then let it cool. I had to improvise for the vegetables, because I didn't have any of the ones the recipe mentioned, so I'll use asparagus, leeks, cauliflower and Chinese shitaki mushrooms. I've prepared my herbs: spring onions, parsley, thyme and mint. I've also got a marinade with shallots, olive oil, coriander, black pepper, white wine, lemon zest, mushrooms, raisins and chopped tomato. You cook it all together, apart from the raisins which you add afterwards. All that's left is the yogurt with grape juice. I'll cook the juice until it's caramelised, then stir it into the yogurt. I add whipped cream as well, and then, seeing there are parts of the recipe that are explained worse than the war in Kosovo, I've made up the rest. I'm going to put the vegetables *al dente* on the platter first, sprinkle the herbs on them, and then add the *foie* seasoned with sea salt. I'll use the yogurt as decoration all round the *foie gras*.'

Biscuter duly turned up at Vallvidrera with all his ingredients, and took over the kitchen with the excuse that Carvalho's dish was very quick and easy to prepare, whereas his needed all the rigour and concentration of a master chef. Carvalho let him get on with it, and in the meantime started to light a fire in the hearth, thanks to *L'Homme et la mort* by Edgar Morin, a book that had tormented him some thirty years earlier, when he had suddenly calculated how old he would be by the year 2000, and had felt he was falling into a well so deep that he was tumbling down and down for ever. He remembered all the deaths that old age heralds, in particular the destruction of the brain cells, the worst beginning of the end he could imagine, and told himself it was pointless writing four hundred pages to reach the conclusion that the only way to defeat death is to welcome it into life, while hoping for some sort of amortality based on a long, slow ageing process which could take you to a hundred or a hundred and fifty if you were obstinate enough and the statistics were with you. What if people stopped fighting death and instead worried more about the quality of life as you got older? But by this time the book was well alight, and Biscuter was complaining he still did not understand the recipe.

'What do I do with the marinade, boss? Where do I put it? On the *foie*, or on the herbs?'

'I suspect it's meant for the vegetables. If not, what's the sea salt doing on the *foie gras*?'

'I'll try it out, boss.'

'Why don't you call the author?'

Never for a moment did he think Biscuter would follow his advice, but in a few minutes he had found the Guggenheim restaurant number thanks to his current gastronomic bible, *La guía de la gastronomia 2000*, by someone called Rafael García Santos, and a short while later he was talking to the chef himself. So the marinade is for the vegetables, no two ways about it, Don Bixente, no two ways, forgive a humble amateur for disturbing you on such a special evening. Then Biscuter came over, rubbing his hands.

'Youth is snapping at our heels, boss. You would never have thought of a dish like that.'

Charo arrived piled high with *turrones, barquillos* and *mantecados,* and several bottles of Rivesaltes muscat wine, which she said she had grown to like when she had been in Andorra. She also had a magnum of Millennium *cava,* because at the end of the millennium you were supposed to drink *cava* specially prepared to catapult you into another dimension.

'Going into a new millennium is like going to a new world. Like travelling to Mars.'

She was determined to spread happiness all around, so she opened the Millennium wine without stopping to consider that Carvalho had filled the freezer with Gramona, the *cava* of his childhood. After all, the celebration was for Biscuter and Charo, and they were the ones who offered Carvalho presents: Biscuter had brought a packet of firelighters, and Charo a strange little case which she handed him with a mysterious smile.

'The firelighters are so you'll have no excuse to burn books. They burn much better.'

'Are you trying to deny the little fascist in my soul, Biscuter?'

Carvalho opened the suitcase and stared in astonishment at its contents, which consisted chiefly of a keyboard and screen for a miniature computer. When he turned to Charo for some explanation, she simply said:

'An MVG 25.'

She handed him a catalogue bristling with information about this kind of case and its variety of gadgets for electronic, video and audio surveillance. The MVG 25 had a completely concealed subminiature colour film camera, a personal video recorder and a powerful hidden stereo microphone.

'It works with rechargeable batteries, and you can also wear it as a backpack or as a ladies' handbag, although I can't exactly see you doing any spying up a mountain or risking your reputation carrying a handbag.'

'Next year you can give me a counter-espionage kit.'

The sarcasm rolled off Charo's back.

'I'd already thought of that. I've seen an APC 99 that can detect hidden cameras and transmitters on telephones, the ones that work on low frequencies. But I didn't have enough savings to buy one.'

Carvalho had no presents for them, and perhaps to avoid an embarrassed silence, Biscuter launched into a Christmas carol in Catalan:

> *A Betlem m'en vull anar.*
> *Vols venir tu rabadà?*
> *Vull esmorzar!**

Charo responded with some traditional songs from her childhood in the southern countryside:

> *My God is born to suffer*
> *let him stay awake*
> *If I am keeping him awake*
> *let him sleep*
> *because those who sleep*
> *are learning how to die.*

Carvalho remembered a Moorish song he had been taught by a teacher called Blecua: *Dance, little Moor, with your little drum, because the pretty boy is Allah's son . . .* but he sang it only under his breath, and smiled indulgently at Charo and Biscuter trying to have a good time, while he drifted off to the island he shared with Yes, a floating island the size of their two bodies, as if they were in the midst of nothingness, as if they gave shape to nothingness. Carvalho was talking to Yes, explaining to her the structure of the song which a Moor who had been forced to convert was using to try to get the mention of Allah as God the Father accepted. He had been hoping for an end to the millennium free of superstitions and irrationality, and yet here he was surrounded by old and new religions which haunted him like premonitions. He walked into an endless kitchen with Yes on his arm, and roasted the lamb tied up in string while she looked on approvingly.

'Pink. I like my lamb nice and pink.'

Yes completely agreed. She also agreed with the Sauterne he chose to go with Biscuter's *foie*, but was surprised at his suggestion of a Soneto de la Rioja red to accompany the lamb stuffed with

---

* I want to go to Bethlehem.
Will you come too, shepherd?
I want my dinner!

ham. But when Biscuter emerged from the kitchen bearing aloft his *foie gras à la* yogurt with grape juice, Charo's applause and exclamations brought him back to reality, so he plunged head first into it, grateful for all the flavours of the food and the fragile happiness he could sense in his loved ones – so fragile that with her fourth glass of Millennium *cava*, Charo burst into tears and eventually confessed why she was so sad.

'I cry every time I think of poor Quimet. He must be having an awful Christmas, while we're so happy here!'

'Why don't we invite him for coffee and a glass of cognac, boss?'

Carvalho shot daggers at him, but Charo's face brightened immediately through her tears.

'Biscuter, you're so kind! But he's gone to Hawaii with his family to see in the new millennium. But thank you, thank you, Biscuter! You're all heart!'

'If only God had given me as much brain as he gave me heart!'

'What God are you talking about? I thought you were an atheist.'

'I'm a Christian atheist.'

'If you're an atheist, you can't believe in God.'

'But there must be some advantage to being an atheist.'

Biscuter fell silent for a moment, pondering his own imponderability, then returned to the charge.

'What I think, boss, is that there are two gods. One who made this world, who is an evil god, but also that somewhere there's a good god who will make everything again, and will use all we know about evil to create good.'

'Biscuter, that's so lovely!'

Charo was full of admiration. Carvalho was upset without knowing why, and left them slicing the *turrón* while he went out into the garden to return to his dream world. The city's altar lights were winning out over the encroaching shadows, pointing out the path of light. The chosen city. Soon the days would start lengthening against the night, until it was summer again, and he could go to the beach, in another century, another millennium. But for how long? Charo and Biscuter were engaged in a loud ideological duet, and Carvalho could hear them parading their theories about death, the millennium that was about to end, and life, the millennium that would arrive in seven days' time. He moved away from them to the far end of the garden, and stared away towards the spot where Yes must be fulfilling her duties as a wife and very loving mother, unless she too had escaped for a moment from her duties to search for Carvalho somewhere in space, the nowhere land that defined them and made them real, both intertwined. When he felt a hand on his cheek he turned, hoping that somehow Yes had materialised next to him and was inviting him to embark on the final journey. But it was Charo who was stroking him, and she gently pushed her head against him, nestling on his shoulder.

'Why are we so sad, Pepe?'

Then the three of them went on drinking until they fell asleep on beds or sofas. Carvalho dozed on and off through all of Christmas Day, until Charo and Biscuter went off to be bored on their own, but not before they had wrung from him the promise that they would all celebrate New Year's Eve together. After they had gone, he had only to put up with the second day of Christmas on the 26th of December as a hurdle to jump before returning to the reality of normal work days.

It was early morning and through the tree branches Barcelona, spread out like an architect's model at the foot of the Collserola hills, confirmed where and who he was. As usual, he switched on the radio. On COM someone was recalling the war in Yugoslavia and how unjust some intellectuals and politicians had been with the former secretary-general of NATO, Javier Solana. His critics must have been post-communists of some ilk, because only post-communists could accuse the secretary-general of the armed forces of the Empire of Good of being a war criminal. The person speaking was a professional of officialised international solidarity, and an MEP. He had recently been elected the universal chairman of Greenpeace, perhaps because there was still something about him of the untypical diplomat who came out with opinions that were not so much intelligent as eminently surprising, more surprising for example than accusing those who did not agree with him of being post-communists. From this globalising debate the radio turned to more regional news, and it was after he had taken a digestive tablet to help prepare the way for his daily dose of pills that he heard, unable at first to take it in, that the body of Jessica Stuart-Pedrell of SP Associates had been found in strange circumstances by a footpath in the Collserola hills: circumstances considerably stranger, it was hinted, than those in which a body with a bullet hole in the side of the head are normally found. When at last the news sank in, Carvalho found himself talking to the head of Yes with the bullet hole in it, asking her: How is this possible? What happened to you? So we'll never see each other again? The saddest music imaginable, the tune he had been whistling when he thought he had said goodbye to Yes for ever, racked his body, especially his brain. He felt as though his hearing were blocked, and could feel a sharp pain in his body between his heart and stomach. He leant over the toilet bowl to try to bring up the food he had not eaten, but only retched up the remains of the first tablet he had just taken. After he had relieved the physical pain, he went back to bed, and pulled the covers right up over his body and his head, hoping to protect his eyes and forget they were his. By now the radio was reporting that the West had called on Russia to stop maltreating Chechnya, although according to the specialist who was speaking, what Russia was doing in Chechnya favoured European interests because Turkey and Iran could be behind any attempt to destabilise the situation in the region, using the Islamic republics of the Caucasus as their kamikazes. When Yes had come to his house for the first time twenty years earlier, she had exclaimed: 'How lovely!' as if she herself did not live in one of the most beautiful houses Carvalho had ever seen. Perhaps she had been generously offering him her envy as a gift, although he had taken it as an attempt to disguise her class origins. On the outside, a class fugitive, on the inside, still part of it, thought Carvalho as he adjusted his bathrobe to hide his nakedness.

'You look like you've settled down for the night. Were you in bed?'

'No, I'd just finished eating. Would you like something?'

'No. Food makes me feel sick.'

Twenty years earlier, Yes had spread her perfectly shaped hips on the sofa and her hair was like a honey-coloured cushion behind her sombre face.

'I behaved like an idiot this morning, and didn't help you at all. I wanted to apologise. I'd like to help you as much as possible.'

'This is out of working hours. I'm not on piecework, you know.'

'Forgive me.'

'Shall we have a glass of something?'

'I don't drink. I'm vegan.'

Carvalho got out of bed, switched off the radio and went over to the sofa where Yes had sat for the first time, and where for the last time she had asked for his understanding.

'Haven't you got anything to say? Don't you like my dream?'

Fortunately, as if the circumstances had dragged it from him, he had at least said 'I love you', in a way that even to him had sounded like it came from someone else. He had not said anything like that since his first love for that unbearable woman he had gone so far as to marry, someone he refused to remember, because to do so meant returning to his lowest days as a domestic animal. He dressed with all the speed and all the pessimism he could muster, and drove his car down to the square on the Vallvidrera crossroad. He bought every newspaper available, and between the kiosk and his car had found the news item about the discovery of the body of Jessica Stuart-Pedrell i Lloberola, the wife of Mauricio Martí González, and the lengthy obituary published in *La Vanguardia* with a raft of death notices from family members, business associates, charities and cultural associations. Like tombstones, these notices gave Yes posthumous membership of the most established patrician families of Catalonia, as if they could somehow shield her from the horror of the event that had raised them:

A forest ranger discovered the body next to a path in the Collserola hills. She was fully dressed, and bore no other signs of violence apart from the bullet wound in her temple. The police are not ruling out any line of enquiry, although everything points to a failed kidnapping in the victim's own car, which was found in the middle of the woods a short distance from the spot where Señora Stuart-Pedrell de Martí's body was found.

He went into the first place that offered a smell of coffee, in Can Trampa. He read all the versions of the story in the different newspapers, and was left not knowing what to do, unable even to drink the coffee before it got completely cold. All around him were the noises of the café, people eating baguettes with sausage or Spanish omelettes, with the smell of onions, coffee or the brandy poured into early morning drinks in the hope of a bit of warmth in the last days of winter, especially for cyclists disguised as Induráin on a bad day, fighting the good fight against the car driver they all carried inside them. So many different ways for the Dr Jekyll and Mr Hyde dialectic to surface! But winter was inside him as well, and he could see no reason to go back out into the square. Never again would he receive a letter from Yes, the shipwrecked woman who sent faxes the way others sent messages in bottles. When finally his feet took him somewhere, it was to the nearby branch of the savings bank. As soon as he was inside he found himself wondering what he had come for. But by then his mouth was already talking to the manager, asking him how much he had in his account, and advice about what he could do with the money he had saved. He already knew the answers, but he wanted to feel depressed for ever, for the whole of eternity.

'You have exactly ten million, one hundred and thirty-seven thousand pesetas in your account.'

'How much is that in euros? I want to be depressed.'

'About sixty thousand.'

'What can I do with an amount like that?'

'If you invest it at a fixed rate, it will only give you around two hundred thousand pesetas a year, about sixteen thousand pesetas a month. Of course, I've no idea what savings you might have in other banks.'

'None.'

'You must have a pension fund.'

'No.'

'So you get a state pension?'

'No.'

'Well, a company scheme, then?'

'No. I once worked for the CIA, but they fired me. Do you think I could ask them for a pension?'

The bank manager did not even blink at this. He was busy eyeing Carvalho not so much as a client, more as a possible suicide.

'We could move your capital around. We could invest some in the stock exchange, for example.'

'I don't believe in capitalist speculation.'

The bank manager's eyes said it clearly: then off you go and commit suicide, brother.

'You own the house in Vallvidrera, don't you? You could mortgage it or sell it.'

'I refuse to sell the family home. I'd prefer to set fire to it. What can I do with ten million pesetas?'

'Spend them carefully when you can't work any more. To survive, you need to calculate around a hundred thousand a month. So if you stretch it out a bit, you've got enough for ten years.'

'What else?'

'Buy something or go on a trip round the world.'

The man had discovered his sense of humour in the safe with the time-delay lock.

'That's an excellent idea. I'll buy a load of rotten caviar from the Russian mafia, or I'll burn books until night falls and travel south for winter.'

He drove back home. Turned all the locks he could find. Went into the bedroom. Switched off the light. Stretched out on his bed, pulled the covers back up over his face, and closed his eyes. He felt as if he were floating in darkness, a body drifting in the most complete nothingness, so complete that there was no possibility of the slightest movement. To move would mean to confirm he existed, to confirm something, to believe. Ignoring the bullet hole in the side of her head and the trickle of blood tracing a dark path from behind her ear to her chin, Yes had turned to look at him. Carvalho tried to scrape off the dried blood with a fingernail, but Yes pulled her head away, as only Yes knew how to pull away her head and her lips, then all at once the adolescent Yes was asking him for a straw or the tube from a Biro to snort the line of coke she had laid on the white tiles around the washbasin. Then Yes was scolding him:

'Why do you always have to talk like a private detective? Can't you give a normal excuse?'

'Take it or leave it, I'm sorry. Besides, it's too much if we see each other so often. Now I'm going to eat here nice and quietly, and I've no intention of inviting you.'

'I'm all alone.'

'So am I, Jessica. Don't use me up all at once, please. Only use me when it's strictly necessary. I've got work to do. Be off with you.'

She did not know how to leave. Her hands fluttered about as though she were looking for somewhere to rest them, but her legs were carrying her off towards the door.

'I'll kill myself.'

'That would be a shame. I can't prevent suicides. I only investigate them.'

The telephone rang until it had exhausted its belief it might be answered. It rang a second time, and again went on and on, as if it were trying to tell Carvalho something vitally important that only he could guess at. Either it was the police, or it was Biscuter ringing to tell him that the police wanted to talk to him.

Biscuter confirmed that the police were looking for him. Carvalho drove down into Barcelona, and when he got to his office worked out a timetable for himself, based on a future allied to Lluquet i Rovelló. With ten million pesetas forgotten as much as saved in the bank and the house he owned, Charo was right: he should grab the last chance of getting a proper paid job, negotiate from a position of strength for a pension on his retirement, and watch from the stalls as what Anfrúns called the Satan of globalised economic forces won his victory. This time he did not even bother to read the follow-up story on Jessica's murder in the papers. He knew that at any moment the story itself would come looking for him, and when he heard a knock on the door, he knew it had arrived.

Two men sent by Inspector Lifante invited him to accompany them to police headquarters in Via Laietana. Police headquarters are never built or destroyed, they simply change façades. Carvalho opened the drawer where he kept the faxes from Yes. He took out the first messages, the ones in which she criticised him for playing only a walk-on part in his own dreams. He stuffed them in his pocket and was indicating to the two policemen that he was ready to go when all of a sudden the fax started to chatter again. Although he tried to pretend he was indifferent or even annoyed at receiving this message, his heart started pounding: it was from Yes. By the time the machine stopped, the climate in the room had fallen below zero, and seemed to have paralysed the two men, who stood there staring expectantly while Carvalho casually sorted the pages, folded them up, and put them in his other pocket. As the police car drove the short distance between his office and Via Laietana, Carvalho touched the pages gently: they felt warm, as if they were still impregnated with Yes's breath as she wrote them, but who could have sent them?

While he waited for Lifante to see him, Carvalho sat on a wooden bench and pretended to pull out the latest fax offhandedly, though he raised it close to his face to protect it from prying eyes.

I/we have already exhausted all the efforts of forensic science, even live dissection; there is nothing to add to the necrological study of this dead body, and besides, studying the remains has brought only a sense of weariness, lack of enthusiasm, boredom even. It is of course a dead body that still looks and smells perfectly fine. That is why it would be best to bury it as quickly as possible; not only because the best thing to do with dead bodies is to consign them to the earth, but because it is the only way to make sure they don't move around. The sparse biographical details I know about you have enabled me to establish the year of our Lord you were born in; I also found out by chance that the month was June, although I have no idea which day. I've been pondering on this and have come to the – irrefutable – conclusion that your birth cannot have been the fruit of a single day, and therefore I would need more of the scarce, secret information about it to draw up your astral chart. At the end of the year, the celebrations were reaching their height, so I decided to send you my present before the 1st of January 2000. I wrote a poem on a parchment for you, trying to combine what I know about you and what I have imagined: in other words, a mixture of real and true information. You are wise and yet fresh as a daisy, deadly accurate and crushing. You have music in your soul. You will doubtless be surprised to learn you also have the soul of a bullfighter. To be a bullfighter, you have to know your profession inside out, to have completely mastered all its elements, to be able to deploy them with precision, decisively, and to switch them or even throw them away, all of them, even those which you can use as an excuse for a show of arrogance, power or colour; with the gentle, harmonious movements of a dance, drawing ever closer to the final embrace, fusing what you know with what you feel, in a funambulesque performance, accepting the risk.

The poem also talks of the sea of joined terraces you saw as a child. It was that kind of view which taught you that to look means to look down. Life goes on inside, on the ground floor, and when you come up on to the roof, you see other human beings like you, the horizon is clear, you can breathe better and see more clearly, you can understand. From that moment on, you acquired the habit of narrowing your eyes to see better, as when you scanned the horizon and the sun hurt your eyes; from that moment on, the heights fascinated you, although it may be that you feel vertigo as well.

Whatever you say, the common denominator will always be an original language, one you have made your own, precise, intimate, knowledgeable, close, new, open to definitions and dreams, seductive yet full of solidarity. Even your silences are a language. It's only when one is aware of your life as a whole that one knows you, and then one knows you completely; it's like a magic trick in which you are each and every one of the parts, all different, irregular, multi-coloured, and then the final surprise is a wonderful mosaic, or rather a rose window. There are not only shapes and colours, but there is light too. I had dared to think that we might write this poem together, and that once I had finished you could play with it, changing and adding words so that this became part of the game too; I would help you face the nightfall, would teach you to welcome the dawn. That was my millennium gift to you, and that was why I thought you might not only accept it but appreciate it.

The poem was as big a mixture as you are, it did not care about techniques – it could incorporate them all, enjoy them all, always hoping to find a new one, it has adopted sympathetic elements, and swallowed up those that were less so. I had written the poem thinking it would only be complete when you cast a glance at it, and the secret green of your eyes would excuse my lack of talent.

Don't worry, this anguish, this schizophrenic behaviour, will soon pass, your memory knows that and perhaps knowing it makes you feel even sadder.

I'm going to give you the news of the year, the century, the millennium.

My husband knows everything.

MY HUSBAND HAS SEEN EVERYTHING.

MY HUSBAND HAS SEEN EVERYTHING.
MY HUSBAND HAS SEEN EVERYTHING.

Last night he told me he was going to show me a really interesting video. He had managed to send the two children to the cinema, so it was logical he would want to show it then. I thought it was something that might harm them.

YOU AND I WERE THE ACTORS IN THE VIDEO. IN YOUR HOUSE, IN YOUR BED, IN YOUR BATHROOM. IN SANT LLORENÇ PARK.

Who could have spied on us like that? Why? What for?

The boy I took with me to Kathmandu has grown up, and had to force himself not to hit me. I know he hates me. I know he hates you. I know he can kill me, but he can never kill what we had, what brought us together again after twenty years and a day and shows what a mistake it was for us to stay apart, a mistake that includes him, and the way I remember him as a youth in glasses, passionate about literature, so shy he couldn't kiss me if I didn't offer him my lips, couldn't love me unless I asked him to, who couldn't hate me until now I have given him reason to. And he has torn up my poem!

No present for you, then.

As Carvalho reread Yes's fearful lines the video was running through his mind as if on a screen, and if he turned his head behind the camera he could see Anfrúns. The screening came to an abrupt halt when the inspector called him into his room. He still had a few more paragraphs to read, but he folded the fax sheets and put them back into the same pocket.

'Anonymous letters?'

'Bills.'

At the far end of the corridor he caught sight of a grim-looking man wrapped up in his own thoughts. He glanced briefly at them, especially at Carvalho. Then he wrapped his scarf round his neck and left the police station.

'Do you know him?'

'No.'

'He's Mauricio Martí, Jessica Stuart-Pedrell's husband. He's a suspect, but there's no proof. And worse still, he has an alibi. What do you know about him?'

'Hardly anything. Just that he travelled to Kathmandu with Jessica in 1979 or thereabouts. When I met Yes again recently we scarcely mentioned him. She was obsessed with what had happened twenty years ago, trying to recover her father, the memory of her childhood.'

'Did she ever seem afraid?'

'No. She had changed a lot. So much so that she seemed a different person, although that was my problem rather than hers, I suspect.'

'Did she ever reveal anything special that could help clarify this for us? She seemed to be a woman with no problems, leading a transparent life. No one has ever seen her with anyone outside the family. She hasn't slept a single night away from her house. There are no gaps in her curriculum.'

Carvalho kept his perplexed expression, while in his mind he roamed through the solitary geography of his meetings with Yes. First, why did she have to tell her husband everything, when that everything was so much part of the past? What point was there to a loyalty that led to the destruction of two human beings, herself and the boy whose life she had transformed by taking him to Kathmandu? Yes had not been the victim of her own sincerity, but of a plot she would never even have understood, of a structural evil capable of filming her giving herself in love and then making it available to her husband, a man scared of his own anger. But Carvalho had also failed to take an elementary precaution: why had he not told her about the photos Anfrúns had shown him? He had hidden his head in the sand like an ostrich. As if the photos did not really exist, or he had been in a position to prevent them circulating, when he himself was the price to pay, and he had not told Anfrúns he would not pay it. And there was something more. A video. Which had been introduced into the fading paradise where Yes, her perfect, vulnerable children and husband lived. Carvalho suddenly realised where the pieces of Dalmatius, the real Dalmatius, Anfrúns, and the enigmatic way Dalmatius had spoken about loyalty and crime, all fitted into the puzzle. The inspector was talking about how the Yes and Mauricio couple was an example, a strange case of success when it came to the union of a girl from a really rich family with a boy who had only his clothes to stand up in.

'A student on a grant who suddenly meets this dazzling young woman.'

'Golden.'

'By which you mean there was a lot of gold around?'

'No, it's like light. It's an aura. It's not even anything to do with the colour of her hair. But if ever there was someone you could call a golden girl, it was the Yes I knew in 1979.'

'She made a man out of him. When the romantic escapade was over and they came back from Kathmandu, he had to fight to deserve her, but by then he was the husband of a Stuart-Pedrell. It's an interesting proposition, Carvalho. From his youth on, he was so dependent on her he could have ended up hating her.'

'That's too literary.'

'Or perhaps he suddenly discovered she could leave him: that he would be without her and therefore without any identity, and so he kills her.'

'That's still very literary, and besides, you have no proof. You have a tendency always to intellectualise things, Lifante. You're a theologian of security, but perhaps things are a lot simpler than that. Perhaps an outsider killed her, if we give the word outsider a metaphorical dimension. Weren't you a semiologist once?'

'I'm still tempted by semiology. But I don't understand what you mean by outsider here. You surely can't be suggesting that Jessica Stuart-Pedrell was killed by a tramp, like in the worst thrillers?'

'In a world where all of us who are on the side of order have already been classified, surely aggression comes from the outsider or the savage, from someone who is not one of us or who has not yet experienced the benefits of civilisation. A barbarian. Yes, the murderer must be a barbarian. An outsider. A stranger. A Slav or Watusi or someone from the Maghreb. They're all the same. I don't see why it has to be the husband. Up to a point, I feel responsible for him. Twenty years ago, it was me who advised Yes to take him to Kathmandu and make a man of him.'

'Why?'

'Some kids look at you as if they're asking for advice, and Yes was one of them. She always seemed to be waiting for advice.'

Lifante sighed. He did not trust Carvalho, but had told him that so often that out of intellectual vanity he did not want to repeat himself.

'It's nothing to do with this, but I warned you not to play at being a spy, Carvalho.'

As he spoke, he threw a pile of photographs on the table. They showed Carvalho coming in and out of Lluquet i Rovelló, or on the beach with Margalida, or meeting Anfrúns. None of them showed him with Yes.

'Did your people take those photos, or have they also been sent you through the good offices of the Holy Ghost?'

'The state keeps watch. None of these groups' activities escapes its attention, and CESID has begun taking seriously the possibility that a European network of intelligence services exists outside the control of governments or institutions.'

Lifante lifted his chin to indicate that Carvalho was free to go, but when the detective was already halfway out of the door, he added:

'One of my colleagues tells me that Jessica sent you a lot of faxes.'

Carvalho slapped his forehead as if scolding himself. He dipped into his right-hand jacket pocket, hoping he was not getting mixed up. No. That was the one, so he retraced his steps to Lifante's desk.

'Here they are, if you're interested. Yes was a critic of other people's conduct. She liked to analyse and criticise the cases I was involved in. It's a strictly conceptual, very literary fax relationship. If you had to choose between literature and life, which would you choose?'

'Literature.'

Carvalho looked scornfully at the inspector and left the sheets of paper on the desk. Then he went out again, making sure the others were still in his pocket. Determined to make sense of his secret eucharist with Yes, there on the opposite pavement was her husband Mauricio, glaring at him angrily like a tortured criminal determined to give the game away. Carvalho refused to look him in the eye, and set off walking, trying at the same time to send him a subliminal message:

Why did you send me the fax that implicates you? Wait until all this has blown over, kid, and set off again to Kathmandu to recover your fondest memory, and remember you're not the only one to blame for Yes's death, I'll always be there as your accomplice, because I abandoned her a second time, I left her naked on the table under the knife of the worst kind of assassin. But it's obvious it was you who accepted, who paid the killers, and who sent me that last fax. Perhaps, though, you have no idea who the real killers are. You'd love me to hand you in. That's the only chance you have to get your revenge on me. To kill me.

Naked on a scornful table. A naked mother. Among all the clothed mothers, a few exceptional women offer themselves to us as naked mothers, and one way or another, we kill them. But the husband with the bloody lance had already stopped following him; he had dived into the first bar he came across, in the hope that alcohol would give him the courage to confess. Carvalho took out the faxes from Yes that he wanted to keep, and read the end of the last one that Lifante had interrupted.

Farewell if it has to be, as the best boleros say, farewell, my love of half an afternoon or half a life, perhaps my work-day love. Perhaps work days are the real thing. Our passion is no longer a secret. In my letters, different times are juxtaposed, interwoven in no obvious order, but deliberately, in other words I have consciously mixed yours and mine. This means that as well as poetry, there's tango music, danced as all tangos are danced – a step, a counter-step – with a syncopated swaying that follows the rhythm, like this one I'm listening to now.

But the fleeing traveller must
sooner or later end his roving . . .

Halfway between a tango and a bolero, thought Carvalho, wiping away the cloud that had somehow got into his eyes, like tangible evidence of the oppression he felt in his chest. He had twice sent Yes off in the wrong direction, but he had done the same to himself, and now all that was left for him was to wander round in circles through old age and death. The first time, evil had killed a poor defenceless dog; the second, it had dared take Yes herself. No. He wouldn't keep his appointment at Lluquet i Rovelló. Having no future meant you could postpone it indefinitely. He didn't want to lay his head on Charo's shoulder to explain Jessica's second death. He walked down Via Laietana towards the cathedral square and the car park in the Ramblas where he had left his car. There were twenty-four hours to go to the first end of the millennium – always admitting the possibility that there could be another celebration on the 31st December 2000 – and the city had merely accentuated the Christmas farce it put on every year. With even more lights and shopping. Although they faced increasing competition from cloth or plaster Santa Clauses, the cathedral square was filled with stalls selling traditional Christmas figures, and there were wonderful cribs made of cork and moss, with metal palm trees and baby Jesuses triumphantly naked in winter scenes taken from a Neapolitan or Empordà landscape. A leaden sky had opened and it was raining on this pasteurised Barcelona, as if its schizophrenic, so often melancholic lustre had not already been tarnished enough. After he reached the Ramblas, Carvalho walked down to the port in search of some sea therapy. In the rain, the sea seemed melancholy, because it was the colour of dark glass, as if it had turned into a foreign, northern sea. Work days are the real thing, not holidays. Winters are real, not spring. He ducked into a phone booth and called Biscuter.

'Thanks for phoning, boss. We were in a real state. Charo is looking for you, but your phone is busy the whole time. Are we still on for New Year's Eve? I've got another fantastic recipe, very baroque, you would call it, boss, that I got from a woman chef by the name of Ruscalleda. Fried breadcrumbs with sausage, ham and pomegranate!'

'Biscuter. Let's get this damned millennium off to a good start. We're going on a round-the-world trip.'

'Have a Bloody Mary, boss. They're an excellent cure for hangovers.'

Next he phoned Anfrúns, and arranged to meet him on the breakwater, opposite the first boat anchored outside the port. It was a final meeting, to talk about Margalida and Albert's escape. Anfrúns laughed.

'Is that all you have to talk to me about, Carvalho? Has nothing else happened?'

Carvalho took a bus to Barceloneta, then walked beyond where the San Sebastián baths had once stood, and continued on until he came to the entrance to the Barcelona Swimming Club. Then he climbed up to the top of the breakwater and walked on towards the lighthouse, with for company only the occasional jogger trying to combat cholesterol and sugar in their blood. He recognised one of them: Xibert, the man in the tracksuit. As he ran past him he slowed down to make sure Carvalho had recognised him, as if to tell him 'I'm here'. For a moment, Carvalho hesitated as to whether to go on and do what he had to, but as the jogger receded into the distance, he convinced himself that there was no going back, whether he was moving or was being moved. When he was opposite the first petrol tanker at anchor in the open sea, Carvalho clambered down the rocks until he was halfway to the water, then sat facing the path so that he would see Anfrúns arrive. He saw him in the distance, the collar of his cheap overcoat whipped up by the salty breeze, his face jutting out like a ship's prow, his ponytail streaming out in its wake. Carvalho waved to attract his attention, and Anfrúns jumped down the rocks with a strictly supernatural agility. He did not understand why Carvalho's first words to him were:

'I've finally worked out what roles you and I have been given in all this.'

Nor did he seem to understand why Carvalho had taken a gun out of his jacket pocket, or his own death when the shot opened a divine hole in the centre of his forehead. Why is it that people react so slowly when it is obvious they are about to be killed? Carvalho agreed with whoever it was who had said: 'Be a relativist about everything that doesn't matter to you.' Who was it who had said that? Looking to right and left to make sure no angler had heard the shot, Carvalho unscrewed the silencer. As he stepped over Anfrúns' spreadeagled body, half-hidden among the rocks, he thought to himself:

For thine is the kingdom, the power and the glory.

When he reached the top of the breakwater, the man in the tracksuit was on his way back from the lighthouse, and ran past him without looking. Carvalho reached for his gun again, but Xibert diverted his gaze towards the scrawl of Anfrúns' corpse down among the rocks. Then he carried on running, without even breaking his stride.

Murder in the Central Committee

'A sharp wit and a knowing eye' *Sunday Times*

'Splendid flavour of life in Barcelona and Madrid, a memorable hero in Pepe and one of the most startling love scenes you'll ever come across' *Scotsman*

'Tightly plotted, very funny, not a one-dimensional character in sight. What more can you ask?' *Tangled Web*

The lights go out during a meeting of the Central Committee of the Spanish Communist Party – Fernando Garrido, the general secretary, has been murdered.

Pepe Carvalho, who has worked for both the Party and the CIA, is well suited to track down Garrido's murderer. Unfortunately, the job requires a trip to Madrid – an inhospitable city where food and sex is heavier than in Pepe's beloved Barcelona.

Southern Seas

'Pepe Carvalho is a phlegmatic investigator. His greatest concern is with his stomach, but when not pursuing delicacies, he can unravel the most tangled of mysteries' *Sunday Times*

'More Montalbán please!' *City Limits*

The body of Stuart Pedrell, a powerful businessman, is found in a Barcelona suburb. He had disappeared on his way to Polynesia in search of the visionary spirit of Paul Gauguin.

Who better to find the killer of a dead dreamer than Pepe Carvalho, overweight bon viveur and ex-communist? The trail for Pedrell's killer unearths a world of disillusioned lefties, graphic sex and nouvelle cuisine – major ingredients of post-Franco Spain. A tautly written mystery with an unforgettable – and highly unusual – protagonist.

An Olympic Death

'Montalbán's Barcelona has a truly great sense of place' *Northern Echo*

As Barcelona prepares for the Olympics, the city is turned over to make way for new roads, new stadia and the giant prawns of Mariscal. Pepe Carvalho who remembers the good old days when a hammer was always to be found with a sickle is forced to work for Olympic entrepreneurs whose only game plan is to make a fast buck.

As Carvalho tries to come to terms with the new values of the present, his life – gastronomic, amatory and professional – confronts the disillusion of middle age.

Off Side

'Magical detection' *The List*

'The mix of political intrigue, Barcelona style, and Catalan cooking tips, makes for a great read' *Venue*

'Because you use your centre forward to make yourselves feel like gods who can manage victories and defeats, from the comfortable throne of minor Caesars: the centre forward will be killed at dusk.'

To revive its sagging fortunes, Barcelona FC has bought the services of Jack Mortimer, European Footballer of the Year. No sooner has Mortimer taken possession of his company Porsche than death threats start arriving. Are they a hoax, the work of a loner or are they connected to the awesome real estate speculation that is tearing Barcelona apart?

In a period of turmoil where Catalan pimps and racketeers are being hustled off the streets by crime syndicates from the Middle East, Pepe Carvalho is thinking of retirement, but the need to save the soul of his beloved Barcelona forces him to take on a case that can only end in disaster.

The Angst-Ridden Executive

Antonio Jauma, an old acquaintance, dies desperately wanting to get in touch with Pepe Carvalho. Jauma's widow has good reason to believe that her husband's death is not what it seems. And who better to investigate than Carvalho, a private eye with a CIA past and contacts with the Communist party.